Blood Axe

By Leigh Russell

The Detective Geraldine Steel Mysteries
Cut Short
Road Closed
Dead End
Death Bed
Stop Dead

The Detective Ian Peterson Mysteries
Cold Sacrifice
Race to Death
Blood Axe

Blood Axe

A Detective Ian Peterson Mystery

LEIGH RUSSELL

WITNESS
IMPULSE
An Imprint of HarperCollins*Publishers*

To Michael, Joanna, Phillipa and Phil

———————

Originally published in the UK in 2015 by No Exit Press, an imprint of Oldcastle Books, Ltd.

EPub Edition OCTOBER 2016 ISBN: 9780062325754

Print Edition ISBN: 9780062325761

16 17 18 19 LSC 10 9 8 7 6 5 4 3 2 1

Acknowledgements

I would like to thank Dr Leonard Russell for his expert medical advice, and all my contacts on the Metropolitan Police for their invaluable assistance.

I would also like to thank the inimitable Annette Crossland for her loyal support.

Producing a book is a team effort. I am fortunate to have the guidance of a brilliant editor, Keshini Naidoo, and I am very grateful to Ion Mills and Claire Watts, along with all the dedicated team at No Exit Press, who transform my words into books.

My final thanks go to Michael, who is always with me.

Chapter One

THE WARRIOR SPRANG on to dry land, shoulder muscles straining as he heaved his narrow vessel against the current. The river flowed darkly beneath the railway bridge. Grunting, he hauled his boat along to the narrow steps that led up a steep slope to the path. Under cover of night it wasn't easy to see the boat lying at the foot of the slope. Bent almost double, he trotted halfway up the steps and looked both ways along the path. Satisfied there was no one in sight he hurried back down the steps, hauled his boat up them and dragged it swiftly over the tract of muddy grass and across the path to a gap in the wall. With an effort he heaved his boat upwards, manoeuvring it right over the top of the wall. Clinging to a rope attached to the boat, he lowered it swiftly to the ground on the other side. Forcing his way through a gap in the wall he made sure the boat was settled in a wide ditch, before pushing his way back through the gap to the path.

Turning, half crouching, he padded towards a nearby settlement. It was a mixed blessing when the moon god lit up the path in front of him. He did not want to be seen as he stole along the deserted river bank. Up ahead, a bridge spanned the dark waters, illuminated at intervals by street lights that cast an orange glow. Even at that late hour a steady succession of cars was gliding across the bridge. He hadn't expected the roads to be so busy at that time of night. He didn't want a confrontation. He could fight with the strength of a bear, but he was alone. A distant humming barely disturbed the quiet of the night as he ran up the steps and on to the bridge. Crossing it, he slipped over the road and up a side street. He rounded a bend and a figure appeared in front of him, only a few feet away. From behind it was impossible to tell whether he was following a man or a woman. It made no difference. If the stranger was armed, a strong woman could be nearly as dangerous as a man. What mattered was to take his target by surprise.

Wolf-like, the warrior ran forward, his leather shoes pounding silently on the hard ground. There was no room to wield a long sword. Having touched his silver amulet for protection, he gripped his axe with both hands and raised it. He had won the axe in battle and had been biding his time ever since, eager to try it out. Now it was about to claim its first trophy. At the last minute his victim looked round. He saw her eyes widen in terror, her lips parting as though to scream. With one blow of his axe he felled her, leaping aside to avoid her spurting blood. She sank to the ground with barely a murmur.

The woman lay at his feet, a pool of blood spreading from a deep gash in her skull. The light overhead illuminated her face and he saw that she was young. There was no time to waste in regret that he had killed her before considering taking her as a thrall. She was beyond his clutches now, already on her journey to the frozen wasteland. Deftly he set to work. Guided by the moon god, he wiped his blade on a piece of her tunic that wasn't drenched in blood. He removed her silver necklace and pulled three gold rings from her hands. They slipped easily from her wet fingers. Dropping them into his pouch he ran on, keeping to the shadows.

After such a kill, the area was dangerous. Once the woman's body was discovered, her people would come looking for him. Until then, the streets were his hunting ground. So far he hadn't found much, just a few trinkets that weighed hardly anything. After all his effort, he had to do better than that. All at once he stopped in his tracks to gaze at a glittering display of precious metalwork, rings and gems, and delicate decorative chains, all skilfully wrought. Trembling with desire, he forced himself to walk past. It wasn't safe to steal such a rich hoard openly in the busy street. People were hurrying by singly or in small rowdy groups. Most of them took no notice of him, but one or two threw curious glances in his direction. With his bloody axe at his side, it was best not to loiter. He spun round and made his way back across the bridge and down to the river. All he had to show for his efforts were a few gold rings and a fine silver chain. He remembered the woman he had killed, and cursed her. If she hadn't appeared in front of him at just that moment, his pouch might have been stuffed with treasure now. The gods had not favoured him that night, but he had no one to blame but himself.

He reached the river and hurried along the path. Dragging his boat from its hiding place behind the wall, he carried it back down to the water and leaped aboard. Silently dipping his oars in the water he made his escape. It was a weary journey, with few spoils to show for it. Next time he would do better. He looked back over his shoulder. The bridge had disappeared, swallowed up by the darkness. From its walkway he too had become invisible. Only the bloody body of a woman showed he had been roaming the streets that night.

Chapter Two

IAN PETERSON WOKE early. His wife was asleep so he went to work straight away, without stopping for coffee before leaving home. Driving to the police station before most people were stirring, he made the short journey in record time. His office was small, but he had it all to himself. That was just one of the many advantages of his recent promotion to detective inspector, another being that he no longer lived anywhere near his in-laws. He cleared his desk before going to the canteen for breakfast. Detective Sergeant Ted Birling was already there, one hand wrapped round a mug of coffee. With black hair and dark eyes, his air of brash confidence made him appear older than his mid-twenties. The sergeant looked up and greeted Ian with a smile as he sat down. Nodding an acknowledgement, Ian tucked into a plate of egg, beans and sausages.

'Wife not feeding you?'

Ian grinned in reply and they sat in companionable silence until he finished.

'Had a good weekend?' Ian asked, putting his knife and fork down.

Ted shrugged. 'Jenny wanted to go to see this new film everyone's been talking about.' He mentioned a name Ian vaguely recognised.

'Was it any good?'

'It was a load of shite, but she enjoyed it.'

'That's all right then.'

They exchanged a resigned smile.

'How about you? Good weekend?'

Ian shrugged. 'We had tickets for the last night of the Viking Festival. My wife's interested in all that.'

Ted nodded. 'I used to go to those events when I was a kid.'

A crowd had gathered the previous day near the west door of the Minster, where a group of people dressed as Vikings were standing on the steps. The men wore round helmets, hooded cloaks and belted woollen tunics, while the women wore long skirts and pinafores fastened with belts and brooches.

'A lot of them aren't wearing replicas of authentic Viking helmets,' Bev told him. 'Nose guards weren't around until the Normans, and the Vikings never had horns sticking out of their helmets.'

'Where do those originate from then?' Ian nodded at a group of men sporting huge curved horns on either side of their helmets.

'I don't know.'

Ian stopped one of the Vikings wearing a horned helmet. 'Where's your helmet from?'

'eBay, mate.'

At a rousing note on a cow's horn, the onlookers surged round the outside of the cathedral to watch a host of costumed Vikings marching past, yelling 'Odin!', and banging their shields with their spears.

'Imagine if you lived here a thousand years ago, and you saw this lot arriving,' Bev said. 'It must've been terrifying.'

Swept along with the crowd following the rowdy costumed Vikings, they followed the procession along Parliament Street to St Sampson Square. There was a crush outside Yorvik before they turned left along Castlegate, round the base of Clifford's Tower, to gather around the green outside the Castle museum. Ranks of costumed warriors lined up on the grass, banging their spears on their shields.

The re-enactment began and the roar of the crowd lifted to a crescendo. A man's voice rang out on a loudspeaker relating the story of the legendary battle. To the accompaniment of cheering from the spectators, the lines of make-believe warriors ran towards each other, slowly swinging swords and waving spears. In their everyday lives bank clerks and teachers, librarians and shop assistants, they joined together to form good-natured armies pretending to hack one another to death. Carefully staged to avoid injury, it looked like a health and safety nightmare. With the battle cries of the victors, and the yells of people pretending to be hacked down, it was an epic show. Bodies fell and lay motionless, their shields protecting their heads. One corpse wriggled away from the stamping feet of a couple of men engaged in combat beside him.

Ian grinned, enjoying the lively atmosphere of so many people out in the open air, engaged in harmless fun. He hadn't seen his wife looking so happy since they had moved to York on his promotion to detective inspector. After so many years, he still couldn't believe his luck. He had fallen for Bev when they were at school together. He had never dreamed then that she would eventually become his wife. She hated living so far from her family and friends in the South. It didn't help that her first job in York had ended disastrously, denting her fragile self-esteem. Ian could never understand how such a beautiful, capable woman could be so lacking in confidence.

'You should have dressed up as a Viking warrior! I always said you look like a Viking,' she shouted up at him.

'Tall, blonde, good-looking,' he agreed with a grin.

In the cheerful shouting, a deep voice roared out in genuine rage.

'Some fucker's nicked me axe!'

A huge, broad-shouldered man with a bushy beard was bellowing about a stolen weapon. He looked like a brute ready for a fight, despite his bare head. Red-faced, with the veins bulging in his thick neck, he towered menacingly over a worried-looking official in an orange hi-vis jacket.

'Cost me a fucking fortune!'

The official stared helplessly up at him. 'I'm afraid there's nothing we can do . . .'

'Nothing you can do? Cost me nearly a hundred quid! I bought it specially. You'd better bloody find it.'

The official muttered about Festival regulations and liability for loss or damage. He looked terrified. With a sigh, Ian stepped forward to calm the aggrieved man before his frustration erupted in violence.

'I'm a detective inspector,' he said loudly. 'Do you want to report something stolen?'

The official threw Ian a grateful glance as Ian led the tall man away from the barrier, and the crush of spectators.

'Someone's nicked me bloody axe,' the tall man said, as soon as they could hear one another. 'Cost me nearly a hundred quid and the guy I bought it from told me it was a one-off. I've never seen another one like it. Unique it was, and it was right here.' He held out his palm, as though his empty hand proved his claim. 'It's a genuine replica. Cost me a small fortune and now someone's gone and nicked it. Bloody hell. I had it right here in my hand. Some fucker just grabbed it off me and disappeared in the crowd before I could stop him. There was no way I could see where he went. Bastard!'

Ian asked him to describe the thief, but the tall man had spotted only a hooded figure who had slipped away before he had registered the theft.

'He was too bloody quick.'

Ian went through the motions of taking the report seriously, just to pacify the other man.

'Do you have a picture of your axe?'

'Picture?'

'Can you describe it?'

'Yes. It's a replica of a real Viking axe. It's got a heavy iron head with a steel edge, and a wooden handle, and there's a rune engraved on the blade, so you should be able to find it.'

'A rune?'

'Yes, a rune, engraved on the blade. It's for protection. It's . . . look, I can draw it for you.'

Seizing the pen Ian offered he drew a capital Y, adding a third middle vertical branch. It looked like a trident.

'So do you mean this pattern's engraved on the axe blade?'

'Yes. That's right. It's a rune. Bloody hell, over a hundred quid it cost me.'

They were interrupted by a loud roar. The battle was over. Promising to contact the man if his axe turned up, Ian took Bev's hand. Together they watched the show draw to a close, in an explosion of fireworks. The battle victims clambered to their feet, brushing themselves down and gathering their weapons.

Above the cacophony of voices, a scream reverberated, shrill and clear. About to walk away, Ian paused and turned to look over his shoulder.

'Wait here,' he told Bev.

'Oh Ian, what now?'

Frowning, he vaulted over the barrier, and ran towards a woman in a belted dress and head scarf. She was standing beside a man who lay motionless on the ground. The woman was flapping her arms and shrieking incoherently, staring down at the prone figure in white-faced horror. Two St John ambulance workers materialised as if from nowhere, racing towards the body. One of them knelt down and felt for a pulse. For a few seconds no one spoke, then she rose to her feet and shrugged.

'He's blind drunk.' She turned to a festival official. 'It's just some sozzled idiot giving everyone a fright. Nothing to worry about.'

Chapter Three

'CHARLES, FOR CHRIST'S sake, we've been over it all before and you agreed to come with me this weekend. It's been in the calendar for weeks. You can't back out now.'

Charles glanced sideways at his wife. 'There's nothing I can do about it, there's no way . . .'

He broke off in mid-sentence as he glimpsed a bloody victim of a hit and run sprawled on the pavement in a side street.

'Charles, you're coming with me and that's that. It's in the calendar.'

She paused, noticing his frown. The car behind hooted as Charles pulled into the side of the road. A few other drivers beeped their horns. One of them wound down his window to shout abuse as he drove past.

'Charles! What the hell are you doing? You can't stop here!'

'Stay in the car!'

Ignoring his wife's shrill protest, he jumped out of the car, slammed his door and dashed back to the side street where he had seen the body. Phone in hand, he turned to check Sharon hadn't followed him. Accustomed to viewing cadavers, he could see straight away that something was seriously amiss. Whatever had happened to her, this girl had not been hit by a car. Just as he got through to the emergency services, Sharon appeared on the corner, yelling at him. He waved at her to stay back, talking quickly into the phone all the while.

'Yes, a woman's body. What?' He listened to the question, still gesticulating furiously at Sharon to stay away. 'Yes, she's definitely dead. In Cambridge Street, near the corner of Holgate Road. What's that?' He gave his name and occupation, registering how the speaker's tone altered as soon as she heard he was a surgeon. 'Look, this isn't a pretty sight,' he went on. 'You need to get a team here straight away to cordon the area off. It's . . . well, it's bloody. She's been hacked to death.' He listened, before repeating carefully, 'Yes, hacked to death, with a large, heavy blade of some kind, a carving knife or a cleaver, something sharp and heavy, I'd say, although that's just an initial impression. Her head's been split open with what looks like a single blow.'

He listened again but before he could respond, the wail of a siren cut across the hum of traffic. At the same time, someone screamed. Turning, he saw Sharon, white-faced, her eyes stretched wide, her mouth gaping.

'I told you to stay in the car!' he snapped.

Judging by the reactions of the two police officers who arrived, it was fortunate Charles had been first on the scene.

'I'm sorry,' one of the young constables muttered, wiping his mouth. 'I just wasn't expecting this.' He glanced at the bloody corpse and winced, his eyes sliding rapidly away again.

Charles nodded. Although his scrutiny of the body had been purely clinical, he could appreciate it was an unpleasant sight.

With one blow the killer had cracked the woman's skull open. Seeping from the gash in her forehead, bloody brain tissue had covered the top half of her face in a macabre eye mask. As far as he could tell, the dead woman had been young, little more than a girl. She was lying on her back, dressed in a short black skirt and denim jacket, the latter streaked with dried blood. One of her shoes had fallen off and was lying nearby in the gutter. He noted mechanically how small her feet were, a hole in her tights exposing a turquoise toenail. Behind him someone groaned. He turned and saw Sharon, propped up against the wall, still vomiting.

'I told you to stay in the car,' he repeated wearily.

Time seemed to slow down while they stood around waiting for someone in authority to arrive and start issuing commands. Just as Charles decided he would have to take charge of the situation himself, a convoy of police cars drew up, sirens blaring, and the street became hectic with activity. People were talking rapidly on phones, a cordon appeared as if from nowhere, and a line of uniformed officers ushered away a crowd of onlookers who seemed to have sprung from the pavement.

Charles approached a portly middle-aged sergeant. 'I need to get to work.'

The policeman shook his head. 'We need you to stay here, sir.'

Tersely, Charles explained who he was, and that he needed to get to the hospital where he had patients waiting. With a nod the sergeant made a note of his contact details and let him go.

'Come on,' Charles said, taking Sharon by the hand. 'Let's get you home. You're in no fit state to go to work.'

Hand in hand they walked slowly back to the car.

'I wonder who she was.'

'It makes no difference to her now. Try to put it out of your head.'

'It'll make a difference to anyone who knew her. She was murdered, wasn't she?'

'It certainly looks that way. But I don't suppose she would have known anything about it,' he added untruthfully.

She must have seen the blade descending; an instant of terror before it cracked her skull and sliced through her brain.

'What about her family?' Sharon was asking tearfully.

'There's no point in upsetting yourself. The police are there. They'll take care of everything. That's their job. There's absolutely nothing we can do about it. Now come on.'

'I suppose we'll hear all about it in the news.'

'I daresay.' He opened his car door.

'Well I hope they catch the sick bastard who did that to her,' Sharon said, sniffing and wiping her eyes, careless of her smudged mascara.

Charles nodded, surprised at feeling faintly nauseous now he was no longer responsible for what happened to the dead girl. Accustomed to working in an operating theatre, even he had been shocked by the horrific sight of a girl who had been so brutally assaulted on the street.

Chapter Four

Back at his desk, Ian was contemplating going home to see Bev when his phone rang. As soon as he hung up there was a knock on his door. It was Ted.

'Ready?'

Ian nodded and they hurried out to the car park without speaking. Ian was pleased to be working with the young sergeant. Not only was Ted efficient and easy to get along with, but he had lived in York all his life. He drove them straight to the address they had been given. Ian sat in the passenger seat experiencing a familiar adrenaline rush mingled with anxiety. Many of his colleagues appeared genuinely unmoved by crime scenes, however bloody. Ian could understand why they were eager to study a victim at the scene of a crime. Viewing a body before it was moved could assist them to ascertain what had happened. The trouble was he had not yet managed to conquer the nausea he felt on seeing a dead body. The only part of the job he dreaded even more than that was speaking to the bereaved.

The body had not yet been taken to the mortuary. Pulling on protective gear, they entered the white forensic tent which had been erected on the pavement near the corner of Holgate Street. If he and Bev had children, he couldn't imagine ever taking them camping. He had seen too many murder victims to enter a tent without experiencing a visceral horror.

'What do we know?' Ian asked, staring at a scene of crime officer to put off looking directly at the corpse.

His white-coated colleague shrugged. 'She was young, female, white; some nutter sliced vertically through the top of her head.'

'Was she carrying any ID?'

She pointed out another white-coated officer who was delicately rummaging through a blue-and-white canvas shoulder bag. As Ian approached he saw that the bag and its contents were stained with blood. Bracing himself, he turned to study the dead girl. The woolly texture of her badly bleached hair contrasted pathetically with the healthy sheen on Bev's blonde hair. Dismissing the comparison with his wife, Ian focussed on the corpse for a moment, before addressing the officer who was holding the woman's bag.

'What have you got?'

'Her name is Angela Jones, sixteen years old.' He held out a student card, the edges stained with blood. 'There's another card, but . . .' He shrugged and held out what looked like a travel card, too badly soiled to be legible.

'Sixteen,' Ian repeated glumly.

'Sixteen last month.'

'Anything else in her purse?'

'A fiver. That's all.'

'No change?'

'No coins.'

Ian forced himself to turn and look at the girl's face. From what he could see she was pretty, with full lips and a button nose. If he squinted until her features were out of focus, she appeared to be wearing sunglasses, because her eyes were concealed behind a mask of dried blood. From the small image on her student card he knew they were dark and assumed she was naturally brunette, as her hair was so obviously bleached.

'Is there a death certificate?'

'Yes. That was a stroke of luck. A doctor was first on the scene.'

'Is he still here?'

'He had to get off to the hospital.'

'Damn. What time did he get here?'

'He reported it at seven fifteen.'

'Out and about early.'

The death certificate wouldn't reveal anything Ian couldn't see for himself: the girl's head had been split open by a violent blow with a large blade. He didn't need a doctor to tell him that death must have been instantaneous. That was some solace.

'Who would do that?' Ted asked, dark eyes solemn behind his mask. 'She's little more than a child.'

'I've no idea,' Ian replied grimly, 'but whoever did it, we'll find them. And that's a promise.'

He was no longer speaking to his colleague. He was speaking to a young girl with dyed blonde hair; a girl who could no longer hear him.

Chapter Five

'ARE YOU GOING to wake her up then?'

'No. Let her sleep.'

'What time did she get in last night?'

'I don't know. I didn't hear her come in.'

Moira put two mugs of tea on the table and sat down opposite her husband. They ate their breakfast in silence: tea, toast and marmalade, the same as every morning. Neither of them spoke. It wasn't the first time they had disagreed about Angela. Moira watched Frank's scowl, waiting for him to calm down, but once he had finished his breakfast he started up again, his pointed beard shaking with every emphatic word he uttered.

'You let that child run wild.'

It was a familiar argument.

'She's not a child, Frank, she's an adult, and she's not running wild. She works hard.'

He snorted. 'She's barely sixteen. That's not an adult. And she certainly doesn't behave like one, out God knows where to all hours, getting up to God knows what behind our backs. It's time she got herself a job.'

'They all stay on at school these days. Would you rather she stopped studying?'

'I'd rather she stopped running around, wasting her time with that wild crowd. What kind of studying is she doing? She'd be much better off going and getting a proper job. One that pays good money. She should at least get herself a Saturday job if she must stay at school.'

'Where's she going to get a job? You know as well as I do there's no work for the youngsters these days.'

'So you're happy to see her pay good money for other people to fill her head with all sorts of nonsense that's never going to get her a proper job?'

'She's trying to better herself, Frank. Would you rather she spent her life cutting hair?'

Frank lowered his heavy eyebrows. His bald head gleamed under the kitchen light.

'It's hardly bettering herself, haring around with other young idiots, all of them getting drunk and getting into debt. And there's nothing wrong with hairdressing. It was good enough for you. I never heard you complaining. There will always be plenty of women stupid enough to pay other women to cut their hair for them instead of picking up a pair of scissors for themselves.'

Moira stood up and began to clear away the plates. 'These days they all need degrees to get jobs.'

'I'd agree with you if she was prepared to do something proper, but a degree in media studies? Don't make me laugh. That's never going to pay the bills, is it? So, are you going to let her sleep all morning?'

Moira waited until Frank went out before she trudged upstairs. It was nearly midday and Angela still hadn't stirred. She seemed happy to lie in bed until all hours at the weekend – and sometimes during the week too, even in term time. It irked Moira as much as Frank, but she would never admit that to her husband. It might have been different if Angela had been his daughter. As it was, Moira couldn't help leaping to her daughter's defence whenever Frank criticised the girl, which happened with increasing frequency. It had become an ongoing source of conflict between them. She knocked on Angela's door and waited, but there was no response. The girl must still be asleep. Really, Frank was right. The way Angela was carrying on was unacceptable. She rapped on the door again, more loudly this time. There was still no reply. Gingerly she turned the handle. Angela would probably scream at her for entering without permission, but, as Frank never tired of pointing out, whose house was it? Moira was entitled to open a door in her own home.

'While you're sleeping in my house, you follow my rules,' he had bellowed at Angela.

'It's not your house,' she had retorted.

That was true, strictly speaking, but pointing that out had done nothing to calm his temper.

'You watch your mouth!'

Moira hated the way they argued. She and Frank squabbled, and he could turn quite nasty, but he had never raised his hand against her. Frank's hostility towards Angela seemed to hold a different sort of menace. Angela wasn't blameless either. She seemed to enjoy goading Frank.

'What you going to do?' she had taunted him only the day before. 'You going to hit me?'

'If you were five years younger, I'd put you over my knee, so help me,' he had fumed, his huge fists clenched at his sides.

Moira peered inside her daughter's bedroom. It was a tip; clothes and underwear spread around the floor in garish disarray, along with brushes, combs, hair ornaments, cheap jewellery, tubes of make-up, shoes and the occasional magazine in which perfectly groomed models stared icily from glossy pages, their hair impossibly sleek. In the middle of the chaos, Angela's bed was empty. Moira frowned. She hadn't heard her daughter go out that morning. She wondered uneasily what Frank would do if he discovered his stepdaughter had stayed out all night without even bothering to phone home to inform her mother where she was. He would call her selfish, and thoughtless, and irresponsible, and a common little slut. There would be more rows. Taking everything into account, Moira wondered whether it would be better to cover up for her daughter. Again.

Hearing the front door slam, she ran to the stairs. If Angela was home before Frank, he would never need to find out that she hadn't come home the previous night. This time, Moira was going to speak very sharply to her daughter and tell her in no uncertain terms that her behaviour was unacceptable. She ran downstairs, but Frank was in the hall. There was no sign of Angela.

'Well?' he accosted her. She could tell he was wound up. 'Have you spoken to her yet, or do you want me to do it? I've been thinking; we need to lay down some ground rules. I want her home by ten every night, and up in the morning before nine at the weekends. That's late enough. She might not like it, but this is our house, and we make the rules. Where is she? I'm going to speak to her right now.'

Moira stepped forward.

'You can't.'

'Don't tell me who I can and can't speak to in my own house!'

'I mean, you can't speak to her right now because . . . because she's not here.'

'She's gone out again?'

'Yes, that is, no.'

'What do you mean, yes, no? Moira, what are you talking about?'

'She didn't come home last night.'

Her relief at telling him the truth was short-lived. Even though she was expecting a reaction, his violent outburst startled her.

'That's it!' he yelled, red-faced. 'Enough! She has to go!'

Seeing her tears, he went on more gently. 'You must see we can't go on like this. It's no good for anyone. It's time we had words with her.'

'Words?'

'Tell her she has to leave, find somewhere else to live.'

'No! Frank, you can't do that. She's my daughter.'

'Well, she doesn't behave like a daughter. She's no good, Moira. Getting up late is one thing, but this . . .' He pulled a face. 'Staying out all night! She did it deliberately to spite us. We can't carry on like this . . .'

He was interrupted by the doorbell.

'Right!' He turned to the door. 'Leave this to me!'

'No, Frank, she's my daughter. I'll speak to her.'

The doorbell rang again. Frank flung the door open. A man was standing on the doorstep. Towering over Frank, he held up an identity card.

'May I come in?'

'Oh shit, now she's got herself in trouble with the police. I knew this would happen,' Frank growled. 'Look, officer, Angela's not a bad girl. She's just fallen in with the wrong crowd. She's only sixteen. Whatever it is, we'll sort it out with her. We were just saying we need to keep a closer eye on her, weren't we, Moira?'

'May I come in?' the detective repeated.

Chapter Six

THE DETECTIVE CHIEF inspector gazed sternly round the room and the assembled team fell silent under her gaze. Eileen Duncan was a thickset middle-aged woman, with a square chin and a determined air. Although he was wary of working with such a forceful woman, Ian had to acknowledge that she achieved results. Her gaze lingered on him in silent acknowledgement of his presence.

'What have we got?' she asked.

With a nod, Ian stepped forward. He wished he was better prepared to brief the team.

'The body of Angela Jones was found just after seven thirty this morning by a hospital surgeon, Mr Charles Everleigh. His wife was with him. They were on their way to work. He was going to drop his wife at the station on his way to the hospital. She works in Leeds. We haven't got the post mortem report yet but the victim appears to have died from a head wound caused by a single slash with a sharp weapon, a cleaver or a large knife of some description. Hence all the blood,' he added, turning to glance briefly at the image on the screen behind him.

'She looks very young,' someone commented.

'Only just sixteen,' Ian confirmed. He paused while a faint sigh whispered around his assembled colleagues. 'The doctor at the scene placed the time of death at between ten thirty and eleven thirty on Sunday night.'

'Just sixteen,' Eileen repeated loudly. She sounded angry. 'And no one noticed she hadn't come home last night.'

Ian wondered if Eileen had a daughter. She wore a plain gold band on her wedding finger, but it was hard to imagine her as a mother. She seemed too fierce to have cared for children, although he realised she must behave differently away from work.

Ian nodded. 'Mother and stepfather didn't notice her absence until this morning. They thought she must have come in after they went to bed at around ten thirty. Mother said she would have waited up but the stepfather refused to allow it. He seems to be very much in charge in the relationship, although possibly less able to control his teenage stepdaughter.'

'Angela Jones wasn't his own daughter,' Eileen commented thoughtfully.

'But she was his stepdaughter,' Ian replied. 'She lived with them.'

'What do we know about the weapon?' Eileen asked, turning back to the evidence.

'Well, not a lot as yet, only it must have been pretty heavy and sharp to slice through her skull.'

'And presumably whoever was wielding it was strong,' Eileen added. 'Oh well, let's not speculate about that for now. We'll know more when we get the result of the post mortem, and hear from forensics.'

After writing up his report, Ian set off to speak to Charles Everleigh. Conveniently for Ian, he worked in the hospital where the mortuary was located. Charles was in theatre, so Ian went straight to the mortuary where he was pleased to see Avril, the cheerful young anatomical pathology technician he had met while he was working on a previous case.

'Hi, Ian,' she greeted him with a ready smile. 'How's things? And how's your wife?'

'She's OK,' he answered vaguely.

It occurred to him that he had no idea about Avril's relationship status. So much for being a detective. She wasn't wearing a ring, but that didn't necessarily mean anything.

'I suppose you're here to see Jonah,' she went on.

He nodded, mentally bracing himself to view Angela's cadaver again.

Avril pulled a mock sad face. 'And there I was, thinking my luck was finally in and you'd come here just for me. Oh well, your loss.'

Ian grinned and followed her into the mortuary where the local home office pathologist was examining the body. Jonah Hetherington was a plump man in his forties. He had pale freckled skin and ginger hair. For someone with such a grim job, he was unremittingly cheerful.

'She's young,' Jonah said, plunging in straight away.

'Yes, I know. Just sixteen.'

'Like the song.' Jonah broke into song in a pleasant tenor voice, beating time with a bloody gloved hand, 'She was just sixteen, and you know what I mean.'

Catching sight of Ian's expression he broke off, with a mischievous grin. Ian couldn't help smiling.

'Right,' Jonah went on in a business-like tone. 'Time of death around eleven on Sunday night. She was killed with one single blow which cracked her skull open like . . . well, cracking it in two. She would have died instantaneously. Her attacker was standing in front of her when he struck, so she may well have seen him. There's no knowing.' He paused, contemplating the dead white face, split open almost as far down as the eyes.

'He?'

'What?'

'You said "he".'

'Did I?'

'Does that mean you think the killer was a man?'

Jonah shook his head. 'To be honest, I'm not sure if we're looking for a man or a woman,' he replied.

'You said "he",' Ian reminded him. 'What gave you the impression it was a man who did this?'

Again, Jonah hesitated. 'Did I say "he"?' he asked. 'I think what I was thinking was that the killer hit her pretty hard, that's all, so it seems more likely she was killed by a man.'

'But it's only an impression?'

'Indeed,' Jonah confirmed. 'At this stage, there's no knowing the gender of the killer, or anything else for that matter. Rest assured, Ian, we're doing everything we can to winkle out more information from her.'

'Is it possible to at least estimate the height of her assailant from the angle of the blow?'

Jonah shook his head. 'If only I could. To answer with any certainty, I'd need to know his arm length, and whether he was standing on anything when he hit her. It seems unlikely, to be honest. My guess is he was an average-sized bloke, quite strong. But that is pure guesswork, and not very helpful to you.'

'What about the murder weapon?'

Jonah frowned. 'A clean cut with a straight, sharp blade. It looks like a very wide knife, something like an axe blade.'

'An axe? Keep that quiet for now, will you?'

Jonah nodded. He understood why Ian wouldn't want the media getting hold of that sensational possibility.

'It was a particularly violent attack,' Jonah went on, 'but I wonder if it mightn't have been a mugging that went spectacularly wrong.'

'What makes you say that?'

Jonah picked up one of the dead girl's hands, spreading the fingers out. Looking closely, Ian could see what he was pointing out. Three fingers on her right hand bore indentations from wearing rings. He saw the same marks on two fingers on her left hand. The skin on one finger had been scraped, as though a ring had been forcibly removed.

'And this,' Jonah added.

He indicated a fine weal on the side of her neck. 'It looks as though she was wearing a chain that was roughly pulled off. This scratch was inflicted after she was dead.'

'Anything else?'

'No, except that this was a particularly violent attack.'

Chapter Seven

SEEING THE TIME, Ian cursed under his breath and rolled wearily out of bed. He had overslept after a late night. Having upset his wife by going into work the previous day, he had gone home in the evening to argue with her and make up, finally taking her out for dinner by way of an apology. After an emotionally disturbing day at work he hadn't felt like going out, but he had felt he owed it to his wife to try and cheer her up. Bev was still snoring gently as he got up. He dressed without opening the bedroom curtains and slipped quietly out of the house. Grabbing a coffee and a roll from the canteen, he went straight to his desk. Uninterrupted, he enjoyed a quiet moment to himself as he ate his modest breakfast. The tranquillity didn't last long. There was a gentle tap, and Ted poked his head round the door.

'Morning, sir.'

'Hi, Ted. Well, you might as well come in now you're here. What is it?'

Although he was a Yorkshire man, born and bred, the young sergeant's dark colouring gave him a Mediterranean appearance.

Shorter than Ian, he was muscular and energetic. With a single-minded focus on the job, he was nevertheless easy to get along with, and Ian was really pleased to be working with him again. He smiled encouragingly at the young sergeant and repeated his question.

'Am I interrupting?' Ted asked, with a nod at Ian's breakfast which was now just a few crumbs on a paper serviette.

'No, no, I was just finishing.' Ian rolled up the serviette and tossed it, just missing the bin. 'Come on in.'

'Crap shot,' Ted said, picking up the ball of paper and dropping it in the bin. 'I just came to see if you'd read the post mortem report.'

'When did that arrive?'

'About half an hour ago.'

'Tox report?'

'Not in yet.'

'Pull up a chair.'

Side by side, they studied the screen. Jonah suggested the force of the attack indicated the killer was male, although he was careful to point out that his findings didn't rule out a female assailant.

'Great that he was able to reach such a definite conclusion about the killer's gender,' Ted said. 'That really helps.'

Ian didn't comment on his colleague's sarcasm. They both understood the pathologist needed to cover himself. The killer had been careful to avoid direct contact with the victim, so had left no discernible DNA traces on the body. Attacking his victim in the street had been risky but although the killer could have been seen, it was impossible to find any obvious trace of his identity in such a public location. The street had given them no clues to his identity, and the post mortem was no help either.

Jonah's conclusion about the murder weapon was more specific. In some ways this was the most disturbing aspect of the
whole report, although it gave the police very little to go on. The
girl had been fatally wounded by a metal blade fifteen centime-
tres in length, with a razor-thin slightly curved edge. Indentations
on one side of the wound made when the blade had been with-
drawn suggested it was not completely smooth. The pathologist
suggested that an edge of hardened steel had been welded on to a
wide metal blade, resembling an axe head.

'Do you think it was sharpened specially?' Ted asked in a low
voice.

Ian didn't answer.

'It sliced right through her skull,' the sergeant went on.

'He says it resembled an axe head. Maybe it *was* an axe?' Ian
said.

Ted grunted. 'I don't see many people going around wielding
axes these days.'

'Do you see many people going around slicing other people's
heads open?'

'People's heads? Do you think there might be more than one
victim?'

'It was just a figure of speech. But I think it's possible he might
kill again. He's killed once. I don't know why, but I've got a bad
feeling about all this.'

'I don't think it would make anyone feel good.'

While they were waiting for the toxicology report, they took
a break.

'It's an odd way to kill someone,' Ted remarked when they were
seated in the canteen.

'Unusual but effective. Was this an attack carried out in anger? It was violent. But then again, who carries a weapon like that around with them? It might suggest a certain element of premeditation. I suppose Eileen's going to bring in a profiler.'

'That's a good thing, isn't it?' Ted asked.

'Depends who the profiler is. But we're going to need to throw everything at this one, that's for sure.'

'You're right there. This killer's completely crazy. But then aren't they all? Murder isn't exactly what you might call sane.'

'You can't imagine ever being provoked into a murderous attack on someone else?' Ian asked.

'No.'

'What if some deranged stranger was threatening the life of your girlfriend, or your mother?'

'That's different. Self-defence doesn't count. I'm talking about unprovoked attacks.'

The tox report came in soon after Ian had returned to his desk. He summoned Ted and they read through it together. Angela had been drinking cider during the evening. Although her intake hadn't been excessive, she had been over the alcohol limit. She had eaten nothing but crisps since lunchtime, and had been smoking cannabis shortly before she died. Jonah concluded that she would have been tipsy and slightly high, but she was unlikely to have been out of control. She had been walking home alone, presumably after socialising on the evening she was killed.

'We need to find out where she was, and who she was with,' Ian said.

If her parents couldn't give them names and details for her friends, they would go through all the contacts and calls to and from her phone. With luck, they would find a message giving them her arrangements for the evening she was killed, and the murder would turn out to have been personal, enabling them to wind up the investigation promptly.

'Let's hope it was someone she knew,' Ted said.

They exchanged an anxious look.

Chapter Eight

ANGELA'S PARENTS WEREN'T much help. Her mother cried, her stepfather blustered, and neither of them had anything useful to tell Ian.

'We thought she'd come home,' Moira wailed. 'She came home late sometimes. But she always came home. She always came home.'

'Have either of you remembered anything she said about where she went on Sunday evening?'

Frank answered gruffly. 'She never told us anything.'

'That's not true. She talked to me. She always talked to me.'

'Much good that did,' Frank muttered. 'So where did she go?'

'I don't know,' Moira sobbed, 'I don't know.'

Ian understood that Angela's stepfather was in shock. It was unfortunate that he expressed his grief as anger, but his wife didn't appear to be upset by his brusqueness. She was probably too far gone to pay him much attention, but Ian couldn't help wondering if such aggression was commonplace, and if so, whether it raised a question about the nature of Frank's relationship with his stepdaughter. As though to compensate for his baldness, Frank had a dark beard and heavy eyebrows. There was something unpleasantly virile about him, a kind of aggression that hinted at a capacity for violence. But Ian appreciated that could have been a response to the situation, a knee-jerk reaction to protect his distressed wife. In any case, there was no evidence to suggest he might have a violent temper. That was merely the impression he gave.

Ian approached the question of relations between Frank and Angela with circumspection.

'Would you describe Angela as difficult?'

Frank shrugged. 'She was a teenager.'

'She wasn't difficult,' Moira burst out. 'She was a happy girl. She was always happy.'

'The thing is, Inspector,' Frank interrupted his wife, 'she wasn't mine. Not my daughter. You could say our relationship was fraught at times, but no more than normal. She was a teenager. I'm not used to dealing with girls her age. I mean, she seemed calm enough when Moira and I started seeing each other, but that was six years ago. Kids change. If I'd known . . .' He broke off, and put his arm round his wife. 'There, there,' he said awkwardly. 'Don't cry.'

Ian hoped he wasn't going to tell her everything would be all right, but he wasn't that insensitive, just gauche. He patted his wife on the shoulder reassuringly. 'There, there.'

Ian spoke as gently as he could. This was a delicate matter.

'Can you remember if Angela was wearing any jewellery when she went out? Any rings, perhaps?'

'She always wore my mother's wedding ring,' Moira said. 'We had it resized for her after my mother died. They were very close. Please tell me it wasn't taken . . .' She broke off, and hid her face in her hands.

'I'm afraid so.'

Behind her hands, Moira sobbed loudly.

'Try not to upset yourself,' Frank urged her. 'This might be a good thing. It could help to find her killer, couldn't it, Inspector? Someone might try to sell the ring. Describe it, Moira. What was it like?'

Moira let her hands fall to her sides and drew in a deep shuddering breath. 'Oh you know, it was an old wedding ring. Just a plain gold band, not very wide. It wasn't much, but it had sentimental value. She never took it off.'

'Did it have any identifying features at all? Anything you might recognise?'

'It was just a plain gold ring, a bit the worse for wear.'

'Was she wearing any other jewellery when she went out?'

Moira sighed. 'She liked to wear lots of rings. They were worthless. The only one that had any value at all was the one my mother gave her. She usually had one on every finger. Even on her thumbs.' She smiled fleetingly, remembering. 'Only my mother's was real gold. Mainly they were silver ones she bought herself.'

'Did anyone else ever buy her a ring?'

'You mean did she have a boyfriend? No, no one special.'

'Not that we knew about,' Frank added.

'Oh Frank, stop that. She would have told me.'

Frank glowered but didn't say anything.

'Could you take a look at her jewellery and see if you can tell if anything's missing?'

Moira nodded and went upstairs.

'Do you think this was all about her trinkets?' Frank asked while his wife was out of the room. 'You think she was mugged and killed for a few cheap rings?'

Ian sighed. 'I'm afraid all I can say is that she wasn't wearing any jewellery when she was found.'

'But you could track her killer through her stolen jewellery, couldn't you?'

Moira returned before Ian could reply. She reported a pendant on a silver chain missing from her daughter's jewellery box, along with one gold ring and a handful of silver ones. As far as she was aware, everything else was there.

She described the pendant, and Ian made a note of the details.

'It's nothing much,' she said wretchedly. 'She didn't have much.'

Neither Moira nor Frank had any idea who Angela had gone out with on the night she died, although Moira mentioned a school friend called Zoe. Angela's phone was more useful. Having tasked a constable with looking into Frank Carter's history, Ian set to work studying the list of calls Angela had made and received before she died. He didn't have to go back very far. There were only two telephone calls, both incoming, both from her home address. She hadn't answered either call. He contacted her parents straight away and asked to speak to Moira.

'Did you phone Angela on her last evening? At half past ten and again at eleven?'

Moira was vague. 'I don't know, I may have done. I usually did call her when she was out, when it was getting late, just to remind her she should be getting home. She never answered her phone. Not to me, at any rate.' She gave a faintly hysterical laugh.

'Could your husband have called her?'

'I don't think so. He never did.'

Frank confirmed that he hadn't called Angela on the evening she was killed. Ian didn't rule out the possibility that Frank was lying to his wife and to the police. The history of texts on Angela's phone was even more revealing. Several messages had been written on the day she was killed, the last one sent only two hours before her death. It was just one word, the name of a pub in Micklegate that was popular with young people. Now they knew where Angela might have been drinking that night, Ian set up immediate surveillance of all CCTV cameras in the area, hoping to trace the victim's journey from Micklegate to Cambridge Street where she was killed. With luck they might be able to catch a clear shot of her killer.

'Go back just over two hours to begin with,' he told the sergeant heading up the team of Visual Images Identifications and Detections Officers.

Watching CCTV was a skilled job, requiring an ability to remain alert for long periods of time. Solving the case might depend on someone spotting one fleeting frame in a blurred film. It could be missed in the blink of an eye.

'You might need to go back earlier to find her arriving at the pub. We need to know the time she got there, and see if you can capture images of any companions arriving with her. And then we need to know exactly where she went when she left, and who she left with, and if she met anyone . . .'

The sergeant nodded impatiently. He didn't need Ian to tell him what was required, and why.

'OK,' Ian said, catching his colleague's expression, 'you know what to do.'

'Yes, sir.'

Ian turned to his next task, going through the list of people with whom Angela had recently been in contact. Nearly twenty texts had been sent and received on the day she died. Most were to the friend Moira had mentioned, Zoe Drayton. Ian studied their exchange. It began with a message from Angela, sent at half past two in the afternoon.

'Sassy wot u doin'

'fa'

'wot you doin later'

'later???'

'later'

'wot'

'wots going on'

'wot'

'WOT U DOIN LATER – TELL ME'

'wot u doin'

'wot you doin'

The messages stopped for a few hours. Soon after five o'clock they started up again. This time Zoe initiated the exchange.

'wot you doin'

'nothin'

'mgate'

'OK mgate'

'OK'

'c u'

There was nothing more until at nine fifteen when Angela contacted a boy she called Gary. Her text said: 'mgate'

Ten minutes later she sent him a second text, with a third one soon after. All contained an identical message: 'mgate'

That was the last time she had used her phone. Gary hadn't replied, perhaps because he had answered her summons in person. Ian decided to go and see him, before speaking to Zoe.

Chapter Nine

BARELY EIGHTEEN, GARY FARR was gangly and ungainly, his face blighted with acne. It was hard to believe any girl would be interested in him. He sat on the sofa in his parents' front room, shoulders hunched, hands between his knees, looking thoroughly dejected. Angela was too good-looking to have any problem finding a boyfriend, yet she had texted him three times in ten minutes, wanting him to join her at a pub in Micklegate. It didn't take a genius to work out the reason for the summons. Gary might be unattractive, but at eighteen he would be served alcohol in any bar.

In response to Ian's demand, Gary held out his ID. Seeing the boy's hand trembling, Ian set out to intimidate him in the hope that fear would loosen his tongue.

'When did you last buy alcohol for your underage friends? There's no point trying to deny what you did. I know all about it.'

Gary bit his lip. He was too scared to answer.

'Gary, you could be in very serious trouble over this, but there's no need for it to go any further. No one else knows about it yet.

All you have to do is give me some information, and we'll say no more about it.'

The boy mumbled something about all his friends being at least eighteen. He sounded close to tears. The boy was more frightened than Ian had realised. There was no point in terrifying him into incoherence.

'Gary, I'm investigating a murder. So believe me, I'm not in the slightest bit interested in whether or not you bought alcohol for your sixteen-year-old friends. You must know it's against the law for an adult to buy alcohol on behalf of someone under 18. And you must have known your friends were underage. I'm prepared to overlook it and you'll hear no more about it. That's a promise. But I can only let you off if you cooperate with me. Otherwise, you'll have to answer for your actions as best you can, and you'll be on your own. Once I report what you did, there'll be no going back. You'll be prosecuted . . .'

'No, no, I didn't know . . .'

'Will you help me?'

Gary nodded his head fervently. 'I do want to help, I do,' he babbled nervously. 'What's it about? What's happened? Who's been murdered? What's it got to do with me?'

Ian watched him closely. 'I'm investigating the murder of Angela Jones.'

The boy's acne showed bright against his sudden pallor.

'Angela?'

'When was the last time you saw her?'

'Angela's dead?'

'Yes, I'm sorry.'

'Oh my God, I can't believe it. Angela?'

'Gary, you need to answer my question. When was the last time you saw her?'

'On Sunday night. We were out together. It wasn't just us,' he added quickly, 'it was all of us; that is, a group of us, we went out, just for a drink.'

'Tell me everything you can remember about Sunday evening, every detail, however unimportant it might seem. What happened?'

Gary frowned. 'Nothing happened. We went for a drink, that's all.'

Bit by bit, Ian winkled information from the scared boy. Angela had texted him on Sunday evening to let him know she was in a pub along Micklegate with some friends. With a little pressure, Gary gave Ian all the names. The list included Zoe. Gary couldn't remember her second name. Ian told him.

'Yes, that's right, Zoe Drayton.'

Gary glanced anxiously at Ian. It did no harm to let him believe Ian knew more than he did. If Gary thought Ian knew about Angela's friends, he would be less likely to lie about them. The boy's account of the evening sounded plausible, and innocent enough. He admitted Angela had summoned him so he could buy her and Zoe a drink, insisting this was the first time he had done it. Ian didn't believe that for a moment. It was pretty obvious when the boy was lying. His face flushed pink, and his eyes darted around frantically.

'It wasn't just one drink, was it? Don't lie to me, Gary.'

The boy shook his head. 'They had a pint of cider each, and then I told them that was enough. They were getting too loud, and people were starting to look at us. I didn't want to get in trouble for getting them drunk. I was doing them a favour, and they never thanked me for it. Not once. Like I was some sort of – I don't know – like a bloody waiter or something.'

Noting a flash of anger in the boy's voice, Ian darted in with a question.

'Which one did you fancy? Oh come on, Gary, no young man buys drinks all night for two girls unless he's after getting his leg over.'

'No, it wasn't like that. We were just friends.'

'You don't really expect me to believe that?'

'But it's true! And I didn't buy the drinks. I mean, I did, I went up to the bar, but they gave me the money.'

Ian remembered a comment he had heard in the forensic tent. It had troubled him at the time.

'What did you do with the change?'

'What do you mean?'

'It's a simple question. They can't have given you the exact money for what they had. What did you do with the change?'

'I gave it to them with their drinks. You don't think I'd want to rip my friends off, do you?'

'Did you give Angela any change?'

'Of course I did.'

'How much?'

'What?'

'Did she give you change or a note to begin with?'

Gary screwed up his face, thinking.

'This is important, Gary.'

'She gave me a note.'

'Are you sure?'

He nodded.

'How much was it? Five? Ten?'

'I don't know. Ten. Yes, it was a tenner. She waved it around like she was made of money.'

'Just to be clear, you bought Angela a pint of cider on Sunday evening with her ten-quid note and you gave her the change?'

'Yes.'

'Was the change all in coins?'

'No. There was a fiver and the rest in change. I remember because I gave the fiver to Zoe by mistake, and she'd given me a fiver in the first place.' He blushed at the memory.

'Did Angela buy anything else? Any more drinks?'

'No.' He blushed again.

'How about crisps or nuts? Anything?'

'No.'

'So it was just the one pint she drank?'

'Yes.'

'So when she left the pub, Angela had drunk a pint of cider, and she had a fiver and a few quid's worth of change in her purse?'

'Yes. I suppose so.'

He shrugged and muttered crossly about not being a bloody accountant. Ian watched him. Gary didn't appear to be lying. Angela had been found with no coins in her purse, only a five pound note. Somewhere between leaving the pub and being discovered, dead, she had lost her change but not her five pound note. It was a bit odd. He wondered if she had given her change away to someone begging on the street. Ian needed to know about any contact she had made with another person that evening.

'Are you sure you gave Angela and her friends any change they were due?'

'Yes, I'm sure. I told you. I always gave them their change.'

'So this wasn't the first time you'd bought alcohol for Angela and Zoe?'

Recovered from his fear, and his shock, Gary had gathered his wits and refused to answer. 'I won't say anything else until I have a lawyer.'

Ian smiled. 'You're not under arrest, Gary. You're not even really under suspicion. Not yet, at any rate. Should you be?'

Chapter Ten

IF ANYTHING, ZOE was even more jittery than Gary had been when Ian turned up at her home asking to speak to her. He went round there after school, careful to take a sympathetic young female colleague with him. Realistically, Angela's friend might be more likely to confide in Detective Constable Naomi Arthur than in him. Mrs Drayton wanted to be present while her daughter was speaking to the police, but Ian wasn't convinced Zoe would be honest about her visit to the pub in front of her mother. He was right. As soon as he explained that he wanted to speak to her about her whereabouts on Sunday evening, she turned to her mother.

'Just go, mum. It's fine, really. You don't need to be here.'

'Don't worry, I won't leave the room,' Naomi added, as though Zoe might somehow be at risk on her own with Ian.

With a worried scowl, Mrs Drayton left. Turning to Ian with large hazel eyes, her skinny hands clasped in her lap, Zoe looked like a trapped rabbit.

'I'd like you to tell me about your evening on Sunday, with Angela,' he said.

'What's happened to Angela? Something's happened to her, hasn't it? That's why she wasn't at school today.' She looked close to tears. 'Something's happened to her, hasn't it?'

'What makes you say that?'

'It has, hasn't it? Why else would you be here?'

Gently Ian explained that Angela had been attacked on her way home on Sunday. He asked if she had left the pub alone.

'Oh my God, is she all right? Where is she? I want to see her. I want to see her right now!'

'I'm afraid that's not possible, Zoe,' Naomi said, leaning forward before Ian could respond, her voice soothing. 'You're going to have to be very brave now. I'm sorry to say Angela died as a result of the attack. She didn't suffer any pain because she died straight away. She wouldn't have known anything about it. But it's very important we find out what happened that night, and who did this terrible thing. So it would really help us if you answered a few questions. Please, Zoe, we need your help. For Angela's sake.'

Zoe nodded dumbly, tears streaming down her cheeks.

'Tell us about your evening on Sunday, everything you can remember.'

Zoe's account tallied with what they already knew. With a little pressure she admitted that Gary had gone up to the bar for them, but he had refused to buy them more than one drink each. He had been afraid of getting into trouble. She was certain the girls had each paid for their own drinks. Hazy about the time they arrived, she confirmed that she and Angela had been together the whole time at the bar, until about half past ten.

'What happened at half past ten?'

'I went home. My mum goes mental if I get in late. If I'm not home by eleven all hell breaks loose.'

'Were you alone?'

'No. I left with Suzy. We always walk home together.'

'Who's Suzy?'

'Suzy's my friend. She lives next door so we always walk home together, unless one of our parents comes to pick us up.'

'What about Angela?'

'We said we'd see her the next morning, at school, and we left. She said she was going home too, but she lives in the other direction, so we left together, me and Suzy, like we always do. It wasn't like it was two in the morning or something. It was only half past ten.'

'Who else was still there when you left?'

'Oh God, everyone I suppose.'

'Who is everyone?'

'I don't know. It was Sunday night. There were loads of people there.'

'Was Gary still there when you left?'

'I think so. But he would never have done anything to hurt Ange.'

'What makes you say that?'

'He was nuts about Angela. He'd never have done anything to hurt her. It wasn't just that he fancied her. You know what I mean, he was mad about her. He thought she was the one.'

Unlike Zoe, Ian thought that made Gary a more likely suspect, a killer who had attacked Angela in a fit of frustrated passion. Before he could probe any further, Zoe's mother opened the door on the pretext of offering them all tea. Ian declined, although he was tempted to accept, in order to send her to the kitchen. Instead, she came in and sat down.

'You mentioned that Gary was keen on Angela,' Ian said.

Zoe burst into tears. When she calmed down enough to speak, she sobbed that she didn't want to get Gary into trouble.

'He's really sweet,' she said, 'he wouldn't hurt anyone, I know he wouldn't. And he was nuts about Angela.'

'Can you be more specific? How do you know he liked her, in particular?'

Zoe gave him a contemptuous glare. 'How do you think I knew? He was always asking her out.' She glanced at her mother. 'He wanted her to be his girlfriend. He said so. He was always on at her.' She glanced over at her mother again.

'Would you prefer it if your mother left the room?'

'Yes, no, oh, it doesn't matter. It's just that Gary comes out with us – that is, he used to come out with us – any time Angela called him and asked him. She'd just tell him where we were, and he'd always come straight away. It was a bit sad. It was like he was always just sitting at home, waiting for her to call. I mean, he never, never said no. Not once in all the time we knew him. But if I ever called him, or one of the other girls did, he either didn't answer, or else he just asked if Angela was with us. If she wasn't he would never join us. He was only interested in her. And that suited the rest of us just fine because no one fancied him. I mean, you've seen him.' She gave a mock shudder. 'Angela couldn't stand him, but . . .'

'But she used to phone him to join you. She took advantage of his feelings for her . . .'

'He didn't mind. He knew he didn't stand a chance with her. I mean, he wasn't angry about it, or anything. He was always saying she was out of his league. But he still tagged along. I think he just liked to see her.'

'Was Angela seeing anyone else?' Naomi asked.

'No.'

'Were you aware of anything happening between her and Gary recently? Anything unusual? Did she say anything about him?' Naomi persisted.

'No.'

Ian sat back for a moment and allowed Naomi to take over the questioning. She seemed very confident, and he wasn't sure what to ask. Teenage girls and their boyfriends weren't exactly his territory. From what he could hear, the questioning seemed to be going round in circles, and he was becoming bored. At last Naomi fell silent. With an encouraging smile, Ian leaned forward.

'Is there anything else you want to tell us, Zoe? Now's the time. Anything that might help us find out who killed Angela after she left you in the pub? We know Gary was buying drinks for you both and . . .'

'Pub?' Mrs Drayton interrupted. 'Zoe wouldn't have been in a pub. She's only sixteen. You've got that all wrong.'

'Yes,' Zoe burst out suddenly, glaring wildly round the room. 'I want to tell you! I want to tell you everything!' She dropped her head in her hands, and burst into loud sobbing.

Her mother put her arms around the distraught girl.

'Come on, Zoe, it's all over. It's all over.' She glared at Ian. 'I think you'd better leave, now. Zoe and I have some talking to do.'

'No,' Zoe interrupted her mother. 'Don't tell him to go. I want to tell him what happened. The police need to know about this.'

Ian waited while Zoe blew her nose and wiped her eyes, her complexion pale and blotchy. Staring at the floor, she said in a rapid monotone, 'He raped her.'

'Zoe!' her mother gasped. Her hands flew up to her mouth.

Even Naomi looked startled.

'It's true, mum.'

'Are you telling us someone raped Angela?' Ian asked.

Zoe nodded.

Ian tried to hide his disbelief. 'Did she report it to the police?'

'The police? No. She didn't want anyone to know. She didn't tell anyone apart from me, and she made me swear on my life to keep it a secret. Only now she's dead, I don't suppose it matters, does it? I mean, it's not her secret any more, is it?'

'You're doing the right thing telling us,' Naomi assured her. 'We need to investigate this.'

'Where did this alleged assault take place?' Ian asked.

Something in his tone provoked Mrs Drayton to round on him as though he had told an inappropriate joke at a funeral.

'It wasn't "alleged". If Zoe says it happened, then it happened. My daughter doesn't tell lies, Inspector, and I'm sure Angela would never have made up something so horrible either.'

'Take your time, Zoe,' Ian said, in as kind a tone as he could muster. 'Tell us exactly what Angela said.'

'She said he tried to rape her.'

'*Tried* to rape her, or raped her? Think carefully. What were her exact words?'

'Raped her, tried to rape her, what's the difference?' Zoe's mother barked. 'You're being very brave,' she added, stroking Zoe's hair.

'What happened?' Ian persisted. 'This is a very serious allegation. You need to tell us why you are making this claim.'

'I'm not making it up!' Zoe protested.

'No one's suggesting you are. But you need to tell us what happened.'

'We were all at a party and he tried to rape her. She was sitting on the stairs. He was going up the stairs and he tried to make her have sex but she pushed him off her and he said he'd tripped and fallen on top of her.'

The two women were gazing at Zoe as though she was some kind of wounded animal. As the only man present, Ian felt constrained from expressing any doubts. He was wary of laying himself open to an accusation of being insensitive or, worse, misogynistic, but he wasn't convinced Zoe's story was based on a real incident. It sounded like the kind of story a sixteen-year-old girl might tell to divert her mother's attention from the fact that she had been drinking alcohol at the pub with eighteen-year-old boys. Warily Ian stepped into the minefield.

'Was Angela all right?' he asked, in preparation for his question.

'Of course not!' Zoe was indignant.

Her mother and Naomi both turned to Ian. Mrs Drayton looked outraged. Naomi wore an expression which clearly stated that only a man could ask so obtuse a question.

'She was terrified of him,' Zoe added, sniffing into a tissue.

'It's all over now,' her mother said soothingly.

But of course it wasn't.

'Did you see what happened?'

Zoe shook her head. 'I was in the kitchen. But Angela told me all about it at school next day,' she added earnestly. 'She made me promise not to tell anyone, but I don't have to keep that promise now, do I?'

'You're being very brave,' her mother assured her again, patting her on the shoulder.

Ian took the plunge. 'Why did Angela phone Gary to insist he join her at the pub on Sunday, if he'd previously tried to assault her? She texted him three times in ten minutes. She was quite insistent he join her. She wasn't really frightened of him, was she?'

'She felt sorry for him,' Zoe replied promptly. 'We all did. And he apologised. He said he couldn't help himself,' she added, turning her head to direct her wide-eyed stare at her mother. 'Some boys can't.'

'The boy's an animal,' her mother hissed. 'You should lock him up. He must have been drunk and tried again, and when she rejected him, he lost his temper. Only this time . . .'

Zoe began to sob loudly.

'We'll investigate this thoroughly, don't you worry,' Naomi said. 'And thank you, Zoe, you've been very brave.'

Or very disingenuous, Ian thought, but he kept that to himself. Zoe was only sixteen. She could have no idea of the problems she was causing in seeking to protect herself from getting in trouble with her mother.

Chapter Eleven

NAOMI WAS PETITE and blonde with a sparkle in her eyes that made her look younger than her twenty-five years, while her ready smile seemed to suggest that life was fun. She wore heavy eye make-up and Ian had overheard Eileen commenting on her skirt being too short for a detective constable on duty. Always careful to look smart and professional himself, he had been embarrassed for Naomi, yet somehow the young constable had succeeded in placating Eileen without conceding the point. The two women seemed to get on well, despite Eileen's didactic comments. With her quietly assertive manner Naomi looked set to do well, a capable young woman who would probably climb through the ranks in any sizeable organisation. She just happened to have joined the police force. She could equally well have forged a career in the civil service, or any large corporation. There seemed to be increasing numbers of young officers who regarded detective work as a career, rather than a vocation. Ian was concerned that they didn't share his passion for their work.

For years he had thrown himself into his job with little purpose other than a dedicated pursuit of justice. Now that his promotion had given him a taste for some measure of independence, he was beginning to resent taking orders from officers who were his superiors only in rank. He could foresee a time when his detective chief inspector would be an officer younger than he was, and the prospect made him restless. He was a skilled detective but he was beginning to wonder if that was enough, both for himself and for his future. He had nothing against Naomi as an individual, but she seemed to epitomise everything he begrudged in such slick youngsters.

'It all points to Gary,' Naomi said, with a confidence Ian resented. 'If he assaulted Angela once he might quite well have done so again, only this time with fatal consequences.'

'That certainly appears to be the case,' Eileen agreed.

'We only have Zoe's word for it that any previous attempted assault actually took place.' Ignoring Naomi's surprised expression, Ian continued. 'I'm not sure we can treat her as a reliable witness. Don't forget, she's only sixteen. She told us Gary's really sweet, and that he wouldn't hurt anyone, and at first she said nothing had happened between Angela and Gary. It was only when her mother came in the room that she came up with this allegation of attempted rape.'

Eileen glanced at Naomi, as though expecting a sharp retort. Ian waited, unsure why he felt the need to defend his position. With a sickening feeling that he might be losing his grip on the situation, he added, 'The pathologist found no evidence of any sexual activity.'

'Now the girl he allegedly assaulted is dead, don't you think it matters any more if he tried to rape her or not?' Naomi asked. 'Is that what you're saying?'

Ian merely shrugged. The question was stupid.

'Well, we may never know if he attempted to rape her, or fell over on the stairs, or if the whole story's a fabrication. Only now he's suspected of murdering her so let's focus on that,' Eileen said.

'We can't just ignore Zoe's statement,' Naomi objected. 'The guy could be a potential rapist.'

'Of course we'll investigate the allegation of rape as best we can, but we may have to accept that there's nothing we can do about it anyway,' Ian pointed out.

'Just because we can't prove anything, it doesn't mean we should just ignore it,' Naomi insisted. She was beginning to sound petulant. 'You seem to think it doesn't matter.'

'It does matter,' Ian replied. 'It matters for several reasons, not least of which is that, even if we can't prove anything, an allegation of rape is bound to influence the jury once they've heard it. And of course it will come out. The prosecution will have that girl up as a witness, crying and accusing the suspect of trying to rape her friend, knowing full well the judge will instruct the jury to disregard the allegation, but it's bound to influence their opinion of the suspect. No smoke without fire and all that. They won't necessarily be swayed by the fact that a teenage girl might be an unreliable witness . . .'

'That's a very sweeping statement!' Naomi objected.

'I'm not saying all teenage girls are unreliable, but I happen to believe this one is.'

'So now you're setting yourself up as jury, are you?'

Ian deliberated. It seemed that challenging a young girl's allegation of rape was too sensitive a topic to be considered dispassionately by other young women.

'I'm not going to argue with you,' he said. 'But if the suspect is innocent, I don't fancy his chances in court, that's all I'm saying.'

He turned to Eileen who had been listening to their exchange in silence. 'It's not clear cut that Gary's responsible. We have another suspect, ma'am. There's Frank.'

Eileen gave him a searching look. 'What's your gut feeling, Ian? You've spoken to all the key witnesses so far. Could either Gary or Frank be guilty, do you think?'

Having worried that Eileen was unimpressed by his spat with Naomi, Ian wasn't prepared for her direct question. On the point of naming Gary, he dropped his eyes from the detective chief inspector's intense gaze. She was shrewd enough to know when he was feeling uncertain. Gauche young Gary was a strong possibility, but two calls to Angela's phone from her home on the night she died raised a worrying question over her stepfather.

'Well,' he replied cautiously, 'I'm kind of guessing here.'

'There's a killer out there somewhere, so I suggest we stop guessing and find enough evidence to make an arrest before the papers go to town about an axe-wielding maniac.'

Eileen asked Ian to stay behind when Naomi left the room. Anticipating a roasting for his brusque dismissal of the constable's concerns, he was relieved when Eileen's face relaxed into a smile.

'Naomi's a capable officer but she's young, and needs firm guidance. You were right to consider both sides of the situation. Hang on to that sense of balance. In our anxiety to get a result, we must never lose sight of the principle that a man is innocent until proven guilty. Our job is as much about protecting the innocent as it is about nailing the guilty.'

'Thank you, ma'am.'

Not everyone seemed to share Ian's high regard for the detective chief inspector.

'We shouldn't be worrying so much about the papers,' Ted grumbled when he met Ian in the incident room later. 'We all know they print unhelpful garbage. The way Eileen bangs on about them, you'd think we were just looking into this murder as a PR exercise when the only thing we should be doing is finding this demented killer and making sure he's put away for good.'

The media was hardly top of Ian's agenda when he was conducting a murder investigation. Nevertheless, he understood the reason for his superior officer's fear of negative publicity.

'The point is, the less confidence the public have in us, the less likely they are to come forward and volunteer information that could result in an arrest.'

Ted gave a dismissive grunt. 'If we focussed more on the case, and less on the media, we might actually catch this killer, and that really would help our public image.'

Ian sympathised with Ted. Immersed in the investigation, at the same time he was observing Eileen's concerns, considering how he might behave if he were to be promoted to detective chief inspector. He wondered if he would be as efficient as she appeared so far. As a young constable, or even a sergeant, he might well have been irritated by Eileen, as Ted was. Now Ian appreciated her concern with public perception. The investigation could be turned around by one witness coming forward. And right now they could do with some help.

Chapter Twelve

ONCE AGAIN THE warrior sprang on to dry land. His bulging shoulder muscles strained with the effort of lugging his long, narrow boat out of the water. He dragged it up the steps and lowered it down behind the wall, until it lay concealed in a ditch. There was little risk that anyone would spot it there. The moon god had left the skies to Freyr with his rain clouds. Before the night was over, the thunder god himself might arrive to hammer out his drum roll across the night sky. Meanwhile the night was dry and dark, fair conditions for a raid.

Silently he stole along the path towards the settlement. Ahead of him, in the distance, a steady stream of cars glided smoothly across the bridge, glowing in the torchlight. Many people were out travelling, even at that late hour, but they were too far away to notice him on the shadowy footway at the water's edge. He smiled grimly and pressed on towards the town.

Turning off the narrow path on to the broader roads of the settlement, he sensed a liveliness in the atmosphere. The night breeze carried warm smells of food and smoke, and the sound of many voices and laughter. Cautiously he concealed his axe beneath his cloak. His powerful hands were ready to seize his weapon if the opportunity arose, or the need. On his previous raid, the outlying streets of the settlement had been disturbed only by a faint hum of cars rattling along nearby roads. Tonight they were alive with the sounds of many people. He frowned. It might be difficult to find a suitable target, preferably a rich old woman adorned with precious jewellery. Even better would be a hoard like the one he had seen on his previous raid. Silently he made his way forwards.

It would be easy for a warrior of his skill and valour to withstand a group of men and women, but he was no fool. There was no point in running towards unnecessary danger. He hadn't come here to prove his worth in battle. Tonight he was seeking treasure, not glory, and only two nights ago he had discovered exactly where to find it. His mind raced ahead of his legs, remembering the hoard he had seen. It was just round the next corner. He had only to wait for the right moment. When the street was deserted he would smash his way in, seize as much loot as he could carry, and vanish into the night. This time, he had brought three large bags with him. The haul would be worth the wait. It was going to make him rich.

He turned the corner and made his way along the street, hardly noticing the shops he passed. His eyes were fixed on the prize on the opposite side of the street. This time lights were on in the shop, illuminating shiny metal and bright jewels. A couple jostled him as they passed by. He gazed around in frustration. The streets were too busy, the pavements too crowded. He would have to return another time when people were indoors seeking shelter, not outside wandering the streets. A group of young women passed him, laughing and shrieking. One of them brushed his arm as she went by. With an involuntary movement his hand gripped the handle of his axe, but the time was not right. Tonight the gods were not smiling on his quest.

He could be patient.

Chapter Thirteen

DANA HAD BEEN working for her uncle for over three years. It wasn't exactly her dream job, standing behind the counter hour after hour, waiting for customers, but what really worried her was that the stock was so valuable. She was terrified when her uncle went out and left her alone. If anything, she was even more nervous now than when he had first left her in sole charge of the shop. She had been younger then, and hadn't known what some of the pricier items were worth.

'Don't look so worried,' her uncle told her as he prepared to go out. 'Nothing's going to happen. I've been here for sixteen years and I've had no disasters yet. I don't intend to start now.'

She mumbled about being afraid someone would come in and steal some of the jewellery on display.

'That's what the alarm's for. But I've never had to use it yet.'

The emergency alarm went straight to the police station, only by the time they arrived, any thief with legs would have scarpered.

Her uncle laughed off her fears. 'Everything's insured,' he said.

'But what if they turn violent?'

'You don't have to let anyone in if you're not happy about them,' her uncle replied.

But how was she supposed to know who was a genuine customer, and who was a brutal robber? Criminals didn't turn up in balaclavas brandishing guns. At least, she didn't think they did. Being left on her own was definitely the worst aspect of the job, but, as her father pointed out when Uncle Tim offered her the job, beggars couldn't be choosers. She hadn't exactly covered herself in glory at school, leaving with no qualifications. Her uncle's offer had been a godsend. It was that, or scrabbling around with everyone else after jobs at Tesco or Sainsbury's, and those were hard enough to come by these days.

'It was different for you,' she had whined to her mother. 'There were jobs around when you were my age.'

'You just have to try harder.'

As it turned out, she hadn't needed to try at all, because Uncle Tim had been looking to recruit an assistant. She had agreed to take the job readily enough, not that her parents had given her much choice in the matter. Tim had taken her on for a probationary period, and that was three years ago.

'At least I know I can trust you, if nothing else,' he had told her when she had accepted his offer. Her mother had snapped at him for being rude, but Dana wasn't insulted. She knew she wasn't exactly Brain of Britain.

For the most part it wasn't a bad job. At least it was a job. Some of her friends weren't earning anything or, worse luck for them, were still at college, and here she was with cash of her own to spend and lovely jewellery to look at all day. Her uncle had given her a gorgeous ring for Christmas.

'They're not real diamonds,' he had told her.

'Who cares? It's beautiful! Are you sure I can have it? Really?'

Tim had winked at her as he removed the price tag. 'I've told you before, Dana, what it's worth and what it can fetch aren't the same thing. But that's between us.'

She wasn't sure she understood what he meant, but she didn't care. She had a lovely new ring to show off to her mates. Life was good. Some of the gems in her uncle's shop were so sparkly she could hardly keep her eyes off them. When he was out, she could try on anything she wanted. One day she was going to have a big real diamond ring of her very own. She had already picked one out. It had tiny little diamonds along the shoulders, and a big princess-cut solitaire in the middle. It was the most beautiful ring in the shop, and one of the most expensive.

'One day I'm going to have one like that,' she had told her uncle, pointing to it.

He had laughed. 'You'll have to find yourself a rich boyfriend first.'

'I'll find a sugar daddy,' she had promised him, and they both laughed.

Uncle Tim was all right, if you caught him in a good mood. Today he was going to visit a client. He packed a selection of rings into a little black bag and tucked it in the inside pocket of his jacket.

'How can you go out with those in your pocket like that?' It wasn't the first time Dana had asked him that.

Tim gave his tolerant smile. 'They're all insured.'

'But what if you get mugged? They could beat you up. A girl was attacked a few days ago and killed just round the corner. They still haven't caught whoever did it. He could be out there now . . .'

Tim burst out laughing. 'For goodness sake, stop fussing. No one's going to beat me up. No one knows what's in my pocket.

Unless you tell them, of course. Now come on, you know you're worse than your mother. I never knew a person to be such a fusser. Don't forget to put the alarm on and lock up properly if I'm not back in time to close up.'

'Now who's fussing?'

As soon as Tim left she checked the door was locked. Her uncle was probably going to be gone for most of the day. She went back behind the counter and stood near the alarm button. After a few minutes, she went over and checked the door again, even though she could see it was properly closed. Then she went and stood behind the counter again. To take her mind off the worry of being there alone, she opened the drawer and pulled out a tray of rings. Enchanted, she tried them on, one by one. Absorbed in studying how lovely they looked on her slim fingers, she didn't notice someone entering the shop. Startled by a noise, she looked up and screamed.

Chapter Fourteen

'SO WHAT YOU'RE telling me is that you think it might have been the boyfriend after all?' Eileen asked.

Ian suppressed a sigh. He wasn't sure the detective chief inspector was really listening to him. He knew there were many aspects of the case she had to keep in mind, but he did think she could be more attentive when he was discussing a potential suspect.

'I'm only putting Gary forward as a possibility, but I'm really not sure. If it was that clear cut, we'd have made an arrest already, but it's not that simple. And in any case,' he explained with exaggerated patience, 'he wasn't Angela's boyfriend. He was just one of the crowd she went around with. She was sixteen.'

Eileen frowned at him. 'I know how old she was.'

'He wasn't her boyfriend. He was one of her crowd,' he repeated. 'But, according to her friend Zoe, Gary was very keen on her. I think that's probably why he was so accommodating about turning up to buy Angela and her friends drinks. He's eighteen, so he could get served.'

'You don't need to remind me of the law on underage drinking. So – are you saying he's now a suspect? On what grounds?'

'Opportunity, certainly. He was there in the pub with Angela and her friends. He must have seen her leave, and could easily have followed her.'

Eileen nodded. 'Do we know if the two of them left the pub at around the same time?'

'It's hard to say one way or the other because no one seems to have noticed exactly when he left. There was quite a crowd there on Sunday evening. Zoe told us she thinks Angela left alone, but we don't know Gary didn't follow her. He could quite easily have left, if not with her, then shortly after, without anyone noticing. He's not the sort of boy people would notice.'

'He could have caught up with her. Presumably he would have known her route home.'

'Exactly.'

'So he had opportunity. What about motive?'

'That's a hard one to be sure about, but Zoe said he was crazy about Angela.'

'So he might have been rejected, disappointed in love?'

'It's possible,' Ian said.

'All of which would give him both motive and opportunity.'

'Yes. In theory, but then the same could be true of Frank Carter.'

'The stepfather?'

'He could well have known where Angela was. Her phone records show two calls from his mobile on Sunday evening. He said he was worried about his stepdaughter, but he might have been checking up on her whereabouts for another reason.'

Eileen looked thoughtful. 'Why would he have wanted her dead?'

Ian shrugged. It was a rhetorical question. There could be a reason.

'So we have two suspects. Good work, Ian. More to do. Let's see if we can narrow it down to one.'

Ian nodded. Somehow they had to uncover evidence that pointed unequivocally to either Gary or Frank and, with a violent killer on the loose, they had to find it quickly. At the moment all they really had was a strong impression and a bit of guesswork.

'It had to be one or other of them,' Eileen said.

'Unless there's someone else involved that we know nothing about. But it was a vicious attack which suggests it was personal.'

'In all my time I admit I've never come across anything like it. Personal or just plain crazy. Let's hope it wasn't a mugging. We already have two suspects, and that's one too many. Let's see if George can shed any light on all this.'

'Who's George?'

Eileen gave one of her rare smiles. 'He's only the best profiler in the business. Bar none. We call him The Wizard. He's coming down from Northallerton. He should be here by midday.'

Ian hoped the profiler warranted her praise. He returned to his desk and reread the statements given by Angela's friends, Gary and Zoe. There were more statements from other youngsters who had been at the pub on Sunday evening. Some knew Angela, others had seen her that evening, laughing and drinking with her friends. Ian couldn't focus on the documents. Leaving Ted to read through the rest of the statements he drove to Micklegate to speak to the bar staff who had been in the pub on Sunday. The landlord hadn't been working that evening. The deputy manager had been on duty. He was behind the bar. The landlord called him over.

'The inspector wants to talk to you about Sunday evening.'

The other man nodded and joined Ian at a corner table. He looked about thirty, thickset, with a Neanderthal brow and sandy-coloured hair. Ian couldn't imagine there would be much trouble in the pub while he was in charge. The landlord left them to it and Ian showed the deputy a photo of Angela.

'Yes, yes, I know, the girl that was killed,' Freddy said, frowning at the picture, his eyes all but disappearing beneath his shaggy brows. 'I don't suppose she looked much like that after what happened,' he added irreverently, 'if what they said in the papers is true.'

Ian grunted. Somehow the local papers had managed to uncover details about the 'Axe Murderer' and were vying with each other to tell the story with as many gory details as possible. For once, their melodramatic accounts weren't exaggerating. The girl's head really had been slashed in two.

'Yes, she was here,' Freddy added. 'I seen her.'

'Did you serve her?'

All at once, Freddy looked uneasy. Shifting his bulk from one side to another, he shook his head. The tendons in his sturdy neck stood out as though he was doing something physically strenuous.

'Freddy, you know what happened to that girl. I need to know what she had in her purse when she left here. So tell me, did she spend any money at all? It's important you tell me the truth.'

Raising his eyebrows in surprise, Freddy glanced over at the landlord who was serving a customer. 'This goes no further, right? I'm only telling you because of what happened to the poor girl. I'd like to help you catch the bastard. But it's more than my job's worth if the boss finds out I'm telling you this.'

'Go on.'

Freddy leaned forward. 'She did come up to the bar, yes,' he admitted. 'She asked for a pint of cider. I could see she wasn't eighteen, and she was already pissed, so I refused to serve her. I let her have a packet of crisps, though, to save face. That way she didn't have to walk away empty-handed in front of all her mates. Like I said, she was only a kid.'

Freddy sat back, seemingly relieved that he had told Ian about his encounter with the dead girl.

'One more question. Did she pay for the crisps in coins?'

'Oh, I didn't take any money off her. I put it in the till myself.' He gave an embarrassed laugh. 'The thing is, I could see she'd had too much to drink. I thought the crisps might help absorb some of it. She was just a youngster. Shouldn't have been in here drinking at all. Not that you can tell these days,' he added quickly, glancing over at the landlord.

Zoe had been adamant they had each been paying for their own drinks. Ian had wondered whether Angela's death had resulted from a mugging that had gone badly wrong, but that didn't add up. A mugger wouldn't have left a fiver in his victim's purse. The more evidence they uncovered, the more likely it seemed that Angela's death had been the result of a personal attack by some-one she knew.

Chapter Fifteen

GEORGE WAS A TALL, thin man with a sharp chin, pointed nose and fluffy white hair. Ian hoped his nickname, The Wizard, had more to do with his skill as a profiler than his appearance. Eileen set great store by him, and although it was early days, they were in need of help in identifying Angela's killer.

'I've read all the statements,' George said, in a clipped voice. 'There are a number of interesting features to this case. Forensics suggest an axe was used to kill the victim. What kind of person carries a weapon like that around with them on the street? It's possible the killer had just bought an axe for a perfectly innocent reason, and happened to have it with him at the time, but that seems unlikely at that time of night, so the weapon used suggests the murder may have been premeditated. The aggressive nature of the attack indicates the killer is probably male. The power of the single blow excludes anyone old or frail. All of which suggests we're probably looking for a man, not too old, out on the street at night, carrying an axe, planning a murder. None of this is neces- sarily the case, of course, but the balance of probabilities suggests such a profile. The target might not have been a specific individual, even if there was an intention to kill. It could have been a random victim.'

Eileen interrupted. 'Enough people knew the victim's whereabouts at the time of her death so it's possible she knew her killer. At the moment her boyfriend and her stepfather are both potential suspects. Either of them might fit your profile.'

'Gary wasn't her boyfriend,' Ian corrected Eileen. 'He was a friend, although according to the victim's girlfriend, he was keen on the victim.'

'The forensic report indicates a particular type of axe head, curved, and possibly decorated in some way. That's odd, isn't it?' George added. 'But distinctive? Where, I wonder, would anyone obtain such a weapon?'

Ian nodded. There was something about the profiler that inspired confidence, perhaps because what he said made good sense. His conclusions were pretty much in line with Ian's own thinking. Understandably, both Gary and Frank had strenuously denied owning an axe, or a large blade of any description. So far the investigation hadn't uncovered anything to indicate that either of them was lying. The whole area was being thoroughly searched but there was no sign of the murder weapon. It was time to take a look at where the suspects lived. Ian had applied for search warrants for both properties, and he set off with Ted and Naomi as soon as George had finished.

First they went to Gary's address. He lived with his mother in a street of rundown terraced properties on the outskirts of town. The door was opened by a short, fat woman who greeted them with a worried smile that faded when Ian asked to speak to Gary.

'Is he in trouble?' she asked.

'Not yet,' Ian replied honestly, 'but we'd like to take a look around the house.'

'Well, I'm not sure . . .'

'We have a warrant to search the premises.'

'What? What are you expecting to find here?'

Naomi stepped forward. 'It won't take long,' she said briskly. 'We just need to take a quick look around the house to eliminate Gary from our investigation, and then we won't need to trouble you anymore.'

She made it sound as though searching the house was no big deal, just a routine matter that might happen to anyone from time to time. With a nervous smile, Mrs Farr nodded and gestured for them to enter.

'Well done,' Ian muttered to Naomi.

She turned to him, with a slightly surprised expression on her face. Feeling as though he had been clumsily patronising, Ian turned to Ted.

'I'll go upstairs, Naomi downstairs, and you take the garden.'

His colleagues set to work and Ian climbed the stairs with Gary's mother wheezing behind him.

'What are you looking for?' she demanded breathlessly as they reached the landing. 'He's not on drugs. He's never done drugs. What do you think you're going to find here?'

Ian reassured her this was merely routine as he asked which was Gary's bedroom.

'I don't want you going in there, not while he's not here.'

Ignoring her indignation, Ian went into Gary's room. It was long and narrow with barely space for a single bed, a built-in wardrobe, and a small wooden cabinet beside the bed. A thin curtain was drawn across the window. Ian switched on the naked light bulb hanging from the ceiling, and began his search by opening the door to the cabinet.

'That's his old phone,' Mrs Farr piped up. 'He never uses it.'

Ian turned it on. The calls had stopped six months previously, and it had no signal. Ian checked his own phone. He had a good signal. Gary's mother was right. The phone was no longer in use. All the same, Gary had kept it in the cupboard beside his bed. Checking the photos Ian found over two hundred images of Angela. He put the phone in a bag and pocketed it.

'You can't take that!' Mrs Farr protested.

There was nothing else of any interest in the room, only a packet of cigarettes in the bedside cabinet, clothes, a towel and a pair of trainers in the wardrobe, and an empty duffel bag on the floor which Ian took. It was possible a small axe could have been carried in the bag.

'What are you doing with that?'

'We just need to get it checked, and then he can have it back.'

'What do you mean, checked? I told you, he doesn't take drugs.'

She didn't appear to realise that Ian was conducting a murder investigation. He went downstairs and waited for Ted and Naomi. Their searches had been fruitless. If Gary did own a blade that matched the description of the one used to kill Angela, he wasn't keeping it at home.

'Does your son own a car?'

'What are you talking about? He's eighteen. He's at college. Where is he going to get the money for a car from?'

'What about your car? Does he drive that?'

'He's insured to drive it, yes.'

'Has he passed his test?' Naomi asked. 'Does he ever go out in your car without you?'

Mrs Farr answered no to both questions. 'Not that I can see it's any of your business.'

'We'd like to take a look at your car.'

'What for? What are you looking for?'

There was no sign of the murder weapon in Mrs Farr's car. Disappointed, Ian and his colleagues left. Although he knew better than to allow himself to be seduced into believing theories that lacked hard evidence, Ian had been desperately hoping that they were going to find something incriminating. The photos of Angela on Gary's old phone were suggestive, but they were inconclusive. As they drove away, it didn't help that Naomi joked about finding a bloody axe under the bed.

Their next visit was trickier. Frank came to the door.

'Keep it quiet,' he warned them. 'She's asleep. The doctor's given her something, and she's sleeping all the time. I suppose it's for the best, for now. Well, have you found out who did it?'

'Not yet,' Ian admitted heavily.

This time Naomi's seemingly casual request to look around the house was not so well received.

'What are you talking about, you want to take a look around?' Frank retorted in a low voice, suddenly red-faced with anger. 'What the hell do you think you're going to find here? No, I won't have you poking your noses in my house. Your lot have already been here, ferreting about in Angela's room. We've had enough of it. Please just go away and leave us alone. And find out who did it. That's what you ought to be doing, not hanging around here, pestering us.'

Ian spoke very calmly. 'We have a warrant to search the premises, so it would be best to let us get on with our job quietly. If you're determined to obstruct us, I'm afraid we'll have to remove you.'

'Remove me? From my own house?' Frank blustered. 'Oh very well then, if you must. Can you at least tell me what you're looking for?'

'I'm sorry, we can't tell you that. Now, if you'll let us get on, we can get through this as quickly as possible.'

'You'd better not wake her up.'

Of course they had to disturb Moira, provoking more protests from Frank, but it was all for nothing. Ian wasn't surprised. While Gary could quite conceivably have kept a murder weapon under his bed, Frank struck him as too clever to be so easily caught out.

Chapter Sixteen

UNCLE TIM THREW his head back and guffawed.

'You should have seen your face when you saw me,' he spluttered.

Flustered, Dana muttered something about being caught trying on rings. The truth was that she hadn't expected him back in the shop until the next morning. Usually when he went out on a visit he was gone all day. Dropping her gaze, she saw that her fingers were still sparkling with gems. Quickly she pulled the rings off, one by one, and replaced them on their trays.

'I was only trying them on. There wasn't anyone here. It was boring. I didn't do anything . . .'

'Caught red-handed,' he said, and burst out laughing again. 'Or should that be caught ring-handed?'

He took a deep breath, still grinning at her discomfort. 'Look, I never said you couldn't try the jewellery on,' he went on, kindly. 'You can try on whatever you want. If anything, I'm pleased. You should be familiar with the stock. You go ahead, try things on as often as you like, as long as customers aren't here to see. Just make sure you put them all back in the right places, with the right price tags. We wouldn't want to sell that for two hundred quid!' He held up a diamond ring with a four-figure price tag. 'Though that might be closer to what it's worth.'

He winked at her and she smiled, relieved that he wasn't cross with her.

'Isn't that cheating customers?'

He laughed. 'We've been through this, before, love. Caveat emptor.'

'What?'

'Let the buyer beware. They can see what they're getting, and they know the price before they buy it. What they do about it is up to them.'

'But aren't we lying about what they're worth?'

'They're worth whatever people are willing to pay. Who is it puts a value on these trinkets? Some little stone dug out of the ground, why should it be worth anything?'

She frowned, trying to understand his point. 'Because it's pretty?'

He laughed. 'How do you put a price on that? It's just what someone's prepared to pay for it, that's all.'

'But you're saying it's worth something.'

He smiled at her. 'Well, obviously I want to get as much as I can for these things. But everyone knows that. I'm here to sell them for as much as I can get. That's what keeps me in business. Everyone knows the rules.'

Dana shook her head. She wasn't sure he was right about that, but she wasn't clever enough to argue with him. She wasn't sure what rules he was talking about.

'Did you have a good day?' she asked, when she had taken all the rings off and returned them very carefully to the right trays.

They chatted for a while, did some tidying up, and then Tim told her she could go home early.

'Are you sure?'

'Yes. You deserve it. You did a great job today, holding the fort while I was out. We're hardly going to have a rush now.'

About to point out that it was the evening they stayed open late, when people sometimes popped in after work, Dana remembered she was going out that evening.

'Thanks, Uncle Tim. You're a star!'

'No worries. Take care on the way home.'

He had never said anything like that to her before. Catching sight of a headline in a newspaper someone had left on the seat at the bus stop, she wondered if there had been a reason for his concern. The headline read: 'Axe Man Still at Large!' Underneath, in a smaller font, it said: 'Police Baffled.'

Dana cast a covert glance around. There were three people waiting at the bus stop, two of them youths in hoodies, one an older man in a long grey raincoat. She had been nervous left alone in the jewellery store, but at least there was an emergency button there. She could have refused to unlock the door to anyone she didn't like the look of, and if someone had tried to smash their way in, which sometimes happened in jewellers, the alarm would have been triggered automatically as she ran out the back. It wasn't ideal, but she had some protection in the shop, apart from the CCTV which was supposed to deter criminals.

Out here on the street, she was alone. Looking around, she caught the eye of the man in the raincoat. The two youngsters were engaged in a good-natured altercation which involved exchanging insulting obscenities. The older man was staring at her. Bald, with a neatly pointed beard and thick eyebrows, he reminded her of the game she used to play as a child where she would stick plastic features on to potatoes to give them funny faces. Abruptly she turned her back, hoping the bus would come soon. If the bald man got on, she would sit as far away from him as possible and jump off at the last possible minute so he couldn't follow her off the bus. When her bus came, the bald man didn't climb aboard. Twisting round to stare out of the window, she caught a glimpse of his back disappearing into her uncle's shop as her bus drew away. Although he hadn't been interested in her at all, there had definitely been something creepy about him.

Fully recovered from her fright at the bus stop, Dana was all dressed up ready to go out when her father stopped her in the hall.

'Where the hell do you think you're going, dressed like that?'

'Dad, I'm an adult. I can wear what I want.'

'You're nineteen, not much older than the girl who was hacked to death not far from here last weekend.'

Her mother joined them. 'They still haven't caught him,' she added her weight to her husband's warning.

'Well, no one's going to hack me to death,' Dana retorted. 'I'm not going to be wandering around the streets alone at night. I'm meeting the others at eight and we're going to share a taxi home. Don't look like that. You wanted me to get a job, and now I can do what I want with the money I earn and you can't stop me.'

'At least put on a coat over that skirt,' her mother said.

'And you can't tell me what to wear!'

Dana flounced out of the house. Her bare legs trembled as she hurried to the station. She wouldn't feel safe until she was with her friends.

Chapter Seventeen

BEFORE IAN HAD finished speaking, Eileen reached a decision.

'We need to try and get to the bottom of this. Let's bring him in.'

'I'd like to speak to Zoe again first,' he replied. 'I'm not sure I believe her story . . .'

'This is an allegation of rape, Ian, from a sixteen-year-old girl. Angela may even have been underage when the alleged assault took place.'

'We heard this from a girl who wasn't present . . .'

Eileen raised her eyebrows.

Ian pressed on. 'I don't believe there was any sexual assault.'

'Whatever we may think, we have received this allegation and it has to be investigated with full rigour.'

'I'm only saying we shouldn't prejudge the situation. This alleged rape might not have actually happened. It could have been a genuine accident. It hardly seems likely he would have attempted to force himself on Angela on the stairs at a party with other kids around – and Zoe wasn't even there.' Eileen gazed at him stony-faced. 'What I'm trying to say is that we don't know what really happened . . .'

'Well, let's find out. One way or another we need to look into It. Bring him in, Ian, and let's put some pressure on him to tell us the truth.'

While Eileen had made it fairly clear she expected Ian to go straight to Gary's house to pick him up, she hadn't issued a direct order to go there right away. He wanted to take advantage of the ambiguity and speak to Zoe again first. He would have preferred to go alone, but under the circumstances that was awkward. He really had to take a female officer with him. He wasn't sure whether he could trust Naomi to be discreet, so decided against asking her to keep quiet about the return visit. He would be completely open about it, recording the details on his decision log. In any case, it was never wise to be underhand in his dealings with members of the public. Duplicity – or even secrecy – had a tendency to backfire. If he failed to record the visit and Zoe or her mother lodged a complaint about it, he could end up in serious trouble.

He was pleasantly surprised when Zoe's mother didn't slam the door in his face. She invited him in quite cheerfully.

'Zoe's fine,' she assured them, as though the purpose of their visit was to find out how her daughter was.

'I'd like to have another word with her.'

'I'm not sure . . . you won't go upsetting her again, will you?'

Ian didn't say that he had done nothing to upset her on his last visit.

'Don't worry,' Naomi responded quickly.

'I only want to ask her if she knows who else was at the party when the alleged incident took place. The more witnesses we can

find the better. We want to make sure we have a watertight case,'
Ian lied.

With a nod, Mrs Drayton led them into a neat living room.
'I'll call her.'

Ian looked around. The living room was, if anything, even
tidier than he remembered it from his first visit. There was a pile
of magazines neatly stacked on a coffee table, around which a sofa
and two armchairs were arranged at right angles to each other.
A coaster had been placed in each corner of the table, in a perfectly symmetrical arrangement. The carpet looked as though it
had recently been hoovered, and every surface – table, television
screen, window sills – gleamed as though everything had been
wiped and polished only a moment before they arrived. Mrs
Drayton was evidently house-proud.

At first Zoe said she couldn't remember who else had been at
the party. Then she said it didn't matter, because no one else had
been on the stairs when Gary had assaulted Angela. As gently as he
could, Ian enquired how she knew that if she hadn't been present.

'Because she told me! Angela told me!' Zoe retorted angrily
before she burst into tears.

'Now you've upset her again,' Mrs Drayton protested.

It was hopeless. Thanking them for their cooperation Ian left,
more convinced than ever that Zoe was fabricating her story, but
unable to challenge her. She had committed herself too far to
retract now, and with Angela dead there was no one to confirm or
refute her account. Ian couldn't put any pressure on her without
her resorting to tears. He was rendered helpless. It was more than
his career was worth to be heavy-handed with her. And it was still
possible that she was telling the truth. There was just no way he
could be sure, one way or the other.

'She's only sixteen,' Naomi reminded him when they were back in the car.

'And we're talking about a man's freedom,' Ian replied tersely.

Gary was at home when they arrived.

'You're lucky, he's just got in,' his mother said, her eyes nearly closing in a scowl. 'What d'you want with him this time? Can't you buggers leave him alone? He's done nothing.'

She turned and bawled at her son who came galloping clumsily down the stairs.

'About bloody time,' he said. His expression darkened when he caught sight of Ian and Naomi standing in the hall. 'Oh, it's you again. What now? I thought she was calling me for my dinner.'

Ian stepped forward. 'Gary Farr . . .' he paused in the act of arresting the boy. At his side he heard Naomi draw in her breath. 'Gary Farr I'd like you to accompany us to the police station for questioning.'

Mrs Farr began a shrill protest. 'Questioning? What's that supposed to mean? What's he supposed to have done? He's going nowhere until he has a lawyer. You stay right where you are, my boy. You're not going anywhere.'

Ian was relieved that Gary was more amenable than his mother. 'Oh leave it out, mum. They're the police. I got no choice.' He turned to Ian. 'I expect you want a statement about Angela, don't you?'

Naomi stepped forward eagerly but Ian held up his hand to stop her.

'What do you want to tell us?'

'I already told you about it, didn't I? You know it was me buying them drinks. Look, I'm sorry. I never meant no harm. She was a nice girl, Angela.' He blushed. 'I really liked her, you know?

If I'd thought she'd get so pissed that she'd go off and get herself killed . . . Look, I'm sorry, all right. I don't know what else you want me to say.'

'Why can't you leave the poor lad alone,' his mother interrupted. 'He's not what you might call bright.'

'I'm sorry,' Ian said, 'but you're going to have to come with us.'

'And we'll be sending a search team to go through your property thoroughly,' Naomi added.

She sounded narked. Ian glanced at her and she frowned up at him. She had been expecting him to make a formal arrest. Ian wasn't sure why he had changed his mind at the last minute.

'I want to do what I can to help you find whoever did – that – to her,' Gary assured him.

'Come on then.'

He took Gary by the elbow. As he did so, he caught a glimpse of the distraught expression on Mrs Farr's face. With a slightly sick feeling, he guided the suspect towards the car. No one spoke on the journey back to the police station. Gary stared disconsolately out of the window, but he didn't look nervous. Eileen set about interviewing him as soon as they had finished the preliminaries. She started out quite gently, but Ian could see a severity in her face to which Gary appeared oblivious. He leaned back in his chair and answered the questions in monosyllables. Only when Eileen raised the allegation of rape did he show any sign of animation.

'We have a witness,' Eileen insisted, somewhat disingenuously.

Zoe had not claimed to have seen the incident. On the contrary, she had admitted she hadn't been there to see what happened.

'Rape?' Gary blinked in disbelief. 'What's that supposed to mean? Someone says they saw me rape Angela? You're having me on. That's the craziest thing I ever heard.' He paused while the lawyer muttered in his ear, then turned back to Eileen. 'Who told you that pack of lies?'

'We have a witness,' Eileen repeated calmly.

The lawyer whispered to Gary again, but he batted him away.

'Why the hell would I ever want to do that? To Angela of all people? Someone's having a laugh. It's sick. I could've had her any time I wanted. I tell you, she was gagging for it. She was all over me. She was always calling me – you check my phone records. You'll see. She was after me. I could've had her any time I wanted.'

Gary sat back in his chair and folded his arms, as though the question was settled. Ian watched him closely throughout his speech. Even if it was all bravado, the Crown Prosecution Service would never try to build a case against him on such flimsy evidence. With Gary denying the accusation so robustly, it was his word against Zoe's. Ian, for one, didn't believe Gary's claim that he could have slept with Angela any time he chose, any more than he believed Zoe's allegation of attempted rape. They had wasted far too much time on a pathetic adolescent drama, when they should have been focussing on the murder investigation. All the same, he appreciated that Eileen had felt constrained to investigate the allegation.

Chapter Eighteen

THE HIGH BRICK wall of a post office faced him across the street. No one would see him leaving the jewellery shop. Turning right he hurried along the pavement, past a baker's and a burger bar. Worried he had been spotted, he crossed the road and slipped into an alley that ran between a grill bar and a restaurant. Pressing himself against the wall, he peered round the edge of the building. No one seemed to be taking any notice of him. Reassured, he returned to the street and continued on his way. At the corner of the road he turned left, opposite the museum. As soon as there was a gap in the traffic he darted across the road. The traffic lights were too far to his right to cross there. Striding quickly past Lendal Tower, he went over the bridge, manoeuvring his way through a throng of Japanese tourists. At the far end of the bridge he took a sharp turn to the right and made his way down a winding stone staircase that led to the river. The sight of the fast flowing water calmed him. The river would carry him out of danger.

He jogged quickly along the path past a rowing club, a small park, and the railings of a car park. Passing through a dark tunnel that ran beneath the railway bridge, the scene became wilder. He stopped and looked around. In front of him were narrow steps that cut through a steep grassy slope to the river. Behind him, concealed behind a whitewashed wall, a deep ditch ran along the bottom of another high slope. He pushed his way through a gap in the wall, to the ditch where his narrow boat lay concealed. Hearing footsteps approaching, he dropped to the ground and squatted, breathing silently, leaning against the wall. It felt clammy against his cheek.

He winced as a bramble caught at his hair. Carefully he shifted position and another thorn pricked the side of his head. He pressed his lips firmly together. The slightest gasp might betray his whereabouts. Gingerly he shifted sideways, but the thorn remained lodged in his skin. Leaves rustled with his cautious movement. He closed his eyes tightly and listened, alert to every tiny sound carried on the night breeze. In the distance he could hear shrill ululations, and roaring, and wondered if his raid had been discovered yet. Shrouded in a long hooded cloak, he had slipped away unseen from the site of his triumph, but he still had to get home. He would wait until the moon hid behind a cloud before pushing his way back on to the path, and dragging his boat down the steps to the water.

He opened his eyes and peered through the gap in the wall. Two people were walking along the path. They stopped when their feet were just inches away from his face. Squinting upwards he saw they were hand in hand so he guessed they were a man and a woman. As he waited impatiently, they both laughed at something the woman said. He held his breath, but they were too engrossed in each other to notice him. They sauntered away, towards the settlement he had just left. They weren't looking for him. He breathed more freely as they moved off.

At last it was safe for him to move around unseen. He ripped the bramble from the side of his head and raised himself up gradually on to all fours. Wolf-like, he sniffed the air, listening, his head tilting slowly from side to side, feeling the sounds of the night. After the excitement of the raid he was so pumped up it had been hard to keep still. He had thought he would burst, hiding in the ditch, terrified to move a muscle. He should be running, and shouting, brandishing his spoils to an admiring throng. Instead, he was painfully stiff from crouching in an awkward position. Gently he arched his back and stretched his feet, rotating his head slowly.

The sudden barking of a dog shocked him into frenzied action. The local people might already be on his trail. Forcing his way back through the gap, he pulled strongly on the rope to drag his boat over the top of the wall. One edge hit his shoulder as he lowered it, but there was no time to stop and examine his injury. Swiftly he carried the vessel down the steps to the rippling water. Tossing his bags ahead of him, he sprang on to the boat before it slid away from the bank. One of his bags fell open to reveal a glittering hoard. A few of his new treasures spilled out on to the damp wooden floor: chains and bracelets, and gold rings decorated with precious gems. Without pausing to pick them up, he continued rowing with a will. After his successful raid, he was determined to make his escape. He would never surrender so valuable a hoard.

The boat glided across the black water, its progress slowed by the current. He glanced back over his shoulder. There were lights, and he thought he could hear voices. Fighting to control his panic, he lunged forward. Seizing one of the heavy bags he tore open a black plastic bin liner inside it and allowed the contents to slip out and hit the surface of the water with a loud splash before disappearing beneath the murky ripples. He didn't look back. His treasure was far more important than the spoils of victory he had abandoned. Resuming his rowing, he looked down at the pieces of jewellery that had fallen out of the bag and were rolling around on the wooden floor of the boat. He would soon be back in the shelter of the abandoned boathouse where he kept his boat in between raids. Then there would be time to gloat over his success. For now, he had to concentrate on making his escape.

Chapter Nineteen

IT WASN'T THE first time Dana had been late for work. At least this time she had a reason for having overslept. Admittedly having a hangover wasn't exactly a good excuse. Her head pounded as she rummaged through her wardrobe. Predictably, her mother started on her as soon as she reached the bottom of the stairs.

'If he wasn't your uncle you wouldn't last five minutes in that job. He's too soft, always has been. No one in their right mind would put up with you.'

She never tired of scolding her brother for spoiling his niece. 'You're not doing her any favours, letting her get away with murder. How's she ever going to cope in a real job?'

Dana's Uncle Tim was so sweet, it was hard to believe that he and her mother were brother and sister. They didn't even look alike. While Dana's mother was tall with straight, dark hair and piercing eyes, her uncle was short and slight, with fairish hair that was almost ginger, and an infectious grin that made him look like a cheeky school boy. Dana sulked whenever her mother put her down like that. If Tim had been there he would have just laughed, throwing his head back until his Adam's apple was visible, bobbing up and down beneath his beard.

'I've only got one niece. If I can't spoil her, who will? Not you, that's for sure. You're too hard on the girl, Jilly. Cut her some slack for God's sake. She's only nineteen. Have you forgotten what you used to get up to when you were her age?'

Whenever her Uncle Tim spoke up in Dana's defence, her mother would give in with an indignant grunt. He always won their arguments as soon as he threatened to reveal his sister's secrets. Dana wondered what youthful indiscretions her mother had committed.

'You'll have to ask your mother about that,' was all Tim would say when she pestered him to tell her what he knew.

With no time for breakfast, Dana ran out of the house. She pelted past the traffic stuck in a queue along Bootham, and along St Leonards Place towards the river. Turning left off Museum Street into Lendal she slowed down, because she could see the shop was still shut. More than ten minutes past opening time, the metal grilles were closed and the interior of the shop looked dark. Surprised and relieved, she reached the shop, still panting from her exertion. It wasn't like Tim to be late. Although he never reprimanded her for turning up to work after opening time, she could tell by the way he pursed his lips at her that he wasn't pleased. She always expected him to morph into her mother and start lecturing her about punctuality, not without reason, but he would just shrug whenever she apologised, and turn away. In some ways that was worse.

Guilty about taking advantage of his good nature, she kept resolving to be more punctual, but it was hard. Of course her mother was right, in theory, but then again, so was Tim. She was only nineteen. Many of her friends were still at college, and they all liked to go out in the evenings. There was nothing wrong with that. Dana's mother went ballistic if she stayed out late, and she never gave Dana any credit for working.

'Do you want to end up like that poor girl who had her head cracked open on the street on Sunday night, right here in York? They haven't caught her killer yet, you know. He could still be out there, roaming the streets. Do you want to be the next victim? A headline in the papers?'

Dana had done her best to explain that she often came home late precisely because she was sensible. Not wanting to be out on her own at night, she usually waited to share a taxi with her friends. Her mother never listened to her explanations.

Dana was still feeling angry about it as she reached the shop. The sign said 'Open', although the lights weren't on. Tim must have forgotten to turn the sign round when he had left the previous evening. With a grin, she rummaged in her bag for her key. When he arrived *she* would ask *him* where *he* had been when she had arrived at nine o'clock. She might even purse her lips at him for being late. Classic! Turning the key, she glanced at her watch, another present from her uncle. She was surprised to find that the door was already unlocked. It was almost quarter past nine. Her uncle must have arrived before her after all.

Before she had even flicked the light switch by the door, she sensed something was wrong. The silence was disconcerting, the darkness unnerving. For the first time she noticed the display trays in the window, some completely empty, others a tangle of pearls and sparkling gems thrown around higgledy-piggledy. Tim would never have left them in such a mess. He was anal about the displays.

Dana had long ago come to terms with her own intellectual limitations. Although she would never admit as much to anyone, it wasn't for lack of trying that she had left school without any GCSEs. But she wasn't completely stupid. She realised at once that there had been a break in. Presumably the burglars had escaped out the back. But it didn't make sense, because if there had been a break in, the alarm would have gone off. As she felt in her pocket for her phone, it struck her that the burglars might still be there, prowling around the premises. She had to get out of there, fast. She turned, her finger already on the light switch. Inadvertently she flicked it and blinked, dazzled by the sudden brightness.

Barely conscious of the phone dropping from her hand, she screamed once, a really loud, shrill scream. She tried to back away, but her legs wouldn't move.

Chapter Twenty

THE SCENE HAD already been secured by the time Ian and Ted arrived, with barrier tape across the front of the shop entrance, and a guarded cordon outside. Several passersby had gathered on the pavement, waiting for information. A reporter was there with a photographer, but all they could see was the outside of the jewellers' shop. There was a sense of desolation as people hung around, waiting. Ian turned his attention to the shop front. The window displays were in disarray but there was no sign of a break in. The uniformed officers standing in the street merely nodded at him, strangely quiet. The usual bustle around a crime scene was absent. Something was wrong.

Ian followed Ted into the shop. Instead of moving forward to allow Ian inside, the sergeant came to an unexpected halt and stood perfectly still, obscuring Ian's view of the interior. Looking over his sergeant's shoulder Ian could see more blood than he would have thought possible. There was blood everywhere: on the carpet, on the counter, on the cabinets displaying rings, chains and watches, on the wall. Normally Ian struggled to control his reaction at crime scenes, embarrassed by his own squeamishness.

This scene was so bloody, he felt only a strange sense of unreality. It looked as though someone had chucked a trough of dark red paint around the room. In front of him, Ted exclaimed out loud and half turned to stare back at Ian, wide-eyed. He looked unusually pale. Until this, Ian had never seen his colleague shocked at the sight of a body, and they had seen a few on their previous case together. Impatiently, Ian stepped forward. He manoeuvred his way past Ted who moved aside wordlessly.

The body lay on its back, feet pointing towards the door. Automatically, Ian registered the fact that the underneath of the victim's shoes were clean. Those shoes hadn't trodden in any blood on the carpet, although there was a mess of blood nearby. It took a few seconds for Ian to register that, where the victim's head should have been, there was only a pool of blood that had soaked into the carpet above the victim's neck and shoulders. Temporarily shocked into silence, Ian stared. He struggled to regain his composure. It was difficult to know what to say.

Ted broke the silence. 'Bloody hell! I don't believe it. He's been decapitated.'

Ian turned to the nearest scene of crime officer. 'Where is it?'

The officer shrugged one white-clad shoulder. 'What? You mean the head?'

'Yes. Where is it?'

'We'd all like to know that.'

'Bloody hell,' Ian echoed Ted. 'Are you telling me the head's missing?' He looked around the room feeling disorientated. 'What do we know about the victim?'

'Quite a lot, actually, if he's who we think he is. The name's Timothy Granger – assuming it *is* him. He was the manager of the shop. His niece found him.'

'His niece?'

'Yes. She works for him. You can speak to her yourself, but good luck getting any sense out of her. She's completely freaked out. Hardly surprising, considering what she found here. She's sitting out the back.'

He jerked his head in the direction of a door at the back of the shop, before returning to his task of collecting and recording evidence. Alerted to the fact that the body had been discovered by a young girl, Ian had already sent for Naomi. He was beginning to think he ought to request to be permanently accompanied by a female officer specifically trained to question teenage girls. Every other witness on this case seemed to be a girl aged somewhere between fifteen and nineteen. As Naomi wasn't on duty that day, Ian went to tackle the girl himself in the company of a middle-aged female constable in uniform. He felt unaccountably nervous. Even though he had been in a relationship with his wife for years before they eventually married, exchanging a few words with a young female witness had become a worrying prospect.

Ian was in favour of the Police and Criminal Evidence Act, established to strike the right balance between the powers of the police and the rights and freedom of the public. It was common knowledge that in the past all sorts of undue pressure had been exerted on vulnerable people to force confessions, sometimes leading to miscarriages of justice. But while Ian would never want to see a return to such unregulated practices, there was a distinction between coercion and accepting the testimony of witnesses without any evidence to substantiate their claims. He was reluctant to rely on the statement of a distressed teenage girl. In the absence of any other witnesses, the truth became a chimera.

Ian returned to the street, relieved that he didn't have to cross the shop floor to reach the office behind the shop, which could be accessed from a back exit. Ted was outside. His normally slightly swarthy complexion had a greyish tinge. Ian wondered if he had been sick.

'You all right?'

Ted nodded. 'Never seen anything like it,' he mumbled.

'Me neither. Not something you want to see either.'

Ian could see Ted was shaken, and wished he could think of words to lessen the horror of what they had witnessed.

'The head's gone,' Ted added unnecessarily, with a hint of panic in his voice. 'They don't know where it is.'

'At least that should make the killer easier to track.'

'Let's hope so!'

The female constable Ian had been waiting for approached.

'Are you sure you're OK?' he asked Ted before turning away.

'Did you see the body?' he asked the female constable as they walked together round to the back of the premises.

Her relaxed demeanour suggested she hadn't been inside the shop, and he wasn't surprised when she shook her head.

'I heard about it,' she told him. 'What a terrible thing for a young girl.'

Ian nodded. At least he had been expecting to see a corpse, if not a decapitated one. He couldn't imagine what the dead man's niece must be feeling. He struggled to prevent his own horror from swallowing up his sympathy for the witness he was about to question.

Chapter Twenty-one

IT WAS HIGHLY unlikely that two killers would be abroad at the same time attacking people with weapons that were very similar, if not identical. The second victim having been killed while Gary was in custody made him an unlikely suspect for Angela's murder. Ian had never believed he was guilty.

Although he knew it was important to speak to the witness as soon after the event as possible, Ian regretted his impatience the moment he set eyes on the hysterical girl. Her head was buried in her hands while her shoulders shook with her sobbing. He stood awkwardly at the door of a tiny office, looking around. A back door led to the alleyway behind the shop, and a second door was labelled Staff Toilet. On a table next to a small sink were a kettle, and tins labelled tea, coffee and sugar, together with an unopened packet of chocolate digestives. The functional whitewashed walls and untreated wood surfaces formed a stark contrast with the carpeted interior of the shop.

After waiting for what felt like ages for Dana to pause in her crying, Ian called her name softly. She looked up, terrified. Her dark hair had an unnatural reddish tint that didn't sit well with her pale spotty complexion, and her dark eyes were red-rimmed and puffy from crying. She was wearing very dark nail polish on short, stubby nails.

'Dana, we need to ask you about what happened here,' he said gently.

He pulled up a chair beside her, close enough to talk quietly to her, but not so close that he risked any contact. The female constable stood stolidly beside him without speaking. He wished she would take over, but wasn't sure he could rely on her to ask the right questions.

'It's very important we find out who did this. You're the person who reported this to the police, aren't you?'

Dana sniffed and nodded. Blowing her reddened nose loudly on a tissue, she raised her head to look at him. When she spoke, he was relieved to hear her talking coherently, in spite of her distress.

'I was late for work this morning. I'm often late but he never – he never ever –' She burst into tears again. Regaining her composure, she continued. 'He's my uncle. It's his shop, that is, he's the manager, and I work here.'

Ian nodded encouragement. 'So you arrived late this morning?'

'Yes.' She gave a faint smile. 'I'm often late. My mum gives me hell for it, but Uncle Tim . . .' She stopped and blew her nose again, stifling a sob.

'So he's your uncle?'

'Yes. He's the manager here. He gave me the job. He's – he's the nicest man I've ever met – he gave me a job –' She began crying in earnest again.

Ian waited patiently while she pulled herself together. Someone brought her a cup of tea and he sat there while she sipped it. As he was about to resume his questions, the sound of voices erupted in the shop. A second later a woman burst into the office. She was thin, with dark hair and wildly staring eyes. The moment she saw Dana, she flung herself forward to throw her arms around the girl who stood up to meet the embrace. The two women stood sobbing together for a moment. At last Dana drew back.

'Mum, the police are here.'

'I should hope so. What happened?'

Dana's mother sounded furious, as though the shop manager's death was somehow Ian's fault. Her anger was vicious, but he understood she was beside herself with grief.

'That's what we're here to find out,' Ian replied levelly. 'Please, sit down. You're Dana's mother, aren't you?'

The dark-haired woman nodded and collapsed on to a chair. 'He was my brother,' she said. 'My little brother.'

It was a while before Ian was able to question Dana again but at last she calmed down sufficiently to answer his questions. He felt more comfortable with her mother present, and was sure she did too. Dana told him she had arrived at work shortly before a quarter past nine to find her uncle lying dead, on the carpet. It was extremely difficult for her to talk about the body without both her and her mother breaking down in tears.

'How could anyone do that?' Dana's mother kept asking. 'It's barbaric.'

Every time she mentioned the grotesque nature of her brother's murder, she and Dana began crying again. The interview progressed painfully slowly, punctuated by bouts of weeping. Ian struggled to remain focussed on his task. It felt callous to persist in questioning Dana but she insisted that she wanted to continue.

'We could leave this until another time, when you've had a chance to come to terms with – with the shock,' he suggested feebly.

As he was speaking, he wondered if it was ridiculous to talk about coming to terms with what had happened. He wasn't sure he would ever fully recover from the sight of the headless corpse. He couldn't imagine how terrible the sight must have been for the people who knew and loved him.

The girl flapped her hand in the air at him. 'No, no, this is important, I know. I want to help find who did that – that horrible thing,' she managed to stutter before she became incoherent again.

At last Ian was able to continue with his questions. Both Dana and her mother were sure the body was Tim. When Ian asked for the third time whether they could be a hundred per cent sure it was him, Tim's sister recalled a birthmark on her brother's chest.

'I should have thought of it before. It's like a third nipple, although it isn't. It's a mole.'

No longer crying, she was suddenly alert, excited by the possibility that the body might not be her brother after all. With a heavy feeling, Ian summoned a constable and sent him to check with a scene of crime officer, as the doctor had already left the scene. He could have wept himself, seeing how Dana and her mother sat, holding hands, their tear-streaked faces bright with a desperate hope. The presence of the blemish exactly where Tim's sister had described it was conclusive. This time, she was inconsolable.

Dana carried on resolutely answering questions, but for all her determination to be of assistance, she was able to add very little to what they already knew. The door had been unlocked when she had arrived just after nine, the alarm switched off. Only Dana and the shop manager knew the code, which had recently been changed.

'I want you to think very carefully now. Are you absolutely positive you couldn't have shared the code with anyone else?'

She nodded. 'I'm sure.'

The doctor had confirmed that the murder had taken place between eight and nine o'clock the previous evening. It appeared the killer had entered the shop before closing time, with the intention of carrying out a robbery. Something had gone badly wrong, resulting in Tim being killed in the confrontation. After that, the killer had made his escape with his loot, and the door must have been left unlocked all night.

'One final question. Can you give us any idea at all of the value of the jewellery that was taken?'

Dana shrugged. 'I've no idea, but the robber must have taken about half the stock.'

'But why do that to him?' Dana's mother asked again. 'Everything was insured. Tim would never have risked his life to save his stock. Why would anyone do that to him?'

It was a good question. With Dana and her mother in the room, no one asked the other question that was bothering Ian and probably everyone else in the shop. No one asked where the missing head might be.

Chapter Twenty-two

'IT DOESN'T MAKE sense,' Ian insisted. 'Why cut off the victim's head? It couldn't have been to hide his identity because he was left there, on the floor of the shop he managed. There was no attempt to conceal who he was at all, really. His sister and niece recognised him from his clothes straight away. They knew it was him, even before the birthmark.'

'The killer probably didn't know about the birthmark,' Ted pointed out. 'So it could have been a clumsy attempt to hide the victim's identity, by removing the most obvious identifying features.'

'But then why kill him there, leaving the body in the shop where he worked? It makes no sense.'

Eileen intervened. 'The killer might have intended to remove the body but run off, because he was afraid of discovery. Perhaps he panicked and just took the head, in the heat of the moment.'

'Yes,' Ted agreed. 'Don't forget this was a robbery that went wrong. It wasn't a planned murder.'

Ian nodded. That at least could be true. But he had a feeling they were missing something vital. This didn't strike him as a simple case of a robbery that had gone wrong, and he said so.

'When do robbers steal people's heads? Really? It doesn't make any sense.'

Eileen frowned. 'Let's not overcomplicate matters. Focus on the actual robbery for now. The shop was robbed. It was a jewellery shop, full of valuable stock. What was the total value of the missing items?'

Ian shrugged. 'The insurers are still working on their figures, but they reckon the total stock was worth well over a million and a half, but the jewellery store chain are going to come up with another figure of their own.'

'Well, let's say it was something over a million pounds,' Eileen said. 'The robber must have got away with something in the region of half of that value? What do we think?'

Ian grunted. 'We don't know yet.'

'Ballpark figure,' she insisted.

'Something like that, all right,' he agreed, 'if we have to make a guess.'

'The exact amount doesn't concern us at this stage,' Eileen went on. 'The point is this wasn't a premeditated murder, but a violent robbery that ended in a brutal killing. So we can't spend time debating *why* the body was left there. The killer was interested in getting away with his booty. He probably didn't give the victim's body a second thought.'

'But why remove his head? That makes no sense,' Ian was aware that he was repeating himself, but he couldn't control his perturbation at the macabre nature of the incident. 'And why take it away and hide it somewhere we haven't yet been able to trace?'

Whichever way they looked at it, the missing head was weird. They all saw the sense in consulting a profiler about so extraordinary a murder. Soon after their frustrated exchange, Eileen summoned Ian and Ted to her office where Ian was pleased to see George's fluffy white hair. Eileen outlined the details of the killing to George who listened intently.

'And the head, you say, has simply disappeared?' he asked quietly when she finished.

'We're still looking for it,' Ian admitted. He didn't add that nothing about this seemed simple to him.

'I doubt you'll find it easily,' George responded promptly, 'not if he's taken it.'

'What do you mean?' Eileen asked.

'The killer must have taken the head deliberately. It's not the sort of thing you slip in your pocket by mistake. That means he wants to keep it, perhaps as a kind of trophy. Why else would he have gone to the trouble of taking it away? This wasn't a crude attempt to mask the identity of his victim, because the body was left in the shop the victim managed. Find the head and you find the killer.'

There was a faint murmur of agreement. They had all worked that out by now.

Ian felt an uneasy sense of déjà vu as George continued. 'This is a strange case and this new incident raises a number of questions.'

Eileen frowned. It had not yet been confirmed that the two recent murders were connected.

'It seems clear that the murders are linked in some way, even though there are differences. First, both victims were killed by a blow to the head, one vertical the other horizontal. Is this pattern giving us some kind of message?'

'Should we look out for someone waving an axe in a diagonal plane next?' someone asked with a grin.

A few of the young constables sniggered. No one else took any notice. Everyone understood it was sometimes necessary to release the tension with flippancy. With a pang of regret Ian remembered indulging in such fooling around himself before he attained the rank of inspector and felt he ought to conduct himself with more dignity.

'It's an unusual murder weapon,' the profiler continued in his clipped tones, 'if for no other reason than that it can't be easy to carry around without attracting attention.' He paused. 'No one carries an axe around without reason. It's not a particularly easy weapon to use at close quarters. The bearer needs room to swing it. So it wasn't carried for self-defence. Does this weapon suggest an element of premeditation? And yet – this was undoubtedly a targeted robbery.' He paused again. 'A murdering thief, or a thieving murderer? What is going through his mind?' He paused again, but no one answered. 'I merely ask the question.'

Ian decided he rather liked George's manner of raising questions. He had encountered opinionated profilers in the past. It was far better to adopt a collaborative approach.

'You keep saying "he",' Eileen said. 'Are you sure we're looking for a man?'

'Aggressive; wielding a heavy weapon capable of splitting a skull; severing a spinal cord with a single blow.' George seemed to be talking to himself. 'Removing a head while carrying loot.' He nodded slowly. 'Yes, I'd say this is a man. I may be wrong, of course, but I can only give you probabilities at this stage. Like you, I have absolutely no idea about the actual identity of this killer.'

'You seem very sure we're dealing with one killer?' Ian asked.

'Well, we may be looking for a copycat killer, of course. The first death was all over the papers, wasn't it? That would explain the difference in the attacks, if the papers reported a head injury.'

'Oh great. Now we're looking for two crazies,' someone muttered.

'I'd be surprised if this wasn't the same killer,' George said. 'As you say, it's completely crazy. The chances of two such maniacs hitting the streets at the same time have to be slim.'

'But that's just the balance of probabilities,' Ian said.

'Indeed.'

'You mean . . .' Naomi stared at George, wide-eyed, 'you mean this could be a serial killer?'

No one spoke. It seemed to be tempting fate to point out that the emotive term 'serial killer' technically referred to someone who had killed three or more people.

Chapter Twenty-three

A TRACKER DOG had been brought in to try and trace the killer's route from the shop. It wasn't proving easy to establish the relevant scent from the mass of potential evidence at the scene. Many people had visited the shop the previous day. When Ian arrived, a handler was leading a German shepherd round the shop where it was sniffing at all the display cabinets that had been disturbed.

'We've already followed a couple of false leads,' the dog handler told him cheerfully. 'But they did take us to customers who visited the shop yesterday,' he added in defence of his animal. 'We're going to try the victim. It might be easier to track his head, assuming the killer carried it away with him. And if it doesn't get us to the killer, we might at least recover the missing head.'

He dragged the dog over to the patch of blood that had dried on the carpet. After sniffing at the stain for a minute, the dog raised his head and barked.

'Here we go again,' the handler said, smiling as though he was off on a ramble. 'Want to come along?'

Ian nodded. Together they followed the dog out of the shop. It wasn't easy negotiating the streets with the dog straining at its lead. It led them away from the centre of town, down towards the river. Reaching the path, the dog gathered speed so the handler had to tug at its lead to slow it down. All at once, the dog halted and barked.

'Something happened here,' the handler said, as though he could interpret what the dog had communicated.

Looking down beside the path, Ian saw straight away what the handler meant. The grass had been disturbed. A few twigs had been flattened and shattered by some heavy object that had been dragged across the ground, down to the water.

'The bastard got away by boat,' the handler said. 'There's no way we can track him beyond this point. Bugger. Pluto's the best, nothing gets past him, but this killer's no fool. He knew we'd be on to him and he's covered his tracks, escaping on the water.'

Ian frowned. It looked as though they were going to have to dredge the river. He called Eileen to let her know what had been discovered, and suggested the killer might have discarded the stolen head when he reached the river.

'I can't see why,' she replied. 'I mean, why take it away with him if he was going to chuck it away?'

Although he suspected Eileen might be concerned about the cost of dredging, Ian agreed it was unlikely they would find the missing head abandoned in the water. There was no point throwing money at the case for no reason. But at least they now knew how the killer had escaped, even if they were no closer to finding him. In the meantime, an expert boat builder had arrived to examine the site where they believed the killer had entered the water. A wiry grey-haired man, he stared at the muddy ground beside the river and shook his grizzled head.

'Well, I can't tell you much from this,' he concluded at last. 'From the tracks it looks like he used a flat bottomed boat, some sort of dinghy I'd say. That's just an informed guess, mind, from the ground cover being crushed smooth like that. It doesn't look like a rudder was dragged through it. But it happened last night, didn't it? A lot can change overnight. This evidence here could have been seriously compromised since the killer made his get away.'

Listening to his jargon, Ian suspected the boat builder was a fan of detective series on television.

'Can you be more specific about what sort of boat it was?'

The boat builder laughed gruffly. 'You don't want much, do you? You'll be asking me who owned it next.'

'Wouldn't it have to be registered?'

The boat builder scowled. 'You should know that. I thought you were a police officer. No, privately owned open boats like dinghies don't need to be registered, unless they're carrying more than a dozen passengers, and this one would have been too small to do that without attracting notice.'

Ian seized on the snippet of information, casually thrown out.

'How small? Can you estimate the size of it?'

The boat builder shook his head. 'You'd need to measure the deeper indentation here, and here – it looks as though the boat was left standing right here for a few minutes, maybe longer, whereas over here, see, it was just pulled across the ground without resting in any one place.'

He pointed to the traces by the path, and a deeper indentation further away that indicated the boat's dimensions were approximately five metres long. It was a very rough estimate, but it gave them something to go on. All officials on the river were notified to be on the alert for any suspicious crafts matching that description.

'Suspicious how?' the officer sending out the message wanted to know.

Ian hesitated. 'We're looking for a boat that might be concealed . . .' He paused, aware how ridiculous that sounded.

'In a boat house, you mean?' she asked patiently.

'Yes, that's certainly a possibility.' He paused. 'We're specifically looking for a boat that has blood stains.'

It was just feasible that someone on the river might have noticed something unusual. Meanwhile, it was hardly reassuring to realise that the killer was clever enough to make his escape from a crowded city centre, not only without attracting attention, but without leaving any tracks. He had simply slipped on to the water and vanished. Realistically, unless he had somehow drawn attention to himself in the darkness, there was no way of telling in which direction he had made his escape. Even if an observer recalled seeing a boat slip into the water at this precise location along the bank, no one was going to be able to give a description of the boatman, or tell where the vessel had ended up. It was hopeless, but they had to explore every possible avenue.

'Send out an urgent message,' Ian said.

For all the good it would do, he might just as well have asked the officer to cast a line in the river and fish for the missing head.

Chapter Twenty-four

IT WAS A GOOD haul, not bad for one night's work, a great addition to his stock of treasures. It was a pity he had been forced to jettison the third sack. In some ways that bag had contained the most precious cargo of all, but that particular trophy wouldn't have lasted long. He had done well to abandon it, keeping only the loot that would endure. Having stowed the boat out of sight, he carried his spoils home, doing his best to prevent the metal items from jangling against each other inside the bags. Any clue might lead to his downfall, but no one saw him hurrying along the street, or spied him on the stairs inside his house. That was the most dangerous place of all, because the staircase was well lit and there was nowhere to run if he was seen. Concealed beneath his cloak, he hoped the bags would be mistaken for shopping. He had slipped them inside plastic carrier bags for that purpose, but there was no way of knowing what other people might suspect. He was relieved when he reached the safety of his own room unseen.

As soon as his door was shut, he leapt in the shower and scrubbed his face. All the blood vanished down the plug hole, along with the blood he washed off his hands. Not his own blood. Stepping out of the shower he scrutinised himself in the mirror: sturdy, muscular, triumphant. Satisfied that he had removed all traces of his night's work he returned to his own room, checked the door was locked and settled down to check his haul. It turned out to be even better than he had realised. In the heat of the raid he had snatched whatever he could get his hands on, without pausing to examine what he was taking. Now at leisure, he studied each individual item.

With a thrill of possession he gazed at intricately wrought pieces of shiny metalwork. Bright gems glowed in the electric light. He had never seen so many beautiful ornaments before, and they all belonged to him. His battle-scarred hands trembled. It was a beautiful sight, well worth all his exertion, and the risks he had taken. On a crazy impulse, he tossed a handful of gems in the air and watched them spin twinkling to the floor in a gorgeous array of gleaming colours. He picked up a sapphire ring and slipped it on his little finger. It shone brightly, winking up at him. Fishing through the pile, he found a gold ring large enough to fit on his index finger. One by one he selected rings to fit each of his fingers. They shone golden and silver. A slow smile relaxed his jaw. It was over, his glorious mission accomplished. He had succeeded.

He hid his loot in a round tin concealed under the floor beneath his bed. He had loosened a floorboard for the purpose. With difficulty he manoeuvred the tin out from its hiding place and put it on his bed. Lifting the lid, he stared at the contents stolen from a woman on the street: a watch, a chain, coins and a few rings. That was a small hoard compared to what he had gathered in tonight's raid. If this carried on, he would soon need a larger tin. Laying his spoils gently back in the tin, he closed the lid and returned it to its hiding place. Muttering a quick prayer in thanksgiving and celebration, he flopped back on the bed. Only his aching muscles and a stinging scratch on his temple remained as mementoes of his glorious exploits that night.

Chapter Twenty-five

THE FOLLOWING MORNING, Ian left for work before Bev was up. For a moment he stood by the bed, watching her familiar profile as she slept. She looked so calm when she was asleep, and so vulnerable, he felt guilty for having made her unhappy. They had barely exchanged a word since the weekend. All week he had returned home shattered and distracted, going out early in the mornings before she was up. Although she had known about his career when they married, this was the first time she hadn't complained when he returned home late in the evenings too tired to pay her the attention she wanted. He began to hope she had finally accepted their lifestyle when he was on a case.

'I'll make it up to you when this is over, I promise,' he whispered to her sleeping figure before he left.

Half an hour later he was sitting at his desk examining his reasons for believing Gary was innocent, when Eileen summoned him to the incident room. As he made his way along the corridor, he felt more convinced than ever that Gary had neither attempted to assault Angela, nor killed her. The first allegation made no sense at all, given how eager Angela had been to persuade Gary to join her in the pub a few days later. Added to that, he could see no reason to believe Zoe's fanciful tale, and good grounds to suspect her of lying. Ted and Naomi were already in the incident room, waiting.

At first Ian wasn't sure how to react when he heard that the same axe had been used to kill both Angela and Tim. There was no longer any room for doubt. A trace of blood from a different blood group to Tim's had been isolated from the tissue in the edges of the wound on his neck. The trace was so miniscule as to be virtually impossible to identify, but sophisticated DNA testing confirmed it was Angela's. Not only were they now looking for a double murderer, but they had lost their suspect in the investigation into Angela's murder. Gary had been securely locked in a police cell the previous night, when Tim had been killed.

'You never thought he was guilty,' Eileen said to Ian. 'Well, you were right.' She paused. 'Of course, there's still that rape allegation, but we're never going to make that stick, are we? Oh God, we're not getting anywhere with this. Still, we'll have to let him go. You thought he was innocent all along. You can tell him.'

Eileen seemed so tense, Ian hoped stress wasn't going to affect her judgement. However dreadful a crime might be, it was vital the investigating team remained rational. All the same, a decapitation was enough to upset anyone's equilibrium.

If Ian had felt sorry for Gary before, his pity was heightened when he saw him in his cell. He had been locked up for less than twenty-four hours, but he looked as though he hadn't washed for weeks. Perhaps he hadn't. There was a stale stench in the cell, and his greasy hair shed flecks of dandruff whenever he moved his head. He was eighteen, legally old enough to be treated as an adult. The custody sergeant had been perfectly correct in the way he had dealt with him. Yet Ian couldn't help wondering whether the right course of action had been followed. Eighteen-year-olds could be quite immature, and Gary didn't appear to be very bright. It hardly seemed fair to treat him as a responsible adult. If he had been just a few months younger, he would have been offered the company of an appropriate adult when he was questioned, someone who could give him support and advice. As it was, he looked pathetically solitary, sitting on the bunk in his cell.

'You're free to go.'

'What?'

Ian repeated his announcement, adding a brief explanation. Gary's response was predictably ungracious but also unexpected. He didn't even appear pleased to be told he was being released

'You mean you locked me up in here, and left me to rot, and all you can say is it was a mistake. I should be compensated for this. You did this, you fucking arsehole. This is your fault.' He sat back on his bunk and folded his arms. 'I'm not leaving until you agree to compensate me for . . .'

'For putting you up for the night?'

'For wrongful arrest!'

Ian pointed out that the young man had never actually been arrested. He had merely been detained for a night.

'I demand to be compensated for the mental torment you put me through!'

Ian stared impassively at the angry youngster for a moment. He really wasn't very clever. Ian couldn't resist the temptation to call his bluff.

'Well, I suggest you seek legal advice. But you can be sure you won't be receiving any compensation, so if you choose not to leave, that's up to you. Only I have to warn you that you could be charged with wasting police time, if you insist on staying here.'

Gary leapt clumsily to his feet in a panic as Ian pretended to leave the cell.

'All right, all right, fucking hell, don't leave me here! I'm going, all right. But you'll be hearing from me – from my lawyer – I got a lawyer – and we're going to see you go down for this. You personally, Mr High-and-Mighty Police Inspector. I know what your name is, I made a note of it, you can be sure of that, Inspector Peterson. You're for the chop all right.'

Given the circumstances, the angry young man's choice of phrase was slightly disturbing. With a sigh, Ian turned and led him to the custody sergeant's desk.

'Now then,' the sergeant addressed Gary cheerily, 'let's see what you handed over.' He glanced down at Gary's feet. 'Shoes, and was there a belt and a wallet to go with them?'

'Yes. And you'd better not have nicked anything. I know what you lot are like. I'm going to complain and you're all going to be in trouble for what you done to me. Especially him,' he added, turning to scowl at Ian.

The sergeant had heard such ranting many times before. 'You have the right to complain, sir, if you're not satisfied,' he responded stolidly, 'but I think you'll find we acted within the law and you were treated fairly. Now, if you'll just sign here, you can be on your way.'

'And we can get on with the job of finding the real killer,' Ian thought.

Releasing Gary had focussed all of their minds back on the case. There was a lot to do. They were looking for a murder weapon, a disembodied head, and an axe-wielding killer. It was a grisly list.

Chapter Twenty-six

THE DETECTIVE'S PARTING words were bothering Dana.

'If you think of anything else that might help us to find out who did this, anything at all, let me know.'

She had been too upset to think of it at the time, but afterwards she had begun to wonder if she did know something. The more it troubled her, the more convinced she became that she could help the police to find her uncle's killer. She had remembered something as soon as she and her mother had left the shop. Normally her mother would have been embarrassed to be driven home in a police car, but she had been so distraught, they could have been dragged home through the streets chained in a cage and her mother wouldn't have noticed. With all the shock of discovering the body, and the fuss and bother with the police, and all their questions, Dana hadn't been able to think.

It wasn't until after they had left the detective that Dana recalled seeing a creepy man at the bus stop. At the time, when she had noticed the man, she had assumed he was watching her. The truth had turned out to be even worse than that, because he hadn't been interested in her at all. His attention had been focussed on the shop. Standing at the bus stop so it looked as though he was waiting for a bus, he had actually been observing people coming and going in and out of the jewellers. Why else would he have let the bus go without getting on? Riding away, she had seen him enter the shop. Once she had left, he would have known Tim was in there on his own. It could just as easily have been her, left alone in the shop. In that case, Tim would have been safe, and she would have been lying somewhere without her head. The thought made her feel dizzy. It was all so horrible; she almost wished it had been her, not Uncle Tim, who had been killed.

At first she was too scared to tell anyone. What if the man found out she had told the police about him? As soon as he realised she was on to him, he was bound to come after her to silence her. The police might not catch him in time to save her. On the other hand, if she didn't go to the police, he might never be caught, and she would still be in danger. It was all so horrible, and so frightening, that she couldn't sleep. Her mother thought she was in a state because she was upset about her uncle, which of course she was. But there was more to it than that. In the end she felt she had to tell someone or her head would burst.

She decided to go and see the fit detective who had spoken to her and been so attentive at the shop. He was nice.

'Mum, I'm going out.'

'What do you mean, you're going out? Where are you going?'

Dana considered for a moment. Her mother could hardly stop her going to the police station.

'You're going to the police station dressed like that? Don't be ridiculous. Go and get changed into something decent. You look like you're going to a night club! And I'm coming with you.'

'I'm fine as I am,' Dana protested, pulling her short skirt down over her chunky thighs.

'Dana, you're not going out dressed like that.'

Grumpily Dana went and put her jeans on before they left the house together. Arriving at the police station she asked for Inspector Peterson.

'He said to ask for him if I remembered anything.'

There was a sudden flurry of activity. Although there were several people ahead of them waiting in the entrance hall, a smiling woman led Dana and her mother straight to a special room with comfortable chairs, where they were given cups of tea. It was the first time a stranger had treated Dana as though she was very important. If it wasn't for her poor uncle, she would have enjoyed the attention. As it was, she could barely control her distress. At last the good-looking inspector arrived and she cheered up a little, especially when he remembered her name. Overweight and homely, she wasn't used to men paying her attention.

'It was Wednesday evening,' she stammered. 'My – he – my uncle let me go home because he'd been out and left me on my own in the shop most of the day. It was our day to stay open until six and then he said he had to stay late after that because he was doing some stocktaking, but he said he didn't need me. He said he'd be there for a while . . .'

The inspector nodded. 'Go on. What was it you wanted to tell me?'

Dana explained about the man who had been standing at the bus stop watching the shop. She hadn't realised at the time, but he had been waiting until she left so that he could find her uncle alone in the shop. It could have been the other way round.

'He might have been waiting for another bus,' her mother pointed out.

'Well, he wasn't,' she snapped, 'because as I was going off, on the bus, I saw him go into the shop.' It was true, every word of it.

The inspector took her seriously. 'Can you describe this man?'

'Yes. I had a good look at him. I remember him really well.'

She was eager to impress the detective. She might not be pretty, or clever, but she could help him find her uncle's killer. He must want that more than anything, just as she did.

'He was quite tall, and really ugly. He was bald, and he had a stupid little beard, and he looked really creepy.'

The inspector went out and returned a moment later.

'Is this the man you saw?' He showed her a photo. 'Take your time, Dana. Look very carefully.'

She could sense a suppressed excitement in his voice. She knew what he wanted her to say.

'Yes!' she shouted, although she wasn't really sure if it was the same man or not.

'Are you sure?'

She couldn't go back on her word now, not without looking stupid. In any case, it looked like the man she had seen at the bus stop. It probably was him, and she was going to help make sure he was caught and locked up.

'Yes, that's him. That's the man who was waiting outside the shop on Wednesday. You know who he is, don't you?'

With luck, the inspector would ask her back to look at an identity parade. As she gave him what she hoped was an alluring smile, she heard her mother burst into tears at her side.

'The bastard,' she sobbed, 'the vicious, crazy bastard! How could he do that?'

At once, the inspector turned his attention to her mother. Dana really hated her sometimes.

Chapter Twenty-seven

IAN WENT TO FRANK's house himself. This time he had no hesitation in setting off to make an arrest, armed with the knowledge that Dana had seen Frank outside the jewellers' shop on the night Tim had been killed. Only as he drove to the suspect's house did he begin to wonder how reliable a witness Dana was. Putting such reservations aside for now, he rapped smartly at the door. After all, he was only pursuing a lead. It wasn't as though he was judge and jury in the matter. After a moment Frank came to the door. He was clearly startled when Ian announced the purpose of his visit.

'What are you talking about? She was my daughter. All right, she was my stepdaughter, but I brought that girl up, from a child, and in all the time I knew her I never touched a hair on her head. I might have yelled at her for her wild ways – she used to go out drinking to all hours, even when she was only fifteen, and her poor mother at home worrying herself sick. There were times I would have liked to give her a good slap, given half a chance, but her mother was too soft. I tell you I never lifted a finger against her and that's God's truth. As for anyone thinking I was responsible for what happened – that's outrageous. It's sheer spite. Who was it told you I had anything to do with Angela's death? Who was it?'

Moira came to the door. She burst into noisy weeping when she learned what was happening.

'That's crazy!' she screeched. 'Leave us alone! Frank was with me, he was with me.'

By the time they reached the police station, Frank had recovered his composure. He remained calm throughout the process, waiting for a lawyer to arrive, listening patiently to the convoluted preamble that had to be read at the start of the interview. At last they were ready to begin. He stated his name and sat staring stonily straight ahead.

'Where were you last night?' Ian began.

'Last night?'

'Between six and seven in the evening.'

Frank frowned at the unexpected question, but he answered readily enough.

'I was on my way home from work.'

'Do you have any witnesses?'

Frank's frown deepened. 'There were other people at the bus stop . . .'

It occurred to Ian that Dana might have seen Frank waiting for his bus, without him being in any way involved in Tim's murder.

'It's not a crime to travel on a bus, is it?' Frank added, as though he could read Ian's mind.

'What time did you arrive home?'

'Oh Jesus, I don't know. I didn't make a note of the time in case you came round asking questions. Look, I left work at the usual time, about five thirty, quarter to six, and waited at the bus stop for about five or ten minutes. But it was a nice enough night so I changed my mind and decided to walk.'

'So you didn't take the bus?'

'No, like I just said, I walked. It's only two miles. Sometimes I get the bus, sometimes I walk. It depends.'

'Depends on what?'

Frank looked puzzled. 'On the weather, on how tired I'm feeling, on how long I have to wait – what does it matter? Sometimes I walk, that's all. It's no big deal. I should walk home every day, of course. For the exercise.'

Frank's voice was steady. He sounded as though they were engaged in a friendly chat about ways to keep fit. His face gave a different impression. Although it was fairly cool in the interview room his forehead and upper lip were shiny with sweat, while his sharp, little eyes darted rapidly from Ian to Ted and back again, as though he was trying to weigh up how much they really knew about his movements that evening.

'Did you go into any shops on your way home?' Ted asked.

Frank shook his head. 'No.' He frowned. 'I'd just finished a day's work. I wanted to get home.'

'Yet you didn't wait a few minutes for the bus.'

'No. It was a nice evening. I wanted to clear my head, I guess. Look, I can't really remember what was going through my mind. It's not a crime to take some exercise, is it? It just helps.'

'Helps with what?'

'I've not been sleeping well since we lost Angela. The doctor said exercise would help.' He sighed.

They took a break shortly after that to check the bus timetable. The schedule confirmed Frank's account, establishing that he could have caught a bus home from the stop outside Tim's shop.

Leaving work shortly after five thirty he might well have just missed one bus, meaning he would have had to wait about ten minutes for the next one. It was perfectly reasonable to believe he had decided to abandon waiting for the bus in favour of walking home. Dana's accusation proved nothing.

'No, it proves nothing,' Eileen conceded, 'but it's a bit of a coincidence. He was a possible suspect for Angela's murder – he knew her, at least – and now he's admitted to being in the street outside the shop just about the time Tim was killed, and we have a witness – reliable or not – who saw him go into the shop. And he's strong enough to carry an axe.'

Ian had to agree Frank was a viable suspect.

'It's too much of a coincidence,' Eileen repeated. 'I don't buy it. Let's keep him in overnight, and see if we can persuade him to talk in the morning.'

Ian wasn't sure why he didn't go along with her suspicions. Although he had been unconvinced by Dana's statement, he was as disappointed as the rest of the team when the evidence failed to show anything that supported her account. Grainy CCTV at the bus stop showed a figure that resembled Frank walking in the opposite direction to the jewellers' shop at six o'clock. For a while the street had been almost deserted until at nearly seven CCTV from the shop doorway revealed a cloaked figure entering. Dana might well have seen Frank at the bus stop, noticed his bald head, and maybe even remembered his face sufficiently to recognise his picture the next day. But under the cloak, there was no way of identifying the person going into the shop after a lapse of almost an hour.

'I don't think she was deliberately lying,' Ian told Eileen. 'Eye witness statements are notoriously unreliable, and she's only a kid who's just discovered her uncle's decapitated corpse. It's understandable she might be a bit hysterical about it all.'

Eileen's dismay was emphatic, but she had to accept that Dana's account wasn't borne out by the CCTV evidence. While they all agreed it was a suspicious coincidence, Frank being outside the shop at that time, they had no proof he had gone into the shop, only the confused account of an unreliable girl. They focussed on Angela's murder, checking into Frank's background in even finer detail than before, and questioning everyone who knew him. It was a mammoth task. The results came back fairly uniform. Frank was a steady sort of a man who had never been known to react violently to provocation. His marriage to Moira was, as far as they could tell, stable.

'I love my wife,' he told Ian, speaking with a quiet dignity that Ian found convincing. 'She needs me now more than ever. Angela meant everything to her. It's not right to leave her on her own just now. Please, let me go home to my wife.'

Ian went home that evening, hungry and disgruntled, to find his own wife upstairs placing neatly folded clothes in a suitcase. More of her clothes were laid out on the bed, as though she had been choosing what to pack.

'What's going on?'

She turned to him with a tentative smile. 'I'm going away.'

'Going away?'

'Yes, I told you, I'm going to stay with my parents for the weekend.'

He didn't remember her saying anything about it but resisted saying so. She would accuse him of never listening to a word she said, and the conversation would threaten to end in a row.

'That's nice.'

She turned back to her packing.

'When are you off?'

'Tomorrow. First thing. I've booked a taxi to the station . . .'

'A taxi? Don't be silly. I'll drop you.'

'It's OK.'

She sounded annoyed. He wondered if she had been expecting him to remonstrate or at least tell her he would miss her. Going to her parents for the weekend was a perfectly reasonable thing to do. They had talked about it several times, in general terms, and he had always supported the idea. They were her family, after all, and he knew she missed them.

'I know how busy you are right now,' she added. 'I just thought you'd be off really early or, if you weren't going out at the crack of dawn for once, then you'd want to lie in. You must be knackered.'

He sighed. She was right. He was worn out, and the end of the case was nowhere in sight.

'Well, give your parents my best, won't you? When are you coming home?'

From behind, he saw her shrug her shoulders. 'I thought I might as well stay a few days, while I'm there.'

'Yes, I suppose so.'

There wasn't really anything more to say.

'Are you going to stand there watching me pack? Why don't you put the telly on? As soon as I'm finished here I'll get the dinner started.'

He went downstairs, his thoughts already back on Frank, weighing up the possibility that he might be guilty. First thing in the morning a team would set to work, checking Frank's movements, and looking into whether he could have acquired an axe anywhere. A knife would have been impossible to trace, but this killer had inadvertently offered them a possible lead. Not many people carried axes. With any luck the unusual weapon would lead them to the killer.

Chapter Twenty-eight

ON SATURDAY MORNING Ian overslept. He woke with an uneasy feeling that he had forgotten something. He couldn't grasp what was hovering at the edge of his consciousness, like a half remembered dream. Only when he was up and dressed did he remember that Bev had gone away for the weekend. He hadn't been awake to say goodbye. He called her at once to wish her a good trip, but she didn't answer her phone. His words sounded forced, but she would appreciate the message. At least, he thought she would. In the first few years of their relationship he had sensed a quiet harmony between them. He wondered now if that had been a fantasy. Ironically, since their marriage, he seemed to have become increasingly divorced from her feelings. After all this time she should have become used to his job, but she still seemed to resent the long hours he worked when he was on a case. He wondered if there was something else troubling her, and whether he should challenge her about it when she returned.

Driving to work he tried to put Bev out of his mind. He had to focus on the case. As soon as he reached the station he checked with the officers researching Frank's background. A team had been at work for hours searching for a loophole in Frank's alibi, or a credible reason why he might have wanted to kill his step-daughter. Both teams had drawn a blank. Although his wife was the only person who could give him an alibi, he had no obvious reason to want to kill his stepdaughter.

'Keep looking,' Ian insisted, but they all knew it was hopeless.

By midday they had to accept that they couldn't hold Frank any longer without charging him. Ian faced him across the table once more in an interview room. Frank looked dejected, but he met Ian's gaze steadily enough.

'I want to go home,' he said miserably.

'You're free to go, but don't leave the area without letting us know.'

'Does that mean I'm under house arrest?'

'That's not what I said. You're free to go, get on with your life, go to work, but don't move from your address without telling us where you are.'

'Get on with my life?' Frank repeated bitterly.

'I'm very sorry about your stepdaughter. We're doing all we can to find her killer.'

'By locking me up and spending your time questioning me, and leaving Moira all alone?'

Frank's voice rose in anger. His brow lowered threateningly and his face turned a darker shade. Ian wondered whether he might be driven to violence, given enough provocation. There was no question that teenage girls could be extremely annoying. He pictured Frank coming home from work, downing a few beers, or perhaps whiskies, while his wife wound him up about her absent daughter.

'She's barely sixteen, Frank.'

'Well, what do you want me to do about it?' Gulp of beer or whisky. 'You don't seriously expect me to go out at this time of night and search the streets for her?'

'Yes. It's what any father would do.'

That might have touched a nerve. Angela wasn't his daughter. Perhaps he resented that. Ian imagined Frank, drunk, goaded by his wife into going out. He might have come across Angela on her own in the street and seized her furiously by the arm.

'You're coming home with me.'

'You can't tell me what to do. You're not my father.'

Again, that raw nerve. Drunk and enraged, Frank might have lashed out wildly, giving the girl a fatal injury . . . with an axe. That was where Ian's theory fell apart because it made no sense. Frank might have had an inkling about where to look for Angela on a Sunday night, but why would he carry an axe with him when he went out looking for his stepdaughter.

Meanwhile, Frank's irritation appeared to have dissipated. He leaned back in his chair, his expression calm and his face paler than it had been a few seconds earlier. He was waiting. Slowly his heavy-lidded eyes closed. A faint sheen of sweat shone on his bald pate. He looked as though he was dozing off. With a start he woke up and glared around in surprise, as though he couldn't remember where he was. His eyes met Ian's and he gave a resigned shrug.

'Nearly dropped off there,' he muttered. 'Sorry. I didn't sleep well last night. It's not exactly comfortable in there.'

He jerked his head in the direction of the cells. He could have been making conversation with a mate in the pub. The idea that he might have lashed out in anger against his daughter didn't ring true. Ian stood up.

'You're free to go, Mr Carter,' Ian repeated. 'Just don't leave the area, or go too far from home, without letting us know or you could find yourself in trouble again.'

'Again?' Frank echoed. 'I haven't done anything.' He sounded weary, but not angry.

Ian sighed. For the second time in two days, he had released a suspect. Although he hadn't believed either Gary or Frank was guilty, it was always disappointing to learn that they didn't have enough evidence to charge a suspect and the investigation was right back at the starting blocks. As long as they had no idea who had killed Angela or Timothy, there was no way of knowing whether the axe murderer might strike again.

Having dealt with Frank's release, Ian made his way to the major incident room where the profiler was discussing the case with the rest of the team.

'This is no ordinary killer,' George was saying as Ian entered the room.

'What's an ordinary killer?' Naomi muttered.

Ian nodded in agreement with her. The more he saw of his young colleague, the more impressed he was with her proficiency. All the same, her attitude bothered him. She didn't appear to take the work seriously. Looking for a dangerous killer who had killed twice in four days, they were under pressure to find him quickly. Ian hoped that her seemingly blasé approach was simply her way of dealing with the horror of what they were facing.

George, meanwhile, was speaking in his gentle, clipped tones. 'What concerns me first and foremost is the nature of the weapon. It's unusual, quite ridiculous in practical terms.'

They all nodded or murmured in agreement. No one in their right mind would choose to use an identifiable axe as a murder weapon.

'It's odd, which makes it more difficult to try and work out with any degree of certainty what he's thinking, and almost impossible to predict what he might do next,' George went on, 'but I suspect he's going to kill again.'

'What makes you say that?' Eileen sounded tetchy.

'Because he's playing a role.'

'Playing a role? You mean he's deluded, or schizophrenic? That kind of thing?'

'Yes. My guess is that he's fantasising that he's some kind of SAS soldier.' George hesitated. 'It might sound crazy, but I think that's his rationale. The truth is, I'm afraid he's enjoying this violent killing spree, or at least he's somehow convinced himself he's doing the right thing. Either way, he's not likely to stop.'

'Then it's up to us to stop him,' Eileen said.

'How are we supposed to find him?' someone asked.

Eileen nodded. 'We could do with some help right now.'

Ian sighed. The detective chief inspector was right. With two victims brutally killed, they still had no suspect in the frame. The killer remained at large, and if George was right, he wasn't going to stop at two murders.

'We have to find this maniac,' he said aloud, speaking to himself as much as to anyone else who might hear him. 'We have to.'

Chapter Twenty-nine

'WHAT THE HELL's that?' Jem called out suddenly.

'What?'

'What's that, just over there, by the bridge?'

'Can't see anything!' Tommy shouted back, his thin face twisted with exertion. 'Don't stop – hey, watch out!'

'Look, over there!' Jem insisted, ignoring the warning.

Their oars clashed again, and Tommy swore. They were supposed to be practising for a race. Jem couldn't even row properly. He never took anything seriously. Muttering a curse, Tommy twisted round in his seat to stare in the direction his friend had indicated.

'Now we've lost our rhythm . . . bloody hell! What is it?'

Tommy swivelled round. He felt his hands tighten on his oars as he and his friend stared at each other in silence for a second.

Without exchanging another word, they began sculling gently towards the bank to take a closer look at the object Jem had pointed out. It took them a few seconds to establish a rhythm and pull together again. Slowly they drew closer to a large furry object trapped in the weeds and rushes on the river bank.

'It's a dead rat . . .' Tommy began.

'It's a bloody big rat!'

'Or a water vole.'

'It could be a cat.'

'Or a dog . . .' Tommy broke off with a yelp of alarm.

'What is it?' Jem whispered.

Tommy was closest to the ball of fur. He craned forward to gain a better view of the object bobbing gently up and down on the rippling water. As he stared, the ball of fur rolled over. Entangled in river weed at the water's edge, a human face appeared, seeming to stare back at him. It was virtually unrecognisable, the flesh bloated and ragged, the eyes wriggling.

'Oh fuck. That's disgusting!'

'What is it?'

'It's a dead body.'

'This is so cool!' Jem said. Further away from the floating object than Tommy, he couldn't see the face clearly. 'Where's the rest of it?'

'What do you mean, the rest of it?'

'I can only see the head above the water.'

'That's all I can see.'

'But can you see if it's a man or a woman?'

'I can't see the body under the water.'

'It's probably been here for weeks, and it's all been eaten, and just the bones are left.'

'That's disgusting,' Tommy repeated lamely. He was beginning to feel sick.

'Who do you think it is?'

'How the hell should I know?'

'Let's go closer and get a better look.'

'No,' Tommy protested. He couldn't think of anything worse than having a clearer view of the decomposing face. 'We mustn't contaminate the crime scene,' he added, doing his best to sound grown up.

'Don't be so pathetic. I've never seen a real dead body before. We might never get a chance to see one again. Come on! It'll be fun!'

Tommy shook his head.

'Anyway, we can't just leave it there, someone might be looking for him. Or her,' Jem pointed out, screwing up his eyes and trying to peer through the murky water.

'We have to tell the police,' Tommy said firmly.

'Go on then.'

'What?'

'Go ahead and tell them if you really want to spoil it.'

'You have to come with me.'

Jem launched into a long account of how his cousin who had reported a crime to the police had ended up going to prison.

'All he'd done was tell them the shop had been broken into,' he explained indignantly. 'He hadn't done anything wrong. All he'd done was be a good citizen and because they couldn't find out who did it they locked him up instead. They have to get a conviction. It's part of their targets. He was just a statistic to them. Best steer clear of getting into trouble with the pigs, that's what my dad says. You could end up as one of their statistics.'

They passed the decomposing body and drifted over to the bank, still squabbling about what to do. In the end, Tommy prevailed. Pulling out his phone, he dialled 999 with fingers that shook with excitement. By now the dead body was out of sight, hidden in the river weeds. It was hard to believe they had really seen anything so gruesome but Tommy was on his phone, gabbling to a voice on the other end of the line. He gave his name. Jem shook his head, flapping his free hand in the air too late to stop Tommy giving his friend's name as well: Jem Nichols.

'No,' Jem mouthed, with an anguished grimace, 'leave me out of it.'

Ignoring his friend, Tommy tried to explain what they had seen, and the precise location where they had seen it. It sounded unlikely. He wasn't sure the woman on the other end of the line believed him, she asked him to repeat what he had seen so many times. He did so, with increasing anxiety. At last Tommy hung up. Jem wanted to go back and have a closer look, but the police had instructed Tommy to remain where he was.

'Come on,' Jem urged him. 'Let's go back.'

'She said we had to stay exactly where we are.'

'No one will know.'

'I'm not going back.'

'Chicken.'

'I just don't want to look at it again, all crumbly and maggoty. It makes me feel sick.'

'Wimp.'

Tommy no longer cared about Jem's insults. He had no intention of looking at the dead body again. It was going to give him nightmares enough already. He clung to his excuse for not moving.

'The police said we have to stay where we are. You don't want to get in trouble, do you? Remember what happened to your cousin.'

A few moments passed in uneasy silence before Tommy was startled to hear a voice hail him by name. Looking up he saw a uniformed police officer standing on the bank staring down at him. As he answered, another officer appeared. Tommy and Jem gestured eagerly towards the bridge. One of the officers hurried away and returned a few moments later, talking busily into his phone. He nodded at his colleague who also began talking rapidly on his phone. Within a few minutes, a few more policemen arrived, followed by a team all dressed in white spaceman suits.

'It's just like on the telly,' Tommy said, 'only this lot are so slow.'

Chapter Thirty

NOT LONG AFTER lunch the duty sergeant rapped sharply on Ian's door. 'DCI wants you down by the railway bridge right away, sir. SOCOs should be there by now, with a diving team.'

'What's going on? I thought we weren't going to search the river bed. Has something happened?'

He was on his feet as he spoke, pulling on his jacket. The killer had escaped on the river. Some new evidence must have turned up. There could be no other reason to search the river just then. He hoped another body hadn't been discovered. He never slept well when a multiple murderer was at large. It was hardly surprising, really. The pressure to solve the case became unbearably urgent. Already they were looking for an axe-wielding maniac who had killed Angela and Timothy. That was bad enough. A third victim would mean they were officially looking for a serial killer. The papers were already full of the two victims and their gruesome deaths. Another murder would send them into a complete frenzy.

The duty sergeant confirmed that new evidence had been found that might relate to Timothy's killer.

'But surely the killer didn't leave anything in the water?' Ian asked, puzzled.

'Well, yes, he did leave something, sir. Everyone's very excited about it.'

Ian frowned. 'How come everyone's so certain whatever they found was left by the killer?' The duty sergeant just shook his head. 'I mean, couldn't it have been left by someone else?'

The duty sergeant spoke up. 'Not this time, sir.'

'I don't see why. Yesterday we weren't getting a diving team, today we are. What's going on? Sounds like a lot of fuss about nothing.'

'A couple of kids were messing about on the river,' the sergeant went on agreeably, unperturbed by Ian's bad temper. 'You're not going to believe what they found!'

By the time Ian reached the river, a team of scene of crime officers were hard at work scrutinising a section of river bank; two divers were in the water, and a forensic tent had been erected on the path which was cordoned off in both directions. It was an inconvenience to the locals, but everyone understood the need to avoid contaminating the site where a murderer had been busy. All the same, Ian sympathised with a fat woman who shrieked every time a uniformed officer walked past her, demanding to be told what was happening, and to know when the path would be open again.

'No one tells me where I can and can't walk! I walk along this path every day. It's a public right of way. No one has the right to stop me walking here. It's doctor's orders. I have to walk every day. You! You're supposed to be upholding the law, not breaking it.'

A uniformed officer approached and did her best to pacify the irate walker. Ian hurried past, averting his eyes. He never relished

going into forensic tents at crime scenes. Although he anticipated this one being particularly gruesome, given what he had
been told, surprisingly it was less disturbing than many he had
seen. On the ground a head lay, worm-eaten, the flesh shredded
and falling away. It didn't look human. There was no need for a
medical examiner to sign a death certificate. The identity of the
head had not yet been confirmed but no one was in any doubt that
this must belong to the headless jeweller. There was even some
macabre satisfaction in knowing the body parts would soon be
reunited. It hadn't taken long to establish what had happened. The
head had entered the water at the point where the tracker dog had
lost the scent it had followed from the jewellers' shop. That much
at least was clear. After a brief look around, and a desultory chat
with a scene of crime officer, Ian left.

The head was taken to the mortuary but there was no point
in following it there. The pathologist wouldn't arrive until the
following morning. Despite his impatience, Ian knew they were
lucky Jonah was willing to go in to work on Sunday at all. In the
meantime, Ian returned to the police station, where he spent a
few hours at his desk reading through statements. He was in no
rush to go home to his empty house. He was not used to spending
the night alone there. When he finally packed up work and went
home, the house seemed strangely quiet.

Stacking the dishwasher, he found himself enjoying the mind-
less task. Bev never liked him to potter around in the kitchen;
that was her territory. His chores done, he phoned her, but she
didn't answer. He supposed she was either out with her parents,
or already asleep. It made him slightly uneasy, having no idea
what she was doing, yet, at the same time, it felt liberating. He
tried her phone once more, then gave up. There was no need to

be concerned about her. It wasn't as though she was crossing a war zone by herself. She was with her family. If there were any problems, they would contact him. He could relax, secure in the knowledge she was being well looked after. All the same he slept fitfully that night, and dreamed about his absent wife. They were in a shopping centre but he had lost sight of her. He searched in every shop but couldn't find her.

On Sunday morning Ian drove straight to the mortuary. Avril threw him a shrewd glance.

'Are you OK?' she asked, her blue eyes solemn. 'You look like death warmed up.'

'I've come to the right place then,' he grinned.

'Well, I'm not sure about the warming up.'

'With you here? It's positively hot.'

She slapped his arm playfully. 'Go on in. You'll find him in there, examining your head.'

'My head? I still had it last time I looked.'

Jonah looked up as Ian entered, and a grin spread across his freckled face.

'We've found our missing head. It's a perfect fit!' He stepped aside to give Ian a clear view of the decapitated victim, head carefully set in place above the shoulders. 'It took a few strokes to hack it off completely. I'll give you one guess what was used to cut it off.'

Ian stared at the reconstructed corpse without answering. It was a rhetorical question.

'There is one more thing might interest you,' Jonah added. His voice rose slightly with excitement. 'With luck it might even help you identify the murder weapon.'

Ian raised his eyebrows. He waited, not daring to interrupt.

'Wait.'

Jonah sent one of his assistants to fetch a blown up photograph. Ian looked at it. The lab assistant shone a bright light on it. Jonah pointed to a large darkish blotch being displayed. Ian frowned and leaned closer, trying to see any significance in the discoloured patch.

'What is it?' he asked at last. 'I don't get what it is.'

'That's a bruise on one of Angela's temples. But look at the marking on it.'

Ian stared then shook his head. 'No,' he said, 'I don't get what you mean.'

'It's not easy to make out with the naked eye,' Jonah explained, 'but there's a logo of some sort, and the shape of the bruise suggests it was made with the flat of the axe head, as though the killer whacked her on the side of her head, maybe by accident. We'll send you an image that shows the pattern more clearly. It looks like the letter y.'

Ian nodded, puzzled but faintly excited. Although he couldn't see how it was going to help much, any new information might possibly be the lead they were waiting for.

'Send me the image as soon as you can.'

Chapter Thirty-one

BEV ARRIVED HOME late on Sunday evening. After trying her number without success in the afternoon, Ian had picked up some fish and chips on the way home and was slouched on the sofa, his feet resting on her sewing box, when he heard her key in the lock. The regional news had just begun. For a few days the local media had been dominated by the Axe Murderer. In a way, Ian sympathised with their interest. No one could deny this was a particularly gruesome case. The murderer had used an axe to kill first a young woman and then a man, within the space of three days. He might strike again at any time. No one in the area, man or woman, felt safe.

Murder of any kind was worrying enough, but the weapon used in this case had caught the public imagination. Fears were fanned by media hysteria. 'Axe Man Strikes Again', screamed the headlines in the local papers. Unusually, their sensationalist language was accurate. The killer had used an axe, more than once, and no one knew when he might strike again. It was still unclear who had disclosed the nature of the murder weapon to the press.

Eileen was furious about the leak. Privately, Ian thought she was making an unnecessary fuss. The media would have found out about the axe sooner or later. All that really mattered was to focus on finding the killer. It was even possible that someone had seen a neighbour or acquaintance carrying an axe. The press coverage might prompt a witness to come forward.

The media had been busy over the week since Angela's murder. Not only had they learned about the axe, they had discovered the identity of the man who had been taken in for questioning. Frank's release the previous day seemed to have whipped them up into a frenzy of hyperbole. One of the television reports appeared intent on causing a public panic. 'Police Stumped' the strap line announced, as the presenter described how Frank had been taken in for questioning, only to be released after a day. According to the reporter, the police were at a loss and the public at risk. This was followed by a discussion in the studio between a news presenter and some kind of psychologist, picking over the fact that Frank was Angela's stepfather.

Ian scowled at the screen as a clip of a young, happy Angela was displayed laughing in a garden. Nothing that had been stated was untrue, but the reporter had put an unfortunate spin on the news item, implying the police were incompetents casting around helplessly for clues. He leaned back on the sofa and closed his eyes, irritated by the criticism. Anyone with any sense knew that murder investigations couldn't be conducted hurriedly. He would like to see that smug-faced reporter working round the clock to try and solve the case, instead of criticising the people who were actually doing something to try and track down the killer.

'Ian! I'm home!' Bev called.

With a sigh he heaved himself off the sofa and went out to the hall to greet her. 'How was your weekend?'

Bev shook her head and pulled off her dripping raincoat. Her short fair hair was plastered to her scalp making it look absurdly small, like a child's head.

'It's raining. You should have called me from the station.'

'It's bloody pouring out there.' It sounded like an accusation. 'You knew what time my train was getting in. I texted you this morning. When I didn't see you at the barrier, I assumed you were at work. You usually are. So I took a taxi. I still got soaked though.'

Apologetically, Ian said he must have dozed off, and not realised the time. It was a pathetic excuse. Expecting her home that evening, he ought to have checked the time of her train and been at the station to meet her.

'It doesn't matter,' she said, shrugging off his apology.

He put his arms out.

'Not now, Ian,' she said, avoiding his embrace, 'I'm all wet. I just want to get dry and go to bed.'

'Why don't I make you a cup of tea?'

She shook her head. 'I had something on the train.'

He trailed after her up the stairs but she insisted she was too tired to talk.

'I'm going to have a hot shower and go to bed.'

Ian returned to the living room to wait for the national news. It wasn't encouraging. Although this particular reporter didn't utter a word of complaint against the police, the implication was clear. An interview with a strident woman demanding the police do more to protect the public seemed to go on for a long time. There was no answering interview with the police to balance the report. An uninformed member of the public might well conclude that the police were dragging their heels. However hard the team was working made no difference. All the public were interested in was the outcome, and so far the police had only managed to eliminate a couple of suspects. Two down, several millions to go. With the interviewee's unhelpful comments ringing in his ears, Ian went upstairs.

Bev was already in bed. Wearily he undressed.

'It's good to have you back,' he mumbled.

He kissed the side of her head, feeling the visceral comfort of her warm body beside him. Her hair smelt damp. The familiar scent of her shampoo made him want her. Pulling her towards him, he told her he had missed her.

'You haven't wrapped up the investigation?' she asked, resisting his embrace.

'We're making headway, but we haven't found him yet.'

'Your Axe Man.' On her lips the nickname sounded like a sneer.

'We're doing our best.'

'What happens when the best just isn't good enough?'

He frowned at her, uncertain what she meant. 'Then he gets away, I suppose. Is everything all right?'

It occurred to him that he hadn't enquired about her parents, hadn't gathered anything at all about her weekend. Afraid she was offended, he asked how her family were. She turned her back on him.

'Not now, Ian. I'm tired. Leave it till tomorrow.'

He suspected she would be fast asleep when he left for work in the morning, but there was no point trying to talk to her when she was going to sleep. Somehow he had missed an opportunity to reach out to her. He closed his eyes and whispered, 'It's good to have you back.'

She didn't answer.

Chapter Thirty-two

FEAR WAS AN unwelcome companion to a warrior of his stature. It was unfitting, but he struggled to control his terror when he saw the news on the television. Somehow the police had stumbled upon the contents of the bag he had emptied so thoughtlessly into the river. He had never considered the possibility that it might be discovered. His enemy's head should have sunk down to the riverbed, or else been carried far out to sea by the current. Instead the head had turned up, bobbing about, very near to the place where he had thrown it in the water. The gods were playing with him, but he was strong enough to withstand whatever trials they sent him. Many more would fall at his hand before he carried his weapon to Valhalla.

The police were searching for him. A policeman on the local news said they were following several leads. It would be wise to wait indoors for a while before planning another raid, and keep out of sight. He tried to think if there was any way they could track him down. They were using dogs, but that was no cause for panic. He had outwitted them so far. Dogs couldn't track him on the water. That was good. The gods had protected him. They wouldn't abandon him now, not so long as he remained steadfast in his prayers and kept his wits about him. The treasure was safely stowed in its hiding place but the bags – one bloodied – were still lying on the floor of his living room where he had dropped them three nights ago. In his triumph he had forgotten about them, focussing only on his spoils. The bags were of no value. He folded them, and squashed them into two black plastic bin liners which he crammed into the massive waste bins at the back of his block of flats. The refuse collectors were due to clear the bins the follow-ing day, when the evidence of his victim's blood would be crushed and pulped. No one would recognise the material that had once formed bags. The detritus would never be tested for blood or DNA. It could never be traced back to him.

Next up was his cloak. Back in his bedroom he sat staring at it, undecided what to do with it. The cloak was long, not quite reaching the ground, and voluminous, with a loose hood, perfect for his purposes. He was loath to let it go. Wide streaks of blood down the front had dried so that it looked uniformly black. There was no reason for anyone to suspect it had been present when jets of blood had spurted from a dying man's throat. But the police had ways of testing for such evidence, and a tracker dog could scent blood from far away. He would be playing with danger if he kept it at all, let alone risked wearing it out on the street. He could just imagine the scene. Walking innocently along the pavement he would be assaulted by a baying dog. Within seconds he would be surrounded by men in uniform, slammed up against a car and handcuffed. His cloak would be torn from his shoulders and sent away for forensic examination, the results of which would con-demn him to decades in a prison cell. It wasn't worth the risk. The cloak had to go. It barely fitted inside a bin liner. He carried it out to the waste bins. Grunting with the effort of squashing it down, he heard himself begin to sob at the injustice of it all. The cloak had been a part of his routine. His life would never be the same again. He had no idea how he was going to replace it without leaving any traces. At the last minute he changed his mind and pulled the bag out again. Somehow he would wash his cloak, scrubbing away all traces of blood until it was safe to wear again. He had not finished with it yet. Trembling, he slung the black bag over his shoulder and hurried back to his room.

The axe was a different matter altogether. Without his weapon, a mighty warrior was no more than a man. He ought to be brandishing his sharpened axe above his head, shouting aloud, 'Look what I and my trusty blade have achieved!' But no one else understood the power behind his dark desires. He would hide his axe away, like some wild shame, until it was time to glory in using it again. Meanwhile fools would run around, looking for him. While the gods willed him to claim more victims, mere men could never stop him.

Chapter Thirty-three

Ian FELT A GUILTY relief that Bev was fast asleep when he left for work in the morning. In some ways her interest in his work was more wearing than her complaints about his long hours. He could never be sure what his day would hold and suspected she felt excluded when he rebuffed her questions.

'You have to understand that I can't talk about it, not even to you,' he had told her.

'Of course I understand,' she would answer, with a sour expression.

'Most of what I do is really dull,' he might add, to which she would respond with sceptical silence.

That Monday began like most others. He spent a dispiriting hour reading through statements, and writing up his own records. The only encouraging aspect of the early morning was reading Ted's decision log. Ian had done his best to impress on the sergeant the importance of keeping detailed records.

'It's for your own protection. You can never tell when something might unexpectedly blow up in your face, so you never know when you might be called on to justify your actions. It's not always easy to remember your reasoning afterwards, especially when you have to act quickly. It's not about catching you out. We all have to watch our backs. The fact is, there isn't always an obvious course of action in any given circumstance. You just have to do the best you can and as long as you can explain why you did what you did, you'll be supported, even when things go wrong.'

The sergeant's reports were becoming more thorough yet more concise as he grew in confidence and understood more clearly that the decision log was there for his own protection. It was not a platform for self-promotion. Ted's decisions had consistently struck Ian as sound and sensible. As the officer responsible for the sergeant's professional development, Ian had found his log worryingly slapdash when they had first started working together. He felt pleased with the progression in Ted's reporting. In his own way, Ian had contributed to the success of Ted's career.

Soon after nine o'clock, Avril sent through an image of the bruise on Tim's decapitated head. The photograph had been digitally enhanced until the original pattern on the bruise became visible, although it had been impossible to see with the naked eye. Ian stared at it. There was something familiar about the pattern of a capital Y with a vertical line between the two upper branches of the letter. Feverishly he scanned through his notebook until he found the notes he was searching for. He had been off duty and hadn't bothered to log an official record of the reported theft of a replica Viking axe at the Festival. Nevertheless he had noted the incident, more by habit than design. Several possessions had probably gone astray in the bustling crowds. This man had lost his grip on his axe, and someone else had taken it. At the time it had seemed unimportant, hardly a matter for a police investigation. Now Ian was glad he had kept a note of the theft.

The new information from Jonah placed an entirely different complexion on the incident. Whoever had taken the axe appeared to be using it to kill in earnest. This information was an additional piece of the puzzle. Ian just wasn't yet sure of its significance, or how it was going to help them track down the killer. After writing up his notes, he decided to speak to Andrew Hilton, the man whose axe had been stolen at the Viking Festival. Although they hadn't found the murder weapon, they might be able to gather more information about it.

Andrew Hilton lived in Driffield. It was a pleasant drive there along fast roads, to a small house in a rundown back street. A plump woman opened the door. She narrowed her eyes when she saw Ian.

'I thought you were Ellie,' she said, as though Ian ought to know who Ellie was. 'Whatever you want, we're not interested.'

Ian stepped forward quickly to introduce himself, before she could close the door.

'What do you want with him?' she asked suspiciously when Ian asked for Andrew.

Once Ian had explained the purpose of his call, she turned and yelled out. 'Andy! Come here! They found your axe!'

A few seconds later Andrew appeared.

'Do you remember your axe that was stolen at the Festival . . .' Ian began.

He was loudly interrupted. 'Of course I bloody remember. So, have you found it?'

Ian faced the other man calmly. He wasn't about to be intimidated by this aggression. Quietly he explained his interest in the missing axe.

'What I'd like to know is where you bought it. We need to discover how common such axe heads are. It seems possible the killer might be using your stolen weapon.'

'Oh bloody hell! You're telling me I'm not going to get it back? You're going to need it for evidence?'

Ian swallowed, momentarily taken aback. Andrew genuinely appeared to be more interested in recovering his axe than in assisting the murder investigation. Having taken down details of the missing axe for a second time, Ian learned that it had been purchased from a stall holder exhibiting at the Viking Festival three or four years before. Andrew couldn't remember the name of the stall holder, and had no paperwork relating to the purchase. He wasn't sure exactly when he had bought it, and said he had paid cash. Ian thanked him for his help. It might be possible to trace the stall holder who had been selling replica Viking weapons at the Festival three or four years previously, but the chance that there would be any record of other sales of similar axes was slim. In any case, if the killer was using a stolen axe, which seemed likely, then there would be no way of tracing him through the purchase.

'All I remember is that I was chatting to some people who said they worked at the Viking museum. There was a woman and a couple of blokes, I think. It's difficult to remember. It was such a ruck there, and it's a long time ago. So with them saying they worked at the museum I showed them my axe. I mean, there was no reason not to. Next time I looked, it had gone.'

It wasn't much of a lead, but Ian decided to go to the Jorvik museum. He had been intending to go there anyway. It was a popular tourist attraction in York, and had been recommended by a colleague as offering an insight into life in the Viking settlement.

Bev had been there and had described the place to him, but Ian hadn't really listened closely to her enthusiastic account of her visit. All he really knew was that a significant hoard of coins buried in the tenth century had been discovered in York in 2007. Known as the York Hoard, it was on display in the museum, along with other artefacts, and a complete reconstruction of a Viking community. Bev's imagination had been particularly captured by one of the figures in a model village, which had been created using facial reconstruction from an authentic Viking skull.

'You can tell what he actually looked like, all those centuries ago!'

'Amazing.'

'Ian, you're not listening, are you?'

'Of course I'm listening.'

He wasn't.

'Well, you ought to go there,' she had replied, peeved at his lack of interest. 'Then you'd understand. Really, it's amazing looking at that face. The only trouble is, you're on this little train thing, and it moves along too fast to really study the face. But they weren't the aggressive raiders everyone thinks, they were traders and settled peacefully here. Only they were better looking than the locals, and many of the local women preferred the Viking men. That's why they got such a bad reputation for raping and pillaging, because the indigenous population resented the tall blonde invaders taking their women.'

'Tall and blonde, eh?' Ian smiled. 'Perhaps I've got Viking antecedents.'

He was joking, but Bev took him seriously. 'Yes, I've always thought so.'

Ian had promised to go to the Jorvik museum with her, but somehow they had never found the time. Now he was going there with a different purpose in mind. Ignoring the queue waiting patiently to enter, he rang the bell by the door to the right of the public entrance. Once he had been buzzed in, he went straight up a narrow flight of stairs to a carpeted corridor of offices above the museum. At the top of the stairs a young receptionist asked him to take a seat. He explained that a team of officers would arrive shortly to speak to the entire staff, and the receptionist hurried away to speak to her boss.

'The head of operations will be with you in a minute,' she told him when she returned.

A moment later, a tall man in a dark suit appeared around the corner of the corridor.

Chapter Thirty-four

EXTENDING A HAND, the man greeted Ian with an easy smile. 'Good morning, I'm Ralph Grey, head of operations here. How can I help?'

Ralph was tall and thin, and would have been good-looking if he hadn't been slightly cross-eyed. He led Ian along a narrow corridor, past several whiteboards and peg boards, to a small office with three pine desks and shelving, and a large window. It was bright and airy, though small.

'Now,' Ralph said, 'what's the problem?'

Ian explained that he wanted to question staff at the museum, following a suspicion that the weapon used in the recent spate of murders was a replica Viking axe.

'The axe murders, you mean?'

Ian nodded, acknowledging the name the press had given to the case.

Ralph's eyes narrowed. 'But it was a replica,' he repeated. There was no reason why a copy would be in any way connected to the museum. 'Anyone could get hold of a replica,' he added, as though the implication might have been lost on Ian.

'Indeed,' Ian agreed. 'What I'd like to know is how many of these axes there are around, where they are made, and where they can be obtained.'

Ralph nodded slowly. They both knew the question was faintly absurd. 'We have a description,' Ian added.

'If it's specifically an axe you're interested in, you could talk to Ollie. He has a particular interest in the weapons here and probably knows more about them than anyone.'

Ralph picked up the phone and made a quick call. A few moments later, there was a tap at the door. It opened to admit a skinny young man whom Ralph introduced as Oliver. With straw-coloured hair and pale blue eyes, Oliver Hemmings looked younger than his twenty years. He explained diffidently that he had spent a year studying at the university in York. He had dropped out at the start of his second year, after which he had been lucky to find a job at Jorvik museum.

'And here I am,' he added simply.

A shy smile played on his thin lips as he spoke, but the expression in his eyes remained sharp. Like Ralph, he had noticed no strange activity in the museum recently, and he wasn't aware of any problems in the shop. As far as he knew, the weapons cabinet always remained securely locked and no one had paid any unusual attention in it. He leaned forward and stared intensely as Ian described the rune on the bruise that had shown up on the second victim's head. Ian said nothing about the axe that had gone missing at the Viking Festival. For a moment Oliver was silent as Ian held up an image of the bruise on the side of Tim's head. Ian watched the young man closely. There was a brightness in his eyes and the tip of his tongue flickered in and out, wetting his lips as though he was nervous. Eventually he lowered his head, making his fair fringe flop forward over his eyes.

'Algiz,' he said.

'What?'

'The symbol you just showed me.'

'The sign on the bruise?'

'Yes. It looks like algiz, the rune for protection.'

Ian wondered if it might be significant that Oliver recognised the particular symbol straight away.

'You must know all the runes? That's pretty impressive.'

Oliver shook his head. His expression was difficult to read. 'It's only another alphabet really,' he explained, 'although each symbol represents something, not just a sound like our alphabet.'

'So do you know them all?' Ian pressed him.

Oliver sighed softly. 'I used to,' he admitted. 'I was a bit of a geek in a way, I suppose. I still know all the major ones, but I'm a bit hazy on a few of them now.'

Ian didn't push the point. Apart from confirming what the owner of the missing axe had told Ian about the symbol on its blade, Oliver was not much help. He had no idea where a blade like that might have been obtained and claimed to know nothing about the theft of a similar weapon at the Viking Festival. When Ian expressed surprise, telling him the theft had been reported in the press, Oliver merely shrugged his shoulders.

'Well, I never saw it.'

'We're all sort of experts in one way or another here, but weapons and fighting aren't really my thing. What interests me is the way the people lived, what they wore and what they ate, things about their everyday lives. That's what I've been researching mainly. Of course I'm not really what you'd call an expert. I've just studied Viking society enough to talk about it to members of the public, and to be able to answer basic questions. It's part of our job, being able to tell visitors to the place about the exhibits and where they come from. That's what makes working here so interesting. I'm learning all the time. But weapons aren't really my thing.' He gave an apologetic grimace.

Ian didn't tell him that Ralph had referred to him as the weapons expert. The young man barely hesitated when Ian asked him where he had been on the two evenings when the murders had been carried out.

'I don't know what I was doing that Sunday,' he said straight away, 'I just can't remember.'

Oliver's alibi was inconclusive.

Sophie was next to be questioned. She was twenty-two. Recently graduated in archaeology at the University of York, like Oliver she had found a job there. Originally from London, she hadn't wanted to leave the area.

'I'm settled here.'

'Boyfriend?' Ian asked amiably.

Sophie bristled. 'No.'

Ian studied her. With a face framed by pink hair which faded into blonde strands that hung to her shoulders, she looked like an art student.

'My area is the volur,' she announced.

Ian grunted, pretending to know what she was talking about; something to do with the Vikings no doubt. If it wasn't weapons, he wasn't really interested.

'Magic,' she explained.

'Fascinating,' Ian fibbed. 'You must know just about every-thing there is to know on the subject.'

The flattery worked to some extent.

'We have to be able to answer questions from visitors,' Sophie explained, unbending slightly.

'Tell me about the volur.'

Her face relaxed into a smile. She spoke as though to children, launching into what sounded like a well-rehearsed lecture.

'The volur is the name given to women who practised magic. These women were very influential in Viking society. The peo-ple then had strong beliefs in magic, and almost every story that has come down to us includes an element of magic or the super-natural. These beliefs coloured everything. Although today peo-ple generally think that warriors were the only really important members of Viking society, these women were very powerful. The volur were sort of sorceresses, and were often buried with their metal staffs and amulets. That's how we know so much about them, because of the artefacts that have been discovered in their graves, some of them immensely valuable, and always buried with women. They believed the soul was like a thread which was sent out when people died – or sometimes while they were still alive – and the volur could retrieve people's souls by winding them up on their staffs. Basically everyone had a hamingia, or spirit, that was independent of the person who owned it, as well as having exter-nal spirit guardians.'

'Like a guardian angel,' Ian remarked.

Carefully he moved the conversation round to the missing axe. Sophie didn't seem interested.

'I don't have anything to do with the weapons,' she said firmly. 'The volur are what interest me.'

Sophie readily supplied her alibi for the times of both murders. She had been with her flatmate on the Sunday evening and on her way home from work on the Wednesday.

'Were you travelling alone?'

'Well, I wasn't the only person on the bus that day, but I didn't get the names of the other passengers.'

Her attempted flippancy sat uneasily on her.

Chapter Thirty-five

JIMMY SUTHERLAND WAS the next member of staff to be summoned. A cheerful man of around forty with boyish good looks, he greeted Ian with a grin. His role was to organise the team of curators who worked in the museum, answering questions from members of the public.

'Well, that's an appropriate use for a Viking axe, wouldn't you say?' he responded, when Ian explained about the replica axe. 'Better than being stuck in a glass case at any rate.'

'Better in what way, exactly?'

Jimmy just winked. It proved difficult to get a straight answer out of him. He seemed to find everything amusing. Ian wondered if he was a bit simple. Even when Ian became quite aggressive, Jimmy didn't seem at all troubled. Despite his training in remaining detached, Ian was slightly disappointed to discover that Jimmy had not been in York the day Angela had been murdered. He said he had been away in London for a long weekend, visiting a friend, only returning to York by train on Monday morning, and going back to work on Tuesday. Ian believed him. His alibi was easy enough to confirm so there would be little point in his lying. All the same, Ian made a note to check out Jimmy's alibi. Warning him not to leave York, Ian let Jimmy go.

Apart from the operational staff upstairs who organised marketing and events, as well as the curators who answered questions from members of the public visiting the museum, there were a couple of receptionists, and two girls who served in the gift shop. Ian summoned the operational staff together, curious to observe their interaction. By contrast to Jimmy, Ralph was clearly dismayed by the use of a replica axe to kill people.

'This could be bad publicity for us,' he said.

'Might be a good thing. No publicity is bad publicity,' Jimmy responded. 'These aren't just any artefacts we're talking about,' Ralph insisted earnestly. 'Our artefacts date back over a thousand years. If they're mishandled or used disrespectfully, that's never a good thing. That's why we have to be so careful not to allow just anyone to handle them. They stay locked up where no one can touch them.'

'It's only a replica,' Jimmy pointed out. 'Not even a copy of one of ours. We don't have an axe with that rune carved on it, do we?'

Ralph shrugged. 'It's impossible to say what many of our axe heads looked like originally.'

On the face of it, the staff at the Jorvik museum had nothing very useful to add to what Ian knew about the missing axe. Oliver had explained the significance of the rune carved on the blade, but Ian could have discovered that for himself by looking up runes on the internet. Even so, he left the museum with a faint sense of unease. He wished he had brought Ted with him. A second pair of eyes was always useful, and he couldn't help feeling he had missed something.

Back at the police station Ian sat at his desk trying to think, but none of the information he had gathered seemed to point to any clear conclusion. He wrote up his report and studied what the other officers had found out from the rest of the staff at Jorvik before he summoned Ted so they could discuss what they had discovered. Ian couldn't help feeling there was something odd about Oliver.

'Well, it does seem suggestive that Ralph told you Oliver was a weapons expert, and Oliver denied it,' Ted agreed. 'But expert is a very loose term.'

They agreed that the most obvious suspect wasn't necessarily the right one. There was no reason to suppose the killer had anything to do with Jorvik at all.

Just as Ian began to feel they were going round in circles George, the profiler, wandered into the office. He perched on the edge of Ian's desk and twisted his head round to look at him. With a slow smile he raised an eyebrow interrogatively. Ian just shrugged. With a nod, George spoke.

'Maybe we know more than you think.' He paused. 'Let's go over what you've discovered since we last spoke.'

Ian hesitated.

'We're a bit suspicious of one of the guys who works at the Jorvik museum,' Ted said.

George swivelled round to glance up at Ted, who had stepped forward and was standing beside Ian's desk.

'Why's that? Go on, tell me what you're thinking,' George invited the sergeant.

Ted glanced at Ian who nodded.

'Interesting,' the profiler muttered when Ted had finished his summary of their findings. 'But this is just an overview. What's your gut feeling, Ian? You mentioned a suspicion.'

'We think Oliver Hemmings may be hiding something,' Ted interjected as Ian hesitated. 'Ralph told us Oliver was an expert in weapons, but Oliver denied it. We thought that was significant. And he seemed very interested in the axe. We thought that might mean something, too.'

Ian felt a rush of sympathy for his young colleague who was so desperate to find some clarity in the confusion of an investigation which was, so far, going nowhere.

'It may be significant that he was interested in telling you about the rune on the missing axe. It's often the case that people who have some interest in a case, for whatever reason, are keen to follow the investigation,' George said.

'You mean he might be the murderer, and he wants to get involved with us to find out how much we know?'

George laughed. 'I wouldn't have put it quite like that, but yes, it's certainly a possibility. How strong is his alibi for the times of the murders?'

'We're following up alibis from everyone who works there,' Ian assured him, 'although we're grasping at straws here. There's nothing to suggest anyone who works there had any connection to the murders. They don't have any similar axes there, and none have gone missing. We've been pursuing all the stall holders who were there for the past few years, but so far we haven't found anyone who was selling replicas with runes like the one on the axe head we're looking for. That ties in with Andrew's claim that the one he bought was the only one with that rune engraved on it. From the timing it seems likely that the killer's using the axe stolen from Andrew Hilton at the Festival in February, but even if that's not the case, we haven't yet made any headway tracing other similar axes.'

Stolen from Andrew Hilton, the axe had vanished, leaving a trail of death in its wake.

Chapter Thirty-six

A WEAPON THAT KILLED deserved the honour of a name. Now that his blade had proved its worth, he named it Biter. It was a good name for an axe. Although his arm ached to wave a sword, he knew that a long blade would be almost impossible to conceal in public. Sooner or later it would mean his capture, betrayed by the very weapon that should protect him. Such a fate must be avoided at all costs; falling into the hands of his enemies would result in ignominy. To die in captivity was a shameful end for a warrior whose destiny was a glorious death in battle. He was a mighty warrior, a shape-shifter. Prowling the streets as a wolf, in the heat of battle he became a bear. Why should his axe not change shape too, and become a sword?

It was time to sharpen the blade. Every time he held Biter in his hand he risked discovery, but he had no choice. As a warrior, he was trained to attack; his weapon must be ready for battle too. He had used it several times, concealing it swiftly once his mission was completed. Fear of discovery must not threaten his success. Slashing through bone had blunted Biter's cutting edge. He wouldn't risk his life, and more importantly his honour, by letting the blade rust, dishonoured in a forgotten hiding place. He had to make sure Biter was ready for the next raid. There was no time to waste. The moon god would not help him with this task. It had to be done in darkness. None but his victims would ever thrill at the sight of his weapon outlined against the night sky. With Biter in his grasp he was invincible. Without Biter he was naked.

The wolf ran on its hind legs. Speed and silence were its protection. If anyone attacked the beast, it could slash a man's throat with its powerful jaws. But no one challenged him. He ran swiftly along the pavement, passing unseen through the night. Reaching his destination, he glanced around, peering through the darkness, alert to the slightest sound. Satisfied, he let the wolf slip away and he was a man once more, tall and bold. It was time to feel Biter in his hand again. He was only complete when he had his weapon in his hand. Without Biter he was a cripple, a weak woman.

Quickly he made his way along the river path. Having made sure no one was watching, he pulled at a loose panel in the wall until it shifted to one side, allowing his shadow to slip through. His boat lay waiting patiently in the ditch. He crouched and scrabbled in the earth, until his searching fingers closed on the wooden handle. It felt warm in his palm, the cold blade harsh on his skin. He shivered at its beauty. A warrior was only as effective as his weapon. Biter could not only kill at a single well-aimed blow, it offered him the protection of the gods. But only if the blade was razor sharp

To begin with he had taken Biter home with him and sharpened it in his room. Conscious that every journey he undertook with his weapon beneath his cloak was dangerous, he resolved to take it out of hiding only when using it for its proper purpose. So instead of moving the axe, he packed his tools in a rucksack. Slinging the heavy bag over his shoulder, he stole down to the river and worked on the blade at night, when the path was deserted. No one could hear him working there, concealed behind the wall. It was a lengthy process. First he cleaned and polished the blade with steel wool to remove any vestiges of dried blood and other detritus left over from his last kill. Then he rubbed it firmly with sandpaper. To make sure it was properly clean, he went over it again with a finer, gritty sandpaper until it felt really smooth. Using a rag, he applied metal polishing paste before clamping the blade with a vice to one of the posts on the wall. Even with the axe fixed in position, he was careful, aware of the danger if his hand slipped.

It took hours to file the blade using broad strokes that strained the muscles all the way along his arm. He filed one side, then the other, then repeated the process again. Frowning with concentration, he focussed on his task. Now and again he paused, his heartbeat accompanied by the pounding of footsteps as occasionally, on the other side of the wall, he heard someone running along the river path. From time to time he heard voices approach and waited, motionless, his arm poised, until the strangers had walked by. Bicycles were the worst threat as they passed without a sound. When he was sure the path was clear, he would resume sharpening his axe. Happy in his task, he felt like singing, but he kept quiet. He could be careful as well as bold. Concealment was essential to his success. The gods would not protect a man from his own foolishness. It took several nights. By the time he was finished, his shoulders and arms ached, but it was worth the effort. Biter was sharp as a razor, sharp enough to slice through bone.

Chapter Thirty-seven

GEORGE'S FACE WAS pinched with worry. His sharp chin and pointed nose seemed to stick out more than ever. Remembering his nickname, The Wizard, Ian wished George would work some magic and come up with an identity, but George appeared to know even less than they did about the killer.

'You think the killer's using an axe stolen at the Viking Festival?' he repeated at last.

'We already suspected something along those lines had been used,' Ian said. 'The post mortem indicated an unusual blade, not quite like axes you can get nowadays. And the missing axe had a rune engraved on the blade that appears to match a pattern found on a bruise on the first victim.'

'So you think the axe used in these two murders was the one stolen from the Festival?' the profiler repeated. 'Are you sure?'

'Yes,' Ian replied. 'As sure as we can be, that is. The evidence points that way. Our research indicates such a blade is unusual. And the murders began shortly after the Festival.'

'We're as certain as we can be without absolute proof,' Eileen added, with a touch of uncertainty.

There was a pause. They could all see the profiler was disturbed by this news, although it wasn't yet clear why it had affected him.

'What's all the fuss?' Naomi muttered. 'An axe is an axe. If we don't know who stole the axe from the Festival, what difference does it make if that's the one the killer used?' She stared out of the window, idly smoothing her hair down.

Ian was disappointed by the constable's apparent lack of interest. He was impressed by George's logical insights, and keen to hear what he had to say. He turned back to the profiler, who had begun to speak again.

'Someone steals an axe from the Viking Festival and starts slicing people up with it,' he said in his clipped voice.

'Yes, that's what we just told you,' Naomi said impatiently.

Ian frowned at her. To be fair to her, George was just repeating what he had been told, but they had to allow him time to piece together the scraps of information they were throwing at him, until he could make sense of it.

'Well, I'm afraid it sounds to me as though our killer may be playing at Vikings,' George said at last.

'What do you mean?' Ted asked, scowling under his overhanging brows. 'What do you mean, he's playing at Vikings?'

George shook his head. 'I've no idea,' he admitted, 'and yet it does all kind of make sense.'

'Go on,' Ian urged him.

He thought he had grasped what George meant, but wanted to be sure. Anyone who thought they could see some sense in what was happening deserved their attention.

George nodded at Ian. 'The killer – let's not try to analyse why at this stage, we may never fully understand it – the killer steals an axe, a Viking axe, in the melee at the Festival. This is a replica Viking axe we're talking about. It may not have been very sharp, but that could be rectified. All the same, stealing it wasn't going to be easy. For a start there would have been some risk of discovery. Then the owner was a big chap. He wasn't likely to let his axe go without a fight if he noticed what the thief was up to. The axe cost him a fair amount. The question is, why would someone want to use that particular weapon, when it might be easier and less risky to get hold of an axe somewhere else. Axes are not that hard to come by. Why steal that one?'

Eileen nodded. 'Go to a different area; wear a hat or a minimal disguise; pay cash.'

'Exactly,' George continued. 'Any adult can get hold of an axe. So, with a replica Viking axe – obtained at some risk – the killer sharpens the blade and brutally attacks his victims, robbing them, like a marauding Viking. The original theft might have been opportunistic, but what happened after that is deliberate. He wanted a Viking axe, one that couldn't lead us to him, because he's acting out being a Viking.'

'Why?' someone asked.

George shrugged.

'That's why he took their metal,' Ian said.

'What metal?'

Ian could hardly contain his excitement. The profiler's suggestion made sense of something that had been puzzling him.

'The killer stole gold and silver from a jewellery shop, and he stole coins from Angela, but left the notes in her purse. He's only interested in metal.'

'Precious metals like gold and silver were valued by the Vikings,' George agreed, his eyes meeting Ian's in mutual understanding. 'That was their currency. Paper money didn't exist.'

Naomi looked up from her phone. 'Paper money was first used around the seventh century in China, but it didn't reach Europe until much later,' she said.

'The Vikings didn't use paper currency,' Ian repeated, turning back to George. 'The killer's playing at being a Viking on a raid. I see what you mean.'

'So all we need to do is find a man in a horned helmet wielding a bloody axe, and the case is solved,' Naomi said with a short laugh.

'The Vikings didn't wear horned helmets,' George said solemnly. 'That's a fallacy.'

'But they were violent,' Ian added. 'They did use axes in battle, and they stole precious metals on their raids.'

Ian and Eileen exchanged an anxious glance.

Ted looked worried. 'Are you telling us we're dealing with a psychopath who's fantasising that he's some kind of Viking on a raid?'

'If my suspicions are correct – and remember these are only suppositions based on the nature of the weapon – but if I'm right, then that might be what's happening, yes,' George replied.

'You mean, he thinks he's carrying out some sort of normal Viking activity by killing people and stealing their money and jewellery?' Naomi asked. Her earlier scepticism had vanished and she sounded interested in the theory.

George looked at her solemnly. 'I'm no expert on the Vikings. You'd have to research the subject. But yes, that's what I'm putting forward as a theory. I have to stress that I'm no expert on the subject. This is just an idea.'

'They know all about them at Jorvik,' Ted said.

'The obvious place for someone to spend their time if they're interested in Vikings?' George asked. It wasn't really a question.

Ian decided to return to the museum and find out if they had any serial visitors.

'It could be someone who works there,' George added thoughtfully.

Ian told them what Andrew had said about talking to a couple of people who worked at Jorvik just before his axe went missing. It was pure speculation, yet it all seemed to fit. Promising to give some thought to the killer's possible motivation, and research the subject of Viking killings further, George left. All he had been able to tell them with any certainty was that they were looking for a strange and violent killer.

'Killing is always strange,' Ian replied.

'And violent,' Eileen added.

After the profiler had taken his leave, Ian and his colleagues strolled down to the pub outside the police station to have a quick pint and continue the discussion. Ian was taken with the notion that they were dealing with a lunatic who, for some reason, had convinced himself that he was a Viking.

'But why?' Ted wanted to know. 'Why would anyone in their right mind do anything so bloody weird?'

Ian shrugged. 'I'd hardly call these killings the actions of someone who's in their right mind.' He understood that Ted was irritated at how little they knew. 'Why would anyone ever want to kill anyone else?'

Ted took the rhetorical question seriously.

'All sorts of reasons. You know that as well as I do. Jealousy, anger, greed, the whole gamut of human vice. But why would someone pretend to be a Viking, and take coins but leave all notes behind? I still don't get it.'

George's answers raised more questions than they answered. But one thing seemed clear to Ian. If George was right, they needed to find the axe man quickly. The reason they hadn't been able to find anything to link the two victims was that the attacks had been random. The killer wasn't selective. He had killed two random strangers simply in order to rob them, and he had done so without any scruples. On the contrary, he probably believed his actions were honourable. That meant that, if they didn't stop him, he was likely to kill again.

Ian turned to Ted. 'It's not always easy to understand why people do these things,' he said.

'Isn't that *his* job?' Naomi asked, nodding her head in the direction of the police station. 'He's supposed to be the profiler, but he didn't tell us anything about the killer.'

Ian didn't agree, and he said so.

'So what you're saying is, the more people he kills, the more likely he is to get to Valhalla or wherever it was the Vikings believed their top warriors went?' Ted asked.

'Something like that, yes.'

'I can't believe you two. You're talking about bloody Vikings for Christ's sake!' Naomi burst out, exasperated. 'This is the twenty-first century. No one goes around committing bloody murders in some crazy belief that it's saving their own souls!'

'I'm not so sure about that,' Ian said quietly.

'All George has told us is he thinks the killer may have some kind of delusion that he's a Viking,' Naomi replied, 'or he's pretending to be one at any rate. So what? How does that help us?

Unless he really is running around with a horned helmet on his head, we've got no way of knowing who he is. It could be anyone.'

Ian sighed. That was the problem.

'We need to go back to Jorvik,' he said. 'There are a few more questions to ask. Only this time we need to be aware that one of the staff there could be our Viking axe man.'

'Anyone could be our Viking axe man,' Ted replied gloomily.

Chapter Thirty-eight

TED SET ABOUT contacting organisers of the Festival to gather a list of the stall holders who had been in York selling Viking memorabilia. While there was a nucleus of people who turned up every year, there was also some movement of one-offs and new stall holders, people coming and going as they joined or went out of circulation. It would take some time to establish a definitive list of stall holders who had attended the Festival every year. Not many would have had axes for sale, but Ian was keen to contact every one of them in case they could recall anyone else selling weapons. It was highly unlikely that the organisers could have overlooked one of the registered stall holders. Nevertheless it was possible other stall holders might remember some snippet of information that had not been officially recorded; someone registered to sell ornaments or other knick knacks who had a few axes on display as well. If one of the vendors could recall selling an axe to Andrew, and give them a lead to help identify the axe with the algiz rune inscribed on the blade, it might assist them in gaining a conviction later on.

On Tuesday morning, Ian returned to Jorvik shortly before the museum was due to open. Ralph led him wordlessly up the stairs to an office where Oliver and Sophie were sitting clutching mugs of tea. Jimmy was nowhere to be seen. Oliver was leaning forward, gazing at Sophie and talking earnestly in an undertone. Seeing Ian enter, he fell silent. Looking around at the faces watching him, Ian thought about what George had said. The killer could be in the room with him right now, waiting for him to speak. He began by enquiring about Jimmy.

'He's always late,' Ralph explained, 'but we'll be able to tell you anything you want to know, and you can talk to Jimmy when he gets here. I can give him a bell if you want and find out what time he's going to be here. He's probably on his way.'

Ralph smiled uneasily, Oliver stared morosely at the floor, and Sophie gazed at Ian, wide-eyed.

'First of all, I need you to give me as much information as you can about the Festival,' Ian said, after a pause. 'Nothing is too small to be of possible significance.'

'What do you want to know?' Ralph asked.

Ian took out his notebook and jotted down their remarks. His earlier shyness forgotten, Oliver became quite animated talking about Viking axes. Even his gaze seemed more direct and his expression grew lively as he talked about the ideal weight of an axe head relative to the length of the handle.

'I haven't memorised the details of all the weapons here,' he added with an embarrassed laugh. 'Of course the Vikings weren't the first people to use axes in battle,' he went on, 'although they were possibly the most skilled in their use, ever, and certainly they were at the time.'

Sophie sat staring at Oliver all the time he was speaking. At last, he fell silent and nudged Sophie with his elbow, nodding at her and jerking his head in Ian's direction.

'What is it?' Ian asked, gathering from the dumb show that Oliver wanted Sophie to say something.

'Go on,' Oliver urged her in an undertone. 'You said you wanted to tell him. Now's your chance. Go on.'

'Sophie, if there's something you want to say, is now a good time?' Ralph asked.

'It's nothing . . .'

'Let the police decide whether it's important or not,' Oliver interrupted her. 'Tell him.'

'Should this wait until after the inspector's gone?' Ralph repeated.

'It's the inspector she needs to tell,' Oliver replied.

There was nothing more galling than to learn a lead had been held back because a witness thought information wasn't important.

Ian turned to the girl. 'Sophie, what is it?'

She glanced at Ian and blushed.

'It's just that I think I might have been followed home last night,' she muttered.

Ralph cleared his throat but he didn't speak, and Sophie's blush deepened. Ian considered what she had said. Sophie was quite attractive, delicate, with shoulder-length blonde hair, wide blue eyes and dainty features. It was possible some young man had taken a fancy to her and was following her home, but he couldn't see what that had to do with the investigation.

'What time was this?'

'We close at four in the winter but I didn't leave until about four thirty. I had to get changed and clear up before I left. I didn't exactly rush, but I didn't have any reason to hang about here either.'

'Were you on your own?'

She looked surprised. 'Yes. And that's when I thought I saw someone following me. I mean, he did, he followed me all the way along the pedestrian path to Clifford Street, but when I got to the bus stop he saw that I'd seen him, so he crossed the road, but he didn't go away even then. He just stood there, watching me.'

Oliver and Ralph were both staring at her now. Ralph was holding his head back, so that he seemed to be looking down his nose at her, as though he found her rather stupid. Oliver looked worried. Before Ian could reach any decision about whether to take her claim seriously, he needed more information. Sending the two men away on the flimsy pretext that they should be opening up the museum to the public, he kept Sophie back for a moment.

'Can you tell me anything about the person you suspected was following you?'

She shook her head. 'I couldn't see him very well, because he kept to the shadows.' She shuddered. 'I was probably wrong. It was just a feeling I had.'

'Can you describe him in any way?'

'No. Only that he was tall. That's all I could see really.'

She was staring very intensely at Ian. Feeling slightly uncomfortable, he rose to leave. He was aware that this was a potential lead, but it would be more appropriate for Naomi to pursue it.

'If you're bothered, please do go along to the police station and make a full report. And if you notice anyone suspicious hanging around again, let us know straight away.'

'Yes, I will. Shall I ask for you?'

'You can do so, but if I'm not available you can leave a message with the officer who takes your call. I'll make sure you get through to someone connected with the investigation.'

They left the office together. Jimmy Sutherland, the other full-time member of staff, had finally arrived and was chatting to Oliver in the corridor at the top of the stairs. He apologised to Ian for being late, and mumbled something about his baby keeping him and his wife awake half the night. Grey pouches beneath his eyes bore out his explanation, although he could just as easily have been out on the town. Ian only spoke to him for a few minutes as the other man was preoccupied with starting his day's work. He was already late. He claimed to know little about Viking weapons, although he seemed quite knowledgeable when Ian questioned him about the types of blades they used.

'You should ask Ralph,' he concluded. 'He knows all there is to know about the weapons. He's the expert.' He lowered his voice. 'He gives them all names and talks to them when he thinks no one's listening. We've all heard him.' He laughed easily, a man comfortable with his life.

He clearly had no inkling that his throwaway remark might be significant.

Chapter Thirty-nine

BACK AT HIS desk in his little office, Ian made a half-hearted stab at writing up his notes. He didn't want to skimp, but he didn't really know what to make of George's revelation of the previous day. The more he considered the theory of the Viking, the more sense it made. He squirmed uncomfortably. Whatever position he adopted, his legs were somehow too long for his chair. He was reluctant to commit too much of his thinking to paper, because the idea of a modern Viking was quite outlandish. If it turned out to be true, all well and good. If not, he risked appearing, at best, gullible in taking the profiler's comment so seriously. All the same, he couldn't shake off the suspicion that George had given them a glimpse into the mind of the killer and his twisted psyche. A team was tasked with questioning everyone who worked at the Jorvik museum, again. The work would begin first thing in the morning.

Ian drove home, distracted, and barely registered what Bev was telling him.

'Ian, are you listening?'

He trotted out his usual assurance that he was. All he had taken in was that she had been telling him something about her parents.

'So do you mind?'

'What?'

'Oh, Ian, you said you were listening.'

She gave him a playful slap on the arm. He flung his arms around her and gave her a bear hug, pinning her arms to her sides.

'You know what happens to women who physically abuse their husbands?'

She laughed, squirming out of his grasp.

'What I was saying, when you *weren't* listening to me, was that I thought I might go and visit my parents this weekend.'

'Of course I was listening. I always listen to you.'

'So? Do you mind if I go?'

'Can I stop you?'

'But would you mind if I went to see them this weekend?'

'You've only just got back.'

His protest sounded half-hearted. When she had lived near her family and friends, busy with a job she enjoyed, she used to grumble about his preoccupation with his work, but she had coped. Since the move to York, where she knew no one, she had quite reasonably demanded more of his attention. In time, she would settle down and form new friendships, but it was still early days, and she was left on her own a lot of the time. While he couldn't allow her to guilt trip him into neglecting his investigation, he could hardly complain if she wanted to spend time socialising with her family and friends in Kent. Apart from that, for his own part, he would be quite relieved to have a few days alone to think about the case uninterrupted. A brief period of scant attention to his wife could be rectified easily enough once the case was over. But if he overlooked some vital information, and the killer remained at large due to Ian's oversight, another victim might be killed. Nothing could put that right.

'I'll miss you,' he replied, 'but of course you should go and see your family again if you want to. You know I'd come with you only I can't take any leave right now.'

Bev stared at him with an odd expression. She looked almost put out by the idea that he might want to accompany her. In a way he could understand that he would only get in the way if she wanted to spend time with her family. All the same, he was uncomfortable suspecting that she would prefer to go without him. He sighed. If anything Bev seemed to be growing increasingly resentful of his job. It was as though she believed he stayed in it only to spite her. He tried to put a brave face on the situation, but their marriage was a sour disappointment to him. He was pretty sure she felt the same way. He tried not to feel cheated. They had lived together for years before they married, but she had left it until after the wedding to be completely honest about her feelings. In a way, her deception was to blame for the breakdown in their relationship, although she held him responsible for it.

RALPH ARRIVED AT work first the next morning, as Ian suspected he probably did every morning. Ian watched his lanky figure striding towards the entrance, looking neither left nor right, his attention fixed on the museum, as though he couldn't wait to get there. Ian couldn't suppress his own excitement, remembering George's suggestion that the killer could be someone who worked at the Viking museum. Coupled with Jimmy's revelation that Ralph talked to the weapons, it raised a tantalising possibility. Wondering what Ralph could be saying to the weapons when he thought no one was listening, Ian followed him. After a moment, Ralph answered the bell.

'Oh, it's you,' he said cheerily when Ian announced himself. 'Come on in.'

The buzzer sounded and Ian made his way up the stairs.

'For the purpose of elimination,' he said carefully, 'can you confirm for me where you were on the evening of the Sunday before last?'

Ralph nodded to indicate he understood, and said he had been at home.

'Is there anyone who can confirm that?'

Ralph lived alone. He had no alibi on Sunday night. Ian moved on to ask about Wednesday when Tim had been decapitated. The jewellery shop was only a short walk away. Tim had been murdered between eight and nine that evening. Ralph had been at his desk until around half past seven.

'Was anyone else here with you?'

Ralph shook his head uncertainly. 'We have security cameras at the entrance,' he added, 'so you should be able to see what time I left.'

'And did you go straight home?'

Ralph had gone to a local Chinese restaurant for something to eat before heading home. Ian made a note of the details. It should be easy enough to corroborate the time he had left the restaurant since he had paid with a credit card, which would enable them to estimate the time of his arrival. He had no alibi for the Sunday night when Angela was killed, at around midnight, but if a little checking showed that he had been in a restaurant the time of the second murder, then they could discount him.

Once he had finished talking to Ralph, Ian asked to speak to Oliver. The young man smiled shyly at him as he came in.

'Come in,' Ian said.

Oliver sat down, blinking nervously. Ian quite liked the young-ster. Reminding himself that he might be addressing an insane killer, he began to question him gently about his movements on the Sunday evening when Angela had been killed.

'That Sunday, I remembered where I was, after the last time you were asking me. I wasn't here, I was in Leeds.'

Oliver explained he had gone there with a friend from univer-sity. 'There was a group of us. It was his mate's birthday so we all went round there.'

'A party?'

Oliver shrugged. 'Not exactly. There were only six of us. We had a takeaway, got a bit pissed, you know. It was nothing much, just a few guys. We had a laugh, though. It was all right.'

'What time did you leave there?'

'We stayed over. The others are all still at uni so it didn't mat-ter and . . .' He glanced round and lowered his voice. 'I took the Monday off – it was quite genuine. I *was* sick . . .'

He gave Ian a list of names and contact details for friends who could confirm that he had been in Leeds that night. His alibi was less clear-cut for the time of Tim's death as he had left work late that Wednesday, and couldn't remember whether he had gone straight home or not. Ian hoped that either Ralph or Oliver was lying about his alibi. It would make the resolution of the investiga-tion so much easier, and faster. It was imperative they caught this psychopath quickly. While he remained at large there was a pos-sibility he might claim another victim.

Straight away Ian despatched a team of constables to call on Oliver's friends, visit the Chinese restaurant, contact Ralph's credit card company, and check CCTV film from outside the Jorvik museum. The conclusion after all the checking was that none of the staff at Jorvik had been free at the time of both murders, apart from Ralph who would have had to run very fast from Jorvik to the jewellery shop and then straight to the Chinese restaurant. It seemed almost impossible for him to have done all that, and arrive at the restaurant without any sign of a struggle or a weapon.

'What if they're in it together?' Ted asked as they were having a drink that evening after work.

Ian frowned. 'Who?'

'Well, we'd need to look at all of the statements, but take Ralph and Oliver for example. Ralph has no alibi for Sunday night, and Oliver has no alibi for Wednesday evening, so what if they were working together? One did one murder, the other did the other one? I mean, they have alibis for different evenings.'

'That's a point, although is it likely there would be two such lunatics in one place at the same time?'

'Both playing at being Vikings. They could be having a kind of competition to see who can kill the most people.'

'And claim the most booty,' Ian added, catching Ted's drift. 'But they'd have to be sharing an axe, wouldn't they?'

'If you can have one replica, why not two? I know it sounds crazy.'

'Murder doesn't always follow any rules. We're dealing with someone who *is* crazy.'

'Maybe more than one person,' Ted reminded him.

'Madness is unpredictable. We can't rule anything out at this stage, not without cold, hard evidence. And so far all the evidence really shows is that this killer's insane. And it looks like he might be selecting victims randomly.'

'He or they,' Ted reminded him.

Ian nodded. The theory didn't make the investigation any easier. It added to the uncertainty – and doubled the risk of more deaths. All the same, he had to concede that Ted had a point.

'Your decision log's improved,' Ian said as they stood up.

'It's like being back at school.'

'I know. But it's . . .'

'In my own interest,' Ted completed his sentence, and they both smiled.

Chapter Forty

WHILE A TEAM were checking out alibis, Ian spent the next morning scrutinising the connection between Ralph and Oliver. Ted's suggestion that Ralph and Oliver might be working together might seem unlikely, but it was feasible. At least it was something to go on. Of course the two men worked together, but Ian could find no evidence of any special relationship between them. As far as he could ascertain, they had never met before Oliver started his job at Jorvik. The main challenge to the theory came from George, who insisted that a violent killer like the axe man was far more likely to be working alone.

'The chances of discovery would be doubled for one thing,' he pointed out.

'That's a good thing, isn't it?' someone said.

'Not for the killer. What I'm saying is, it doesn't fit the profile. This type of killer typically works alone. He's in it for the thrill and part of that is the secret. Being the only one who knows what's happening gives him a sense of power, and that's an important part of the whole enterprise. Being in the know. He wouldn't want to sit around planning his campaign with an accomplice. You take this night, I'll take that. He wouldn't want to share his knowledge. Alone, he feels all-powerful.'

'Like God,' someone muttered.

'Plus,' George went on, 'if there were two of them committing murders together, they would be unlikely to be working together at the museum as well. It's too risky.'

For once, Ian was inclined to disregard George's reservations. It seemed pointless to apply reason to the actions of this killer. Eileen agreed with Ian.

'Insanity is unpredictable,' she said. 'We need to keep an open mind about Ted's idea that Ralph and Oliver might be working together.'

In the meantime, none of the research teams had come up with anything helpful. There was no record of mental illness or violence in either Ralph's or Oliver's history. Jimmy had a similarly ano-dyne life story. None of the staff at the museum had any recorded trauma or criminal activity, apart from a couple of women work-ing there. Sophie had been arrested once for a drug offence, while in her first year at university. Charges had been dropped. She hadn't even been cautioned. A woman who worked in the gift shop had been accused of stalking her ex-husband about ten years before. An injunction had been served against her and that had been the end of it. Other than that, a few minor traffic offences were the closest any of the museum employees had come to break-ing the law. None of that helped the investigation into the recent atrocities. They were really working in the dark.

The papers had been quick to find the connection between the two murders. Ian swore. Andrew Hilton had been talking to the papers. It wasn't clear whether he was complaining or boasting about his stolen axe that had been used to hack two people to death.

'Cost me over a hundred pounds,' he was quoted as saying. 'So I hope the police catch this maniac soon.'

Whatever happened, there was no way he was going to recover his stolen axe. It would remain in police possession permanently. Ian would make sure of that. One paper had published a sketch of the missing axe, with a caption, 'Have you seen this axe?' The papers were intrusive, and frequently inaccurate. They had published a photograph of Angela's grieving mother and stepfather, alongside the image of the axe that had killed their daughter. But at the same time, he had to concede that the papers performed a useful function. There was a slim chance someone might actually have noticed the unusual markings on the blade. In all the phone calls coming through to the switchboard, there might be one that led them to the killer's identity. It was possible. It seemed that Ian's hopes were justified when Sophie came to the station asking to see him.

'Says she saw something in the paper,' the desk sergeant added.

Ian's heart thumped. She might have noticed someone carrying an axe with the algiz rune engraved on the blade. Working at Jorvik, she was well placed to recognise such symbols. This could be the lead they had been hoping for.

'If it's dripping with blood, that could be another clue,' Ted called out with a grin as Ian hurried from the office.

Sophie was sitting in an interview room twisting a tissue nervously in her thin fingers. Staring across a table at Ian, her eyes wide with anxiety, she looked more like a frightened rabbit than ever. She crossed her legs and leaned forward slightly in her chair, without taking her eyes off Ian's face.

'It was in the paper,' she said, her voice barely more than a whisper.

'There's no need to be nervous. Just tell me what you saw.'

'It was his face.'

'His face? Whose face do you mean?'

'I recognised him. The man who was following me. It was that poor girl's stepfather.'

Not for the first time in the investigation, Ian felt sceptical about a witness. He decided on balance it would be best to challenge her statement straight away, before making a formal report of it. He didn't want to gain a reputation for distrusting young women.

'You stated quite clearly on a previous occasion that you couldn't see what he looked like, because he kept to the shadows,' he reminded her, checking his notes as he spoke. 'Are you sure you recognised him?'

'Yes.' She sounded slightly hysterical. 'When I saw him, I knew it was him. I mean, I'd forgotten . . . I couldn't remember him very well, so when you asked me last time, I just said I didn't see him because I didn't know what else to say. I panicked. But when I saw him in the paper, I recognised his face straight away. You don't think I'll be the next victim, do you?'

'Don't worry. We'll catch him soon.'

She smiled gratefully. 'I hope so. It's so scary, knowing there's a killer on the streets.'

Ian gave what he hoped was a reassuring smile. 'Like I said, we'll catch up with him very soon. Now, I'd like you to make a formal statement about the man you recognised in the paper.'

She seemed very nervy and he suspected she might have an overactive imagination. Even so, he had to accept the possibility that she was telling the truth. It was hard to be sure. Somewhere along the line, things had to start to make sense. The alternative was too terrible to contemplate.

'She looked very disappointed when I walked in. I think you'd better watch out. She kept asking me where you were,' Naomi teased Ian after he had sent her to take Sophie's statement.

He laughed. This kind of ribbing was fine between colleagues, but it wasn't the first time a vulnerable young woman had thrown herself at him in such an obvious way. With a quip about women who fancied men in authority, he hurried back to his desk. Two young women had come forward to cast suspicion on Angela's stepfather. Ian wondered how significant their claims were.

Chapter Forty-one

EILEEN SUMMONED IAN for an informal update on how the case was moving forward. She sat very upright, her fingers drumming an impatient rhythm on her desk. Her jaw looked even more square than usual, her nose sharper, as though she was trying to sniff out the meaning behind his words. Her impatience was almost palpable.

'Between you and me,' Ian said, 'I'm not sure Sophie is a very reliable witness. When I spoke to her at the museum, she was adamant she hadn't seen her alleged stalker's face. Now she's equally positive she recognised Frank Carter in some fuzzy black-and-white image in the paper. It doesn't really stack up.'

'Help me understand this, Ian. Why would she lie about it?'

Ian hesitated to admit that he thought Sophie might be trying to make him notice her. Apart from the fact that he had no real basis for his impression, he was reluctant to sound narcissistic.

'Just attention-seeking,' he replied vaguely.

Eileen nodded. It needed no clarification, really. The police were used to cranks, do-gooders, and out-and-out oddballs. Bored and deluded, desperate for an audience, if they weren't responding to every request the police sent out for information, they would be reporting psychic communications from the other side.

'You think she's a time waster?'

He nodded cautiously. 'She works at Jorvik, so we'll try to keep her on side, but her claim that Frank has been stalking her is just so much guff, if you ask me. Of course we're looking into it. Naomi's gone to question Frank concerning his whereabouts at four thirty on Monday.'

Remembering Naomi's reaction when he had doubted Zoe's second-hand accusation of attempted rape, he didn't add that he thought Sophie was fabricating her story. He was confident Frank would be able to establish he had been at work on Monday when Sophie was on her way home, not hanging around outside Jorvik museum stalking her.

They talked some more about the case, agreeing that, with no reason to target particular victims, the killer was going to prove difficult to track down.

'Sooner or later he's going to make a mistake, and then we'll get him,' Eileen reassured Ian with a show of confidence he suspected she didn't feel.

'Let's hope he messes up sooner, rather than later,' he said.

The longer the case dragged on, the more chance there was that someone else would lose their life to this demented killer. Meanwhile, time was passing. Angela and Tim had been brutally murdered within the space of three days. A week had now gone by without any more attacks. Eileen was hopeful that the killing spree was over. Ian wasn't convinced.

'It's been a week since the last killing. What's he waiting for?' she asked.

'Opportunity.'

Remembering that Bev was going to see her parents the next day, he turned down Ted's offer of a quick one for the road and went straight home. Thoroughly disgruntled by the frustrations of the case, he tried to put it out of his mind. He stopped on the way home to buy some flowers. Despite his exhaustion, he decided to take his wife out for dinner.

'That was a bit daft seeing as I'm going away tomorrow,' she told him when he handed her the flowers, but she looked pleased. 'They're lovely.'

'I thought we might go out for a bite,' he suggested.

He wasn't disappointed when she told him she would rather stay in and pack that evening.

'You don't mind, do you? It's just that I planned to get ready this evening, wash my hair and all that.'

'No. Of course not. To be honest, I'm pretty shattered.'

She could have spent all day packing for her trip, but he genuinely didn't mind. He was content to phone for a takeaway and slouch in front of the television. He tried not to think about the investigation, but it was impossible to shut it out of his mind. Naomi had easily established that Frank had indeed been at work on Monday until half past five. Sophie was, at best, mistaken in identifying him as the man who had followed her to her bus stop. Alternatively she might be a fantasist, lying in a bid for attention.

Bev seemed to be taking a long time to pack. He flicked through the channels on the television. There was nothing he wanted to watch. He went upstairs and found his wife picking her way through a heap of clothes lying on the bed.

'Jesus, Bev, you're only going to see your parents for the weekend. You look like you're packing for a month's cruise.'

She looked up with a guilty laugh. 'You know they always like to take me out.'

'OK, whatever, I'm only saying.'

'You go on down and put something on the television. I'll be down soon.'

'But . . .'

'Go on.'

With a shrug, he turned and went back downstairs. He would never understand women. Bev looked so excited about going back to Kent. He wondered if he had been unreasonably selfish in dragging her away from her home and her family. His relations with his own family were civil, but distant. Things might have been different if his mother were still around. As a teenager, Ian and his brother had gone to live with their birth father in Kent. His brother had clashed with their father and had joined their stepfather in America as soon as he could. Ian had stayed in England because by then he had met Bev. She was always a magnet for men, but there had never been any other girl as far as he was concerned.

With a sigh, he resumed flicking through the television channels, waiting for the takeaway to arrive. It was little comfort to know there were many more patrol cars than usual on the streets. While he sat at home waiting for his dinner, and police cars were cruising the streets, the Viking axe man could be at his grisly business. Making a mockery of the police patrol cars, he could slip unseen along the dark alleys and Snickelways of York, hunting for his next victim.

Chapter Forty-two

As he walked along St Maurice's Road, skirting the city wall, a car pulled into the kerb beside him. When the driver called out, he was so startled he almost dropped his bag. The strap slipped down over his shoulder, dragging his hood back off his face. Quickly he pulled the strap over his shoulder again. Tensed to run, he registered what the driver was saying. As he dithered, she repeated her question. He turned to look at her. She must have been getting on for sixty. Greying hair was pulled back off her face with a plastic hairband, and she wore red lipstick. Looking down at her tentative smile, his fear faded. At the same time he noticed several sparkling rings on her fingers, and a gold chain around her neck.

He shuffled a little closer. 'Did you say Leeds?'

'Yes, I'm on my way there, only I'm afraid I've got myself hopelessly lost. It's this wretched one way system. I've been round it three times. If you could just point me in the right direction?'

He made his mind up. He had come out looking for plunder, and here was a rich woman displaying her treasure to him as she asked for his help. Cunning as well as valiant, he did not walk away from her. The gods might not send him a second opportunity that night.

'Actually, I'm going to Leeds myself. I'm just on my way to the station. I don't suppose – that is, if I come along I could give you directions . . .'

She understood his question and her smile broadened. 'This is a lucky coincidence! Hop in. I've been on the road for two hours. It'll be nice to have some company.'

It wasn't lucky for her. If he had been honest, he would have admitted that he wasn't quite sure of the way, but it didn't matter. The moment he climbed into the car, her fate was decided. She was never going to reach Leeds. The gods had sent her to him. He would not fail. The car bowled along and the driver chattered on, telling him she was visiting her son and daughter-in-law in Leeds.

'I'm not from round here,' she explained. 'My son just moved up here last month, with his job, and this is the first time I've been able to make it to see the new house. I had no idea it would be so difficult to find. The sat nav's been playing up, you see. I think it's out of date. And then there are all these road works and diversions. I might just take the train next time.'

There wouldn't be a next time.

'I was doing so well, and then I took a wrong turning and ended up in York!' she added with a laugh.

At her side the warrior sat still and silent, watching and waiting for his chance. It would be best to carry out his task after they left the busy roads of the city, but he didn't want to travel too far. He would have to make his own way home when it was over. The wolf could run for many miles, but his bag was heavy. All being well, it would weigh a little more soon, with the addition of her gold rings and chains and coins. He was hoping for rich pickings. He couldn't help feeling a tremor of guilt because the woman trusted him, but he had no choice. She had seen his face. The gods had offered him a chance to prove himself. With their help he would return home safely.

It wasn't actually very difficult to find the road to Leeds. As the sky darkened with the setting sun they left the streets of York behind them. Crossing the River Ouse, they drove past a golf club, and Askham Bar Park and Ride, and on towards Tadcaster. Streets of houses gave way to flat farmland. It was almost dark outside. When she turned on her headlights, it was time.

'Are you all right?' the woman asked, seeming to notice his silence for the first time.

'To be honest, I feel a bit sick,' he replied, seizing the moment. 'Do you think we could stop for a bit? I just need some fresh air.'

'Really?' She sounded surprised. They hadn't gone far. All the same she pulled over. 'We can't have you feeling ill, not after you've been so kind, helping me on my way.'

He didn't answer. His next challenge was to get her out into the fields. It would be easier there, with space to swing his axe.

'Do you want to come with me?'

The woman shook her head. 'No, I'll stay here.'

He hesitated, trying to think how he could persuade her to get out of the vehicle, but it didn't really matter. He clambered out by himself.

'You can leave your bag here,' she called out.

Ignoring her suggestion, he ran away from the car and into the fields. Passing through a gap in a hedge he crouched down for a few seconds, out of sight, hoping she wouldn't change her mind and drive off. He didn't want to leave her for long, but if he went back too quickly she might become suspicious. He counted to a hundred before hurrying back. She was still there, waiting. He opened the door and reached across. Before she realised what was happening, he grabbed her by both arms and pulled her towards him.

'What are you doing?'

Within seconds she was lying sideways across the passenger seat, her head almost out of the door. Too late she began to struggle as he flung the weight of his body on top of her to stop her returning to her seat and driving away.

'Get off me!'

Frantically she scrabbled at his cloak, trying to push him off her. There was no time to lose. No time to think. He had to silence her. One of her hands found the steering wheel and clung to it as he seized her by the hair and yanked her towards the passenger door by her head. Losing her grip on the wheel, her arms flailed wildly. There was very little room to manoeuvre. Holding on to her hair with one hand, he raised his axe. Her eyes widened with terror. Before she could open her mouth, Biter swooped, slicing through flesh and soft tissue, carving a passage through the centre of her chest. She writhed helplessly, blood frothing at her lips as her eyes glazed over.

Swiftly disentangling his fingers from her hair, he wrenched the chain from her bloody neck. Seizing her bag, he ripped her purse open and shook its contents out on the tarmac. Gathering up silver and copper coins, he dropped them into his rucksack along with her gold chain. His breath was coming in gasps. Every time a car zoomed by he thought his heart would burst, it was pounding so fast. The woman had stopped moving. Her eyes were fixed in a terrible glare. Satisfied that she was dead, he pulled at the rings on her fingers. Two came off easily. The third refused to shift. Cursing, he thrust the two he had in his bag and turned away. It wasn't much of a haul after all his effort. Next time he would do better. His clothes were relatively unstained, protected from her spraying blood by the car. He wiped Biter's blade quickly on the grass, then turned and fled. He needed to put as much distance as he could between himself and the dead woman. The body would probably not be found before daylight, but there was always the risk that a police car might drive past and stop to investigate a car parked on the verge of a main road out of town. If that happened, he had to be as far away as possible.

The wolf ran swiftly across the fields, towards York.

Chapter Forty-three

ON FRIDAY MORNING, Ian dropped Bev at the station. She refused his offer to carry her luggage to the platform and he dropped her off across the road from the station. Her case was on wheels and she was only going away for the weekend, although, from the size of the case she was taking, she could have been going away for two weeks. They kissed goodbye in the car, a quick peck on the lips, before she jumped out. He watched her crossing the road, her spiky blonde head bobbing along jauntily above a bright red coat, her case bumping up the kerb behind her. He waited, but she didn't turn to wave. With an empty feeling, he drove along Queen Street and left on to Skeldergate Bridge. Fishergate led him to the Fulford Road and the police station. His day was about to begin.

He had barely sat down at his desk when the duty sergeant ran in.

'There's been another one!' he snapped.

Ian didn't pause to ask him what he meant. His colleague's shocked expression told him enough. He hurried to the incident room where Eileen was standing, pale-faced and stern. Ted ran in behind Ian, followed in turn by Naomi who was scowling as though she had been interrupted in the middle of something important.

'As you're probably all aware by now,' Eileen began, 'there's been another attack.'

She flashed up a picture of a middle-aged woman, her face relatively unlined, her hair streaked with grey. A muted gasp went round the room. Ian stared in horror. Naomi's eyebrows shot up, her irritation changed to shock. The woman was lying, face up, across the two front seats of a car. Her face was splattered with blood, her torso drenched in it.

'She was found lying in her car along the Tadcaster Road,' Eileen said quietly. 'She'd been pulled half out of her seat by her attacker, who slashed her chest as you can see.'

'With an axe?' someone asked.

Eileen inclined her head. 'That's what it looks like.'

'What the hell happened to her face?' someone else asked.

'Out in the fields, it was probably crows,' Ted said.

'What?'

'I'm talking about her eyes,' the sergeant explained. 'Birds always go for the eyes first. Scavengers find a target pretty quickly if it's not moving. That's how they survive. And a body along the edge of a fast road isn't likely to go unnoticed from the air for long. Raptors are always on the lookout for small dead animals that've been run over and killed. The eyes are the first to go because they're easy to get at. The hide of some animals is difficult to get through. But not hers,' he added sombrely.

The statement met with silence as the assembled officers digested this information.

'Yes,' Eileen said at last, 'she was lying there overnight, exposed, and part of the morning too. Her chest is slashed open, and, as you can see, her eyes have gone. A patrol car noticed the car first, about half an hour ago. She was in a BMW, too smart to be an abandoned vehicle. They thought joyriders had left it there. Then they noticed the birds, as you said, and they stopped to investigate. This is what they found.'

Ian stared at the pale blood-streaked face on the screen, trying to avoid looking directly at the eye sockets. Somehow they drew his attention, like gaping dark magnets. He had to look. Around the edges of the sockets he could see bone showing through, picked clean of flesh and tissue. Behind him there was a disturbance as someone ran from the room. Ian felt a tremor of pride that he hadn't been sick. He wasn't sure it was a good thing, but he was growing accustomed to viewing damaged corpses. It certainly helped him professionally. When he had started working in murder investigations, his squeamishness around dead bodies had been difficult to conceal. He wondered how many of his fellow officers had experienced similar problems. At least one member of his current team had not yet learned to control his reaction when faced with a mutilated human cadaver.

'Her name is Beryl Morrison, aged sixty-three, living in North London. The car is registered in her name. What was she doing on the road between York and Leeds last night, and how did she encounter the killer? This attack raises a lot of questions and we need answers fast. SOCOs are scouring the site, but what I want to know is, what was our axe man doing halfway to Tadcaster? How did he get there? And why was he able to pull his victim from her car? He must have flagged her down somehow. Was he driving in front of her? Did anyone else see him? Can anyone describe his vehicle?'

She didn't add that someone might have noted down his registration number. That was too unlikely a stroke of luck to dare hope for.

'He might have made out his car had broken down,' someone suggested.

'But why would she stop? She could have phoned for help, or he could have. What made her stop and open her door for him?'

The discussion was inconclusive. This latest murder was puzzling, in many ways. The atmosphere changed rapidly from shocked inactivity to purposeful bustle as they split up to seek out more information. Ian felt ambivalent about his first task as he set off for London, to speak to the victim's husband. It was a depressing task, telling family about the death of a loved one. In some ways it was the worst part of his job. The dead were gone and beyond pain. The living would suffer for the rest of their lives. A Metropolitan police officer could be sent to Mr Morrison's house to give him the terrible news, but it was possible the dead woman's husband might be privy to information that would aid the investigation. Ian wanted to be there in person, to make sure the bereaved family were asked the right questions.

He was already on the train to London when he realised that he had forgotten to phone Bev to check she had arrived in Kent. He called her, but she didn't answer. On the point of calling her parents, he hesitated. He didn't really want to talk to his mother-in-law just then. It was more important to work on what he needed to find out from the dead woman's husband. Speaking to Bev would have to wait until later. An added incentive for travelling to London was that he could take the opportunity to look up his former colleague and fellow inspector, Geraldine Steel. She worked in North London. When he called her on the off chance, she answered straight away.

'How about lunch?' he asked when he had explained he was on a train to London. 'I know it's short notice, but I'm on my way to North London. It's all very last minute. I'll explain when I see you.' He realised he had made it sound as though he was expecting her to drop whatever she was doing to come and meet him. 'If you can spare the time, that is.'

She laughed. 'You're going to be in North London and you think I might not make time to see you?'

He smiled. 'I'm looking forward to seeing you.'

'Me too. It's been a while.'

Chapter Forty-four

IT WAS BARELY midday when Ian rang the bell at the Morrison's house. The victim had lived with her seventy-five-year-old husband in an expensive area just off Totteridge Lane in North London. The door was opened by a white-haired man. He peered short-sightedly at Ian with a slightly puzzled expression. He would have been as tall as Ian if he hadn't been standing with shoulders hunched, his back bowed. His voice was hoarse and he had a peevish expression on his craggy face.

'Whatever it is you want, I'm not interested.'

Ian introduced himself and the old man took a step back, frowning.

'A police officer? Oh dear. Has something happened?'

Ian suggested they go inside. This was not a message to be delivered standing on a doorstep. The old man fussed for a while. After scrutinising Ian's identity card he went inside to call the local police station and check his visitor's credentials. Ian waited patiently outside the closed door. He had travelled a long way to speak to the widower, but he couldn't fault him for being careful. When the front door reopened, Mr Morrison looked worried.

'They told me you've come all the way from York.'

'That's right. Can we go inside? You might want to sit down.'

'It's Beryl, isn't it? Has she had an accident? I don't understand why you've come here from York.'

He was babbling nervously, preventing Ian from answering his questions.

Gently, Ian guided him inside and into the living room where he virtually pushed the old man down on a leather armchair.

'Mr Morrison, I'm afraid your wife . . .'

'I knew it! I knew something like this would happen.'

'Mr Morrison, I don't think . . .'

'Driving all that way, by herself, I knew there'd be an accident. I told her!' He looked angry, but Ian understood he was scared. 'She will be all right, won't she? Where is she? I need to get to York, don't I? Is that what you've come here to tell me? Can you take me to her? I'll get my coat.'

He half stood up. Ian asked him to remain seated and he sank back into his chair again, his expression openly frightened now. Hating himself for falling back on the cliché, Ian began by saying there was no easy way to pass on the news.

'I'm afraid your wife's dead.'

'No! I shouldn't have let her go.'

'It wasn't a car accident. She was murdered.'

'Murdered? I don't understand.' Mr Morrison shook his head, as though trying to clear his mind. 'What do you mean, she was murdered? She was going to visit our son . . .' He gasped. 'Is Luke . . . has anything happened . . .'

'Your wife was on the road to Leeds when she was attacked. Does your son live in Leeds?'

'Yes, yes,' the widower began to gabble, as though talking would bat Ian's words away. 'Yes, Luke lives in Leeds. He only moved there a month ago. Beryl was desperate to go and see him. I've been laid up with a bad back. I didn't want to sit in the car all that time so she said she'd go by herself. Oh God, why didn't I go with her? She should have got the train. I told her. Oh God.'

He dropped his head in his hands and began to cry. Ian wondered whether he had been rash, travelling all the way to London to bring Mr Morrison the news that his wife had been murdered. He had been keen to question the widower himself. Now he wasn't sure that would be possible. He gave the old man a few moments then spoke to him gently.

'Would you like me to make some tea? Then I'll ask you a few questions about your wife, if I may.'

Mr Morrison looked up and heaved a deep sigh. 'I'll be all right, just give me another minute. And don't worry about the tea.'

'Is there someone you can call? Someone who can come and keep you company for a while?'

Mr Morrison frowned. 'I suppose I'll have to tell her . . .'

'Who?'

'Our daughter. She'll have to know, won't she? Luke's in Leeds. Suzy's in Enfield, not far away. I could phone her. But what do I say?'

'Would you like me to tell her?'

'No, no. I'll tell her myself. And what about Luke? Do I tell him this over the phone?'

Ian said he would arrange for a police officer to visit the son in Leeds and tell him face to face.

Mr Morrison nodded. 'Thank you.' He drew in a shuddering breath. 'What happened?'

'It seems she met someone on the road who attacked her. Did she know anyone in the area? She was killed just outside York, on the road to Leeds.'

Mr Morrison shook his head. He looked puzzled as he assured Ian that his wife didn't know anyone living in Yorkshire, apart from their son, Luke.

'Are you sure? Could she have some connection in the area that you were unaware of?'

'Inspector, we've been married – we were married, that is – for thirty-three years. We've never been to the north of England, never. And no one she knows moved there, until Luke went to Leeds. We were married for thirty-three years,' he repeated, tears in his eyes again. 'You don't keep secrets after all those years, Inspector. I would have known.'

Walking back along the road towards the car that had brought him there from the station, Ian thought about what Mr Morrison had said. It didn't make much sense. According to her husband, the victim hadn't known anyone living in the area. Yet she had stopped her car and opened the door to a stranger. With a sigh, Ian instructed his driver to drop him at the nearest station. From Totteridge and Whetstone he took the Northern line down to Kings Cross where he had arranged to meet his former colleague. Geraldine was travelling down a different branch of the Northern line to meet him there. She had been his superior officer back in Kent when he was still a sergeant, before her move to London and his promotion to inspector. Her sharp insights had been legendary in the Kent constabulary, and he still missed working with her. He couldn't wait to discuss his current workload with her. The longer he spent investigating the case, the less sense it seemed to make. Looking at the facts with a fresh eye, he hoped she might be able to make sense of the mystery surrounding the axe murders.

Chapter Forty-five

IAN AND HIS former colleague had arranged to meet in a pub upstairs at Kings Cross station. Geraldine was already waiting there when he arrived. He spotted her as soon as he walked in. She was sitting against the wall, looking out for him. Her short dark hair glistened and her dark eyes seemed to glow with health. She half rose to her feet, and gave a little wave. He raised his hand to show he had seen her and she sank back into her seat, following him with her eyes as he made his way over to her. They didn't shake hands, or indicate through any physical gesture how pleased they were to see one another, but he returned her smile. It was enough.

'It's a bit less hectic up here,' she said as he sat down. 'We'll be able to hear ourselves talk. But let's order first. I'm starving!'

Ian grinned. He hadn't realised how hungry he was until then. While they were waiting for their food, he explained the reason for his trip to London. It was a relief to be able to talk about the purpose of his visit to Mr Morrison without being swamped with expressions of sympathy. Instead of commiserating, Geraldine spoke directly. They had worked too closely together in the past to feel awkward talking about death.

'This is your axe murderer we're talking about, isn't it? The case is all over the news. I thought you must be working on it. I mean, York are going to put their best detective on a case like this, aren't they?'

He smiled at the compliment. She had praised his skills before, usually adding that she took full credit since she had trained him.

'So where does the woman from Tottenham fit into it?' she asked, when he had outlined what had happened so far.

Ian explained they were working on the theory that she had been flagged down on her way to visiting her son in Leeds.

'She was found lying across the front seats of her car. Her feet were still on the driver's side. The passenger door was open and she'd been dragged sideways from her seat head first, and her chest slashed open.'

'With an axe.'

'Exactly.'

Geraldine looked thoughtful. 'So she stopped her car, we don't know why, and either she opened her door to enable him to grab hold of her, or else she left it unlocked for him to be able to open it from the outside.' She paused. 'Was the window open?'

Ian looked up from his soup. 'What do you mean?'

'Was the passenger window open? If she stopped for some reason, and someone came towards her, what would she do? If she didn't drive off again quickly, wouldn't she have opened the window to hear what he wanted, before opening the door?'

Ian closed his eyes, picturing the scene. 'The windows were shut.'

'Are you sure?'

'No. Shall I check? It won't take a moment.'

He made a phone call that confirmed the car windows had all been closed when the body was found.

Geraldine resumed thinking aloud. 'So did she open the door to let him in? Or did the killer open it himself before he dragged her from her seat? Isn't that a bit odd? Someone opens your car door and grabs you. Wouldn't you try to drive away? She didn't get out of the car at all, did she?'

'No. Her feet were still inside.'

They ate in silence for a moment.

'This is all assuming she didn't know him, of course,' she added as she finished her soup. 'Could someone have followed her from London? I don't see why not. Or what about the son who's moved up there? What do we know about his circumstances?'

Ian told her that Beryl's son had been living with his partner for three years and they had a one-year-old. It didn't sound as though the son or his partner would be setting out to murder Beryl.

'And in any case, what about the other two victims? Anyway, we've sent an officer from Leeds to inform the son of his mother's death, and while we're at it, we'll eliminate him if we can. But he seems an unlikely suspect, given the other deaths.'

Geraldine nodded. 'Although he has just moved to the area, hasn't he? And is it a bit of a coincidence that she's killed so close to where her son lives?'

Ian felt a momentary excitement. It was just possible the killer was connected to Beryl and that her murder would offer them the lead they so desperately needed.

'But don't forget, the others were killed in the centre of York. This doesn't feel like a domestic. Beryl's the third victim.'

'She's the third one we know about,' Geraldine reminded him. 'There could be others.'

'Don't say that! Someone outside the car got her to stop before he pulled her out of the car to kill her,' Ian repeated. 'That's all we know for sure. Why did she stop?'

'That's just what I was wondering. It was night. A woman of sixty, out driving alone in the dark. Is it reasonable to suppose she stopped her car for a stranger, and not only that, but she left the passenger door unlocked?'

They discussed the possibility that Beryl's car had broken down. If that was the case, she might have asked another driver for help. But they agreed that didn't make sense either. The car had been checked and nothing appeared to be amiss, and in any case Beryl would have telephoned for help, not stopped a passing stranger. Her phone was working, the battery charged. It was in her bag. As far as they could tell, she hadn't even tried to call anyone.

Over coffee the conversation moved on. Neither of them had kept in close contact with any other former colleagues in Kent so they chatted about themselves. Geraldine was keen to know how Ian liked York. He told her he was pleased with his move, but his wife hadn't settled yet.

'It's early days,' she replied.

'She needs to do something.'

'Yes. Everyone needs to do something.'

They parted with mutual assurances that they would keep in touch. They had worked closely together on several cases in the past, sometimes facing extreme danger side by side. Such experiences were bonding. No longer a colleague, Ian thought of her as a close friend. He hoped she felt the same way about him.

'You know you can always call me if you need to talk about a case,' she said. 'Any time.'

'Same here.' Staring into her unfathomable dark eyes, he added, 'if you need anything at all.'

She laughed at that. 'How about a seriously rich single man with no baggage?'

Usually one for lighthearted banter, Ian couldn't think what to say. He wasn't rich, but for an instant he almost wished he was single. He turned away without answering.

Watching the gently undulating green landscape flash past the train window, fields and trees, occasionally cows and sheep, Ian pictured a woman stopping her car out of town at night to speak to a stranger. Geraldine had raised an important question. Had Beryl known her killer? It was hard to believe she would have stopped for a stranger, but her husband was adamant she had known no one in the area apart from her son and his family.

Chapter Forty-six

IAN WAS WORN out by the time he arrived back at York station. The train journey had passed without any delay in either direction, but travelling was still tiring and uncomfortable. There was never sufficient room for legs as long as his. Tempted to go straight home and soak his aching body in a bath, he drove to the police station instead. There was still time to do a few hours' work before grabbing a takeaway on his way home. Bev was in Kent for the weekend, so he had no reason to go home early. First he wanted to relax over a cup of tea before getting stuck into writing his report on Beryl's husband. It was a depressing task. The trip to London had taken up most of the day without moving the investigation forward. Besides that, he always felt miserable after talking to the bereaved, especially if he was the one to break the news. The highlight of his day had been meeting Geraldine for lunch, but even that left him feeling sad. He didn't know when he would see her again.

Ted was in the canteen, sitting alone with a mug of hot chocolate. Ian joined him. While evidence gathering and report writing was crucial, it was important to make time for mulling over ideas as well. Geraldine had made a few suggestions he and Ted could usefully consider. Ian enquired first whether there had been any developments since he had left for London that morning. Ted looked pleased to see him and told him the post mortem on Beryl's corpse had been completed that afternoon. The sergeant had been waiting for Ian to return before going to speak to the pathologist.

'Come on, then,' Ian said. 'What are we waiting for?'

Without pausing to finish his tea, he jumped to his feet. Casting a rueful glance at his half drunk mug of chocolate, Ted followed him. As they drove to the mortuary, Ian ran through what Mr Morrison had told him. So far it added nothing to their store of information. Ian was keen to check out Beryl's son in Leeds, but first they wanted to see what the post mortem had revealed. Arriving at the mortuary, Ian was pleased when Avril, the young blonde anatomical pathology technician, opened the door for them.

'I thought you'd forgotten all about me,' she scolded him playfully.

'As if any man could forget you! Do you know Ted?'

'Of course. How's it going?'

Pleasantries over, they put on their protective gear and followed her. Jonah glanced up when they entered the room.

'Aha, the cavalry have arrived,' he greeted them with a wave of his scalpel. 'Too late to save this poor soldier, I'm afraid.'

From behind his mask Ted sounded puzzled. 'Soldier?'

'Oh never mind. It was just a manner of speaking. She was no more a soldier than you or I. In fact, she doesn't look as though she's ever done a day's marching in her life. A soft life, by the looks of things. Privileged. Even apart from her expensive clothes, just look.'

He held up one of the dead woman's hands to display perfectly manicured polished nails.

'She didn't put up much of a fight,' Ian remarked, noticing the absence of defence wounds.

'No, she was clinging to the steering wheel of her car before he pulled her off. She was holding on so tightly, a fine layer of skin on the underside of her fingers has been scraped away. SOCOs found her skin cells on the steering wheel of her car, more than you'd expect just from driving, although you wouldn't know it just by looking at her fingers.'

'But there's nothing else on her hands?' Ian asked urgently.

Jonah sighed. Had Beryl let go of the wheel to hit out at her attacker he might have fallen back, giving her time to slam her car door shut and drive off. Failing that, she could at least have scratched his face, leaving a few particles of his skin under nails to be discovered at her post mortem. As it was, her body told them nothing about her killer, other than that he had slashed her body with a long sharp blade.

Ian gazed at the bloodless gash on the dead woman's chest. It looked fake, like a wound effect created for a film.

'She has one deep wound, made with a very sharp heavy weapon. The blade cut across her at a slight angle, presumably because she was half in and half out of the car. It looks as though he was holding her hair with one hand, attempting to yank her out of the car. Her head was forced backwards, obstructing her windpipe and causing her to choke. She was struggling against his tugging, still hanging on to the steering wheel for some reason, probably panic. She would have done better to have let go and tried to fight back, but I don't suppose it would have made any difference. A few tufts of hair have been pulled out and most of the hair has been pulled out of place.' He flicked the dead woman's hair. 'You can see she had some sort of gel or spray holding her hair in position in a certain style, most of which has been messed up. She was killed at around nine o'clock last night. Now I can't say for certain, but she could have been killed by the same weapon that was used on your other two recent victims. So this could well be the third person killed with the same axe.' He looked up at Ian, his expression more serious than Ian had seen before. 'I think it's time you brought this to an end, Ian. God knows I like to be busy, but this is getting out of hand. Three people viciously attacked in less than two weeks. Are any of us safe? What does the profiler say about it? Does he think it's the same killer?'

Ian inclined his head without speaking. He didn't need Jonah, or anyone else, telling him he needed to find this killer urgently. And at the back of his mind he could hear Geraldine's voice. 'She's the third victim we know about.'

Even if the death toll so far didn't exceed the three victims they knew about, until the killer was caught there could still be more to come.

'Is there anything to suggest why she stopped?' Ted asked.

'Yes,' Ian chimed in, 'we were wondering why she would have stopped the car.'

Jonah shook his head. 'Examining her here tells the story of how and when she died, it doesn't offer any explanation as to why. And it tells us nothing about her killer.'

'But she must have been killed by someone pretty strong?' Ian suggested.

'Or by someone wielding a very, very sharp axe.'

'Would using a blade to inflict injuries like this blunt an axe?'

'Yes.'

'So he must have a way of keeping his axe sharp.'

It wasn't much to go on, but they couldn't afford to overlook even the slightest shred of potential evidence. As they drove away, Ian asked Ted to look into sales of whetstones and knife sharpeners. Somewhere in York a man with a razor-sharp axe was hiding his weapon. He had to be maintaining it somehow.

'Get going on that first thing tomorrow,' he said as they reached the police station car park. 'I'm off.'

Too tired to stop for a takeaway he drove straight home and poured himself a large bowl of cornflakes. As he chomped, he tried Bev's phone. She didn't answer. He was dozing on the sofa, thinking that he really ought to get to bed, when she phoned back having noticed his missed call. It was difficult to hear what she was saying. There seemed to be noise in the background.

'Where are you?'

'What?'

'What's all that noise?'

'Oh that, I'm out with my sister. What did you want?'

'What?'

'Did you call for a reason? I had a missed call.'

'No reason, just wanted to see how you're doing.'

'Fine. How's your investigation going?'

'Slowly.'

'Look, I've got a really bad signal here. Shall we talk later?'

'OK.'

He didn't mind. He was tired. 'Let's talk tomorrow. I just wanted to know you're all right, that's all. I miss you.'

'Miss you too,' she said, and she rang off.

Ian went to bed. Even though he was tired, he didn't sleep well. He missed his wife.

Chapter Forty-seven

AFTER A RESTLESS night, Ian woke up late feeling out of sorts. It was unusual for him to oversleep when he was on a case. He had a vague memory that he had been dreaming about chasing a group of women. His wife had been there, fleeing from him along with the other women. Unsettled, he reached for his phone.

'Hello?' Bev sounded sleepy.

'I miss you.'

'Is that you, Ian?'

'Who else would it be?'

'At this time in the morning, you're right.'

He glanced at his watch. It was ten past eight. He was going to be late for work. 'When are you coming home?'

'Give me a chance, I've only just got here. I'm staying a few days, at least. How's your case going?'

He couldn't say they had made any real progress.

'Well, let me know how you get on.' She paused. 'I miss you too.'

'Let me know when you're coming back and I'll meet you at the station.'

Her thanks sounded formal. He had failed to honour such undertakings before, more than once.

He drove to work and had a full fry-up: eggs, sausages, bacon, mushrooms, tomatoes, fried bread, the works. After that, he felt ready for the day, and set off to speak to Beryl's son. The streets of York were always congested but, once he was out of the city, he was able to put his foot down. He had eaten a good breakfast, the sun was shining, the road was fast, and his beautiful wife would be home soon. Life could be worse. Pulling up outside a small house on a residential estate in Leeds, he hurried up the path and rang the bell. A short fat woman came to the door. Once she knew who Ian was, she gestured to him to follow her along a narrow hallway.

'It's the police again, Luke,' she called out.

Somewhere in the house a baby began to cry. The fat woman waddled past Ian and clambered up the stairs as a tall thin man appeared in the hall.

'Have you caught him?' he asked.

Huge boney hands hung limply at his sides, his shoulders were slightly rounded, and he gazed at his visitor with a wretched expression.

'Have you caught my mother's murderer?' he repeated in a quiet voice. He had a slight lisp.

'We're following several lines of enquiry.'

'I don't know what that means,' Beryl's son replied with an unexpected flash of anger. 'Find out who killed her and lock the bastard up. Prison's too good for him.'

His temper appeared to subside almost as soon as it erupted, as though he lacked energy to sustain his anger.

'Mr Morrison, I'd like to ask you a few questions, if you don't mind. It might help us with our enquiry. We're keen to discover who committed this crime as quickly as we can. Not only are we concerned to see your mother's killer brought to justice, but we want to make sure he can no longer pose a threat to anyone else.'

'Is he likely to kill again?'

Ian hesitated. 'There's nothing to suggest he might, but you can never be sure.'

'I knew it,' Luke muttered. 'It's the same one, isn't it, the killer they're calling the axe murderer. It was him, wasn't it? He killed my mother.'

Ian hesitated again, but there was nothing to be gained from concealing the truth.

'We think so,' he admitted. 'It's looking likely. And he has to be caught before he can attack anyone else.'

Luke glared at Ian for a moment before ushering him into a small living room.

'If you'd caught him before this, my mother would still be alive,' Luke said when they were both seated.

Ian didn't answer straight away. There was nothing he could say to lessen the other man's grief. Luke struck him as a bit dim, so Ian spoke slowly.

'We're doing our best to catch him. I'd like to ask you a few questions.'

According to her son, Beryl had no enemies. She had lived an exemplary life, doing voluntary work to support local charities, attending church, and looking after her family.

'Can you think of anyone at all who might have held a grudge against your mother, for any reason at all?'

Luke gave a short bark of laughter. 'You think someone might have held a grudge against my mother? Enough to want to kill her? If you'd ever met her, you'd know how stupid that sounds. My mother was as nice a woman as you could ever wish to meet.'

According to Luke, his mother had lived a saintly life. He spoke of her in such reverential tones that Ian wondered if he was talking to the right person. Perhaps Beryl's tubby daughter-in-law would have a different opinion of the woman Luke seemed to idolise.

'You seem very certain she had no enemies.'

'That's because I knew my mother. In any case, you said yourself it's the axe murderer who killed her, and he's already killed other people, hasn't he? Is he supposed to have held a personal grudge against them all, enough to make him want to kill them all?'

With a shrug, Ian pressed on. 'There is just one other question, Mr Morrison. Where were you at around nine o'clock on Thursday evening?'

Luke had been at work until half past five and had then taken a bus home, arriving back at around six. At around nine he thought he had been in the local supermarket picking up some beer.

'And where do you work?'

After noting down the names of Luke's employers, Ian asked to speak to his wife. She too had nothing but praise for her mother-in-law.

'She was very generous to us,' she added.

'Generous?'

'Yes, she bought so much for the baby, and don't tell Luke I told you this, but she helped us with the house. We could never have managed it by ourselves. We had to sell the car. I'm not sure what's going to happen now. His mother's always looked after him, but his father's a stingy old bastard.'

Although it was logistically feasible for Luke or his wife to have borrowed or hired a car and driven out of Leeds to meet his mother on the road, they certainly had no motive for wanting her dead. On the contrary, they had a vested interest in protecting her, as she gave them financial support. Ian thanked them both for their help and left, after expressing his condolences once again for their loss. There was nothing to be gained from staying there any longer.

Chapter Forty-eight

RETURNING TO THE station, Ian set to work looking into Luke's background. It didn't take long to discover he had been charged with ABH three times as a teenager, as a result of which he had attended a juvenile detention centre. Some doubt remained over whether he had mended his ways because a few years later he had been acquitted of assaulting his first wife. She had accused him of battering her, but had later dropped the charges. Two years later they divorced. Bearing this history in mind, Ian re-examined his initial impression of Beryl's son.

'He did strike me as a bit of an oddball, to be honest,' he admitted to Ted and Naomi, 'but he seemed pretty harmless.'

'He doesn't sound harmless to me,' Naomi interrupted, shaking her head until her blonde curls bounced.

Ian took no notice. She knew perfectly well he hadn't intended to suggest that violence against women was harmless.

'I think he's a bit slow,' he continued, 'and his wife thinks he relies too much on his mother.'

'He sounds like a pathetic creep,' Naomi snapped.

Ian wondered if he had been right to ignore her first comment, given the content of their discussion. Her face was slightly red beneath her make-up.

'Just because all men who beat up their girlfriends are morons, it doesn't follow that all morons are violent,' he said, hoping he wasn't being clumsy in his attempt to mollify her.

Naomi grunted acceptance of his statement and they moved on. The last thing Ian wanted was to fall out with one of his team. Apart from the unpleasantness, there wasn't time to be distracted from the investigation.

'Admittedly it's highly unlikely that he would have killed his mother because, according to Luke's wife, Beryl was helping support Luke and his family. But he clearly has a temper,' Ian went on.

'If he has an alibi for the time of any of the other murders, presumably we can discount him?' Ted asked, his dark brows lowered.

'Well, not necessarily. There's always the chance this could have been a copycat murder,' Ian said. 'Luke's not the sharpest tool in the box. He knows about the axe murderer. Everyone knows about the axe murderer. You can't turn on the television or walk past a paper shop, without seeing it. Luke's mother oversteps the mark, angers him in some way, and he decides to kill her, making it look as though it's another victim for the axe man. It's not very likely, but we can't dismiss the theory out of hand.'

Although Ian hated himself for raising the possibility, it couldn't be overlooked.

'But first, let's see what we can dig up about him, before we start on that line of thinking. And if you can find him an alibi for the time of his mother's death, so much the better.'

'Or worse,' Naomi replied.

Ian nodded. It wouldn't exactly be a positive result if they eliminated Luke from the enquiry, but somehow he didn't believe Luke was guilty. It took a certain type of person to kill their own mother. While they couldn't afford to waste time investigating the wrong suspect, they couldn't simply rely on Ian's impression of Luke. They needed hard evidence of Luke's whereabouts on the night Beryl was killed. Without that, a question mark remained against his name, regardless of his financial reliance on his mother. Without Luke as a suspect, there was no one in the frame for Beryl's murder, only a shadowy axe-wielding psychopath who had so far completely eluded them.

Naomi went to speak to Meena, a detective constable working as a Visual Images Identification Detection Officer. Leaving Naomi in charge of a team reviewing CCTV cameras that could track Luke's journey home from work on Thursday, Ian retired to his own office to write up his decision log. In some ways a waste of time, writing the log did sometimes spark off an idea for a new line of enquiry. Even when it did nothing to assist the investigation, it was essential for his own protection that he keep the log up to date. At any point an investigation could go pear shaped, and he needed to be able to defend his decisions.

With a team checking Luke's movements to and from his house after he left work on Thursday evening, as far as was possible, Ian finished his log. Next he turned his attention to establishing that Luke stood to gain nothing from her death. So far they only had his wife's word for that. It took him a while to track down Beryl's will. Then he had to wait for a sergeant in London to check the details with the firm of solicitors who had drawn it up. Ian was at his desk when the message came through late in the afternoon. Beryl had left everything to her husband. Far from gaining by her death, Luke was likely to face real financial difficulties without his mother's support. He would probably lose his house.

The final confirmation of Luke's innocence came from Meena's team who had been liaising with the VIIDO office in Leeds. Luke had been seen leaving work at five. He was spotted boarding a bus, which he left around twenty minutes later. He was a short walk from his home. At around half past eight he was sighted on a security camera in his local supermarket, where he bought some groceries and a few bottles of beer, confirming what he had told Ian. A quick check around the local taxi firms and hire car firms indicated that he could not realistically have driven out of Leeds in time to have met his mother and killed her by nine o'clock. There was no record of any telephone calls between the two of them on the day she died, so there wasn't even any way he could have arranged to intercept her on her journey.

Ian couldn't decide whether he should feel relieved or concerned that Luke's name had been cleared. A copycat murder was shocking enough, but it now seemed they were looking for a psychopath who had so far claimed three victims. In some ways that was even worse. Having escaped detection so far, there was no reason to suppose this killer would stop. All they needed was one lead, one small clue to the killer's identity. So far Ian had never failed. It was rare, but not unknown, for a murderer to evade capture. Ian hoped this case wouldn't turn out to be his first failure.

It was Saturday. Ian finished reading all the notes on Luke and closed the file. Too tired to start on any new line of enquiry, he resigned himself to having a quiet night watching football on the television, and an early night. As he was thinking of leaving, Ted put his head round the door.

'Some of us are going over to Leeds,' he said. 'You fancy coming? It won't be late. Just a few drinks.'

Ian understood why they were going to Leeds where it was less likely anyone would recognise them. A group of coppers out on the town sometimes attracted unwanted attention. He had been invited to go out drinking with the other lads before, but it hadn't seemed fair to leave Bev at home on her own in the evening. This time Bev was away, and it was Saturday night.

'Sure. Why not?'

They congregated in the car park. After a brief discussion two of them volunteered to drive. Soon after they set off there was a sudden heavy downpour that eased off into steady rain. Ian cursed. He hadn't thought to bring a coat but it was too late to change his mind now. He half regretted having agreed to go. He hoped they wouldn't be out late. On the other hand, it was a useful team-building exercise. He told himself he was doing the right thing, socialising out of work with his colleagues. He could do with a break from work. But as they sped along the road to Leeds, he couldn't help thinking about Beryl and wondering what had made her stop.

They reached Leeds and Ian finally began to relax as the atmosphere in the car grew lighthearted. They were a group of lads having a night out. The conversation drifted round to teasing Ted about his relationship with his girlfriend.

'What's the problem?' one of the constables asked. 'She's a looker. You like her, don't you?'

'Yes, but . . .'

'Oh God,' someone else chipped in. 'Don't do it, mate. Put a ring on her finger and you'll regret it for the rest of your life. Or at least until you get a divorce.'

A few of them laughed. Ted glanced uncomfortably at Ian, but he was laughing along with the others.

'You're married, aren't you?' the constable challenged Ian.

'So am I,' a sergeant piped up.

'Yes, and we know who wears the trousers in your house,' another officer laughed and they all joined in.

'Come on, then, Ian, what's your advice?' the constable said.

Put on the spot like that, Ian couldn't think what to say without sounding either slushy, or disloyal to his wife.

'Shut up, Jones, you're pissed and we're not even there yet,' Ted said.

'Come on,' the constable insisted. 'What made you do it? Why did you tie the knot?'

Ian shrugged. 'I asked her and she said yes.'

They all laughed and the conversation moved on. Ian was relieved. They weren't too drunk to understand that he didn't really want to talk about his marriage on a rare night out. He sighed, envying them their louche camaraderie. He missed his colleagues in Kent, men he had worked with before his marriage, when he had been free to go out regularly with his mates while Bev spent the evening with her sister or her parents, or sometimes an old school friend. Moving to York had been a mistake. He wasn't having as much fun as he had expected on his rare night out. More than anything he wished he was at home with his wife, only she wasn't there.

Chapter Forty-nine

ALTHOUGH IT WAS nearly dark he hesitated to go down to the river. The weather was mild. People might be outside in the evening, jogging or cycling along the river path. It would be better to wait for wet weather before venturing out to clean the blood from his axe. In the meantime, he tried to content himself with staying in and admiring his booty. Taking a leather pouch from the tin he kept beneath the floor, he tipped the contents out on to his bed. Patiently he separated out the different items, picking at the chains with a pin to untangle them. With everything neatly separated, and displayed in rows, he sat gazing at the shiny metal. Handfuls of copper and silver coins, gold and silver chains and rings, many with sparkling jewels set in them. It was a start. With Biter's help the hoard would increase. He reached out and touched one of the thick gold chains, the metal shiny and beautiful. It would be a shame to chop it into pieces. Sliding a forefinger under the chain, he scooped it off the bed and let it swing gently from his finger, glowing in the light from his lamp. He could have sat there looking at it all night, but with a sudden storm Thor's thunder sent people running for shelter.

Heavy rain meant it would be safe to go outside and clean Biter. He wanted to polish the blade until it shone as brightly as his golden chains. He gathered his treasures together and dropped them back into the leather pouch. Soon he would need a bigger bag. The best haul had come from the shop. He had been looking for another jewellers, but they were risky. People out alone at night were easier targets. Despite his fear that easy pickings might bring less honour than a dangerous challenge, he understood the need for caution. His enemies were everywhere. He had barely begun raiding yet had already achieved notoriety. His exploits had made the headlines on the front pages of the papers. Television showed the sites where he had carried out his attacks. He wasn't surprised. It was inevitable that a great warrior's fame would spread quickly. But the gods were with him. No one would penetrate the many disguises of a shape shifter. He was a warrior. A wolf. A mighty bear in battle. He could adopt any shape he chose. They would never find him.

He had studied the descriptions of his exploits. They knew about his long cloak. It would be dangerous to wear the blood-stained garment again, equally dangerous to buy a new one. People would be on the lookout for a warrior of his stature enquiring about cloaks. He was too wily to give himself away like that. All the same, his old cloak had been bloodied in too many skirmishes, apart from which it was torn, ripped in a way that might make it too distinctive to allow him to slip through the streets unnoticed. He would have to get rid of it. In the meantime, he bundled it up and shoved it in the back of his wardrobe. He would drop it into one of the large waste bins the night before they were next emptied to minimise any risk of discovery. The people tracking him were clever, with their dogs and their divers, but he would stay one step ahead of them. For all their science, they were fools, their ignorance his protection.

The gods inspired him to make a new cloak from his blanket. With a cord threaded through one side and gathered to make a hood, it worked well enough. One advantage was that the new cloak looked very different to the old one. It was much shorter, with more material gathered around his shoulders. No one would recognise him from the blurry image the police had published, taken from a CCTV film. Before leaving the flat he returned his bag of treasure to its tin and stored it under the floor. Then he rolled his cloak under his arm and went out. Rain pattered around him. The heavy cloudburst had lightened into a steady downpour. It was enough to keep most people off the streets. Occasional passersby took no notice of him when they scurried by, rushing to escape the rain. As he trotted along the familiar route towards the river, he was filled with a sense of wellbeing. Thor had cleared the way for him to clean his weapon. The gods favoured the valiant.

By the time he reached the river the rain had eased but still the path was deserted. Silently and swiftly he stole through the night. Under the railway bridge he paused to slip on his homemade cloak. Fingers stiff with cold pulled the hood up to hide his face, the woolly fabric rough against his cheeks. If anyone passed him they wouldn't see his face. After a quick look around, he squeezed through the broken wall and his hand closed on the handle of his axe. With a surge of pride he began wiping the razor-sharp blade, lovingly cleaning and polishing. It took a while to clean off the blood but he persisted. A warrior who failed to honour his weapon could have no self-respect, and no success. From time to time he checked the gleaming metal in the light of his torch, shielded by his cloak. At length he was satisfied.

It was late by the time he finished, and the rain had completely stopped. Leaving Biter hidden behind the wall, he pushed his way back on to the path. In the shelter of the railway bridge he pulled off his cloak and rolled it up. Tucking it under his arm, he set off, trudging towards home. Tired from his evening's exertions, he didn't notice a uniformed figure approaching until it was too late to slip into the bushes, out of sight. He was sure the policeman would hear his heart, it was pounding so loudly. Biter was way out of reach behind the wall on the other side of the railway bridge. He was on his own.

'You're out late,' the policeman said, blocking his path.

'Just on my way home.'

'Do you mind my asking what you're carrying under your arm?'

'This? It's a blanket,' he answered, unrolling his cloak and shaking it out. He was careful to keep the gathered hood in his grasp, so the alteration wasn't visible. 'I was sitting on it.'

'Having a picnic, were you?'

At first he didn't realise the policeman was joking.

'Best get off home,' the policeman went on. 'It's not a good idea to be out after dark on your own.'

With lowered eyes he listened to the policeman warn him against wandering around the streets at night. He had to struggle not to laugh, because the policeman was warning him against himself.

Chapter Fifty

On Monday morning Ian was summoned to an interview room. Sophie had come to the station and insisted on speaking to him in person. Wishing he was away from his office, he asked Naomi to accompany him.

'This is probably going to be a waste of time,' he warned her. 'I think she might just be making up an excuse to see me.'

'Ooh, someone has a high opinion of himself.'

All the same, she dropped what she was doing and went with him.

'DC Naomi Arthur is here to observe,' Ian said when they arrived.

Sophie paid no attention to the constable who sat at Ian's side, watching her.

'You asked me – that is, you asked us – if we've noticed anything unusual.'

Ian nodded without speaking.

'Well,' Sophie hesitated.

'Go on,' Naomi encouraged her.

Ian concealed his impatience and waited in silence. He wondered if it was ridiculous to suspect she was disappointed at not seeing him alone.

'You asked if we'd noticed any strange activity in the museum recently,' she repeated, parroting his words back at him. 'Well, I have.'

Her expression grew increasingly earnest, while her fingers fidgeted in her lap. She was definitely nervous. Ian wished he knew why. If it wasn't because she fancied him, then there might genuinely be something amiss. He focussed, determined to take her seriously.

'I've seen the same man in there, and I recognised him from the paper. It's the man who was arrested before, that girl's father, the girl who was killed.'

Ian was surprised. This was the second time Sophie had accused Frank of being involved with the murders. Dana had thought she recognised him too. He proceeded carefully.

'Are you sure it was him?'

She nodded her head vigorously. 'Yes. Absolutely. I recognised him.'

'What makes you think he was doing anything unusual?'

'Strange,' she corrected him, as though that made any difference. 'He was just hanging around a lot. He kept coming back, reading the signs on all the weapons, and studying them. Weapons isn't my thing, my area is the volur, you know, the women who practised magic. It was really important in Viking culture. Anyway, I wasn't in the weapons section all the time, I was just walking through, so I don't know how long he was standing there. It just seemed that every time I walked through he was there, staring at the axe heads. It was weird. He made me feel uncomfortable.'

'How often did you see him there?'

'I don't know, I didn't count. But he kept coming back and hanging around the weapons, as though he was watching them. Like I said, it was weird. He gave me the creeps. I was scared, so I came to tell you straight away, like you asked.'

She blushed and looked down.

'Thank you, we'll look into it. And if you see him there again, please call us immediately.'

'OK. I've got your number.'

'My work number,' he corrected her, conscious of Naomi sitting at his side.

'I see what you mean,' the constable said when they were walking back along the corridor. 'She's got the hots for you all right.'

Ian smiled uneasily. He would prefer never to see Sophie again, but she seemed inclined to confide in him. He couldn't afford to rebuff her. She might be a time waster, but with luck she could turn out to be a star witness in the case. It was possible she had just given them a crucial lead. He and Naomi went to discuss the development with Eileen. Her eyes narrowed when she heard what had happened.

'That's two girls who have seen Frank acting suspiciously.'

Ian was more cautious, pointing out that Dana's description had not been clear cut. She had merely seen a bald man with a beard.

'She recognised his picture.'

'She thought she did.'

'Ian,' Eileen said gently, 'don't let your marital situation cloud your judgement. Not all women are unreliable.'

Remembering his scepticism about Zoe's claim that Gary had raped Angela, Ian felt awkward. Eileen had got him all wrong. He wasn't distrustful of women, and his marriage was fine. He told her so as firmly as he could.

'That's good to hear,' the detective chief inspector replied.

Ian vaguely recalled mentioning to someone that his wife had gone to see her parents for the second weekend in a row. As a result of that one harmless remark, it seemed tongues had been wagging. Mortified to realise he was the subject of gossip at the station he resolved to keep quiet about his private life in future.

'Now, about Frank,' Eileen went on, 'we know he's denied being anywhere near the crime scenes, but how do we explain his interest in the weapons in Jorvik? It sounds as though Sophie has been putting two and two together.'

Ian wasn't sure that needed any explanation. 'Surely a man – or a woman – can stop and look at exhibits in a museum without attracting suspicion. And don't forget, Sophie saw Frank's face in the paper. She must know he was brought in for questioning. Anyone following the case knows that. The bloody papers give so much away, it's criminal. She's young, and she might be suggestible. Probably she saw Frank in Jorvik, but she could be reading too much into it. I daresay she was scared when she saw him. He's been accused, and we let him go. She saw him hanging around the museum and might have been alarmed, but that's no indication he's guilty.'

He thought it was understandable that Frank might want to look at the weapons in an attempt to find out in more detail just what had happened to his stepdaughter. Wanting to know what had happened was a common response to bereavement. Sophie was an observant girl, of a nervous disposition. She might well have put two and two together and come up with the wrong answer. He agreed it looked a bit suspicious, but was reluctant to jump to any conclusions.

'It's possible she misunderstood, but she's the second witness to identify Frank. We need to look into this,' Eileen said. 'Let's have another chat with Frank, and this time I want his alibis scrutinised and taken apart. I want his movements accounted for every second of the time frame for these murders. This killer's operating in a small area. If Frank could have slipped off unnoticed, I want to know about it.'

'He has a car,' Naomi added. 'He could have followed Beryl out of town and flagged her down.'

'It's possible,' Eileen agreed.

Meena and her team set to work scrutinising CCTV footage once again, searching for Frank at the entrance to the Jorvik museum. Another team examined the roads leading to the A64 to Leeds, looking for Frank's car out on the road on Thursday evening.

'If we don't see him, it doesn't mean he wasn't there,' Eileen said. There was a hint of desperation in her voice.

Chapter Fifty-one

FRANK STRENUOUSLY DENIED having spent time at Jorvik museum. To begin with, when they were questioning him at home, he claimed he hadn't been there at all, saying the place was for children. When Ian pointed out that ticket sales and CCTV would confirm whether he had visited the museum, he changed his story. That in itself was suspicious. They took him back to the police station and left him to sweat in a cell while they checked the museum records. He had been to the museum, but only once, after his stepdaughter's death. Eileen wondered if the museum's ticket sales were accurate.

'He could have paid cash.'

'Sophie could have been mistaken,' Ian countered.

They went back to the interview room.

'How many times have you visited Jorvik this month?' Eileen asked.

Frank looked surprised. 'I don't understand why you're still on about the Viking museum.'

'Answer the question please.'

Frank passed his hand over his forehead. He was sweating. 'What was the question again?'

Eileen repeated it.

'I went there, yes. All right, I went there. So what? It's not a bloody crime, is it?'

'How many times did you go there in the past month?'

'Once.'

'Why did you go there?'

According to Frank he had wanted to see what the axe that had killed his stepdaughter might have looked like.

'Why did you want to see it?'

He shrugged. 'I just wanted to. I can't explain why. I don't know.'

Eileen leaned forward. 'You went there on more than one occasion, didn't you?'

'I already told you I went the once, just to see.'

'We have a witness who saw you there several times in the past two weeks.'

He shook his head, puzzled, muttering that Eileen was mistaken.

'We have a witness,' she repeated.

'Then your witness has got it wrong. He's mistaken, or else someone's stitching me up.'

Frank's protest appeared genuine. His denial suggested a new possibility. Eileen and Ian retired to her office to discuss the idea that, rather than being mistaken, Sophie could be deliberately lying to frame Frank. It seemed unlikely, but they had to explore every avenue. Privately Ian thought it was no more far-fetched a notion than to suspect Frank had killed his own stepdaughter, and two other people. Whoever the killer was, it was still hard to believe anyone was out and about in York hacking members of the public to death. Meanwhile Frank appeared outraged by Sophie's accusation.

There was no sign of Frank on the road on Thursday evening. CCTV and ticket sales confirmed that he had visited Jorvik

Museum only once, on the Tuesday two days after Angela had been killed. It was time to put pressure on Sophie. Leaving Ted to look into Frank's background more closely, Ian took Naomi with him to Jorvik. He needed to speak to Sophie again and get to the bottom of her lying.

While Ralph went to fetch Sophie, Ian and Naomi waited in one of the small offices above the museum. They sat in silence. Although he wanted to conduct the interview himself, Ian wasn't quite sure how to handle Sophie. He hesitated to ask Naomi's advice. As an experienced inspector, he was worried it might seem inappropriate for him to be asking for guidance from a young constable. On balance, he decided it was best to tackle Sophie in his own way. He hadn't messed up questioning a witness yet. Still, he felt almost unbearably tense as the door opened.

He led into the conversation gently, assuring Sophie that her information had been very useful and the police were very appreciative of her help. He hoped he wasn't laying it on too thickly. Naomi threw him an impatient frown, but Sophie looked happy. At last he reached the crux of the interview.

'How well do you know Frank Carter?'

'Who?'

'Frank Carter. Angela Jones' father. You might know him as Frank Jones.'

Sophie stared blankly at him. She didn't look worried, just puzzled. Ian explained that he was talking about the stepfather of the girl who had been killed.

'Oh,' Sophie drew in a deep breath. 'Oh, of course. Frank. I wondered who you were talking about. I should have known. I knew his name was Frank because I saw it in the paper. But I didn't actually *know* him. I never met the girl that was murdered. That's why I didn't get who you were talking about straight away.'

'So how can you be so sure you saw him at the museum?'

'I recognised him from his picture in the paper.'

'You must have very sharp eyes,' Naomi interjected.

Sophie spoke to Ian. 'What does she mean?'

'It wasn't a clear picture in the paper,' Ian explained, turning his head slightly to glare at Naomi. 'And it's a few weeks since you saw him at the museum . . .'

'No, he was there again yesterday. That's why I was so sure it was him in the paper. And I saw him again this morning.'

'What time did you see him in the museum?' Naomi asked.

'I don't know.'

Sophie had lost any semblance of self-assurance. Her face had turned pale and her fingers were fidgeting as they had done when she had been at the police station.

Ian leaned forward and spoke very gently. He wanted Sophie to focus just on him. That way he hoped he might be able to persuade her to open up. She was lying and he wanted to know why.

'You didn't see Frank here yesterday, Sophie, because he wasn't here yesterday. And he wasn't here this morning either. We know that. So what I want you to tell me is why you're lying to me.'

'I'm not lying.' Ian swore under his breath as Sophie began to cry. 'I thought it was him. I really did. I'm just so scared. I think I'm being followed, and what if he's the killer?'

THEY COULDN'T KEEP Frank in a cell based on the accusation of a hysterical frightened girl.

'I think she was confused, and she's clearly very frightened about the killer,' Ian said.

'She's a deluded idiot,' Naomi said firmly. 'She's just trying to get Ian to notice her.'

'Like that, is it?' Eileen said. 'Let's not waste any more time on her in that case.'

Ian felt equally dismissive of Sophie. All the same, he still wanted to check on the girl's alibi. The trouble was that a private meeting with a hysterical girl who fancied him could result in awkward allegations. He hated himself for his suspicions, but he had nearly been caught out once before. As a young constable, he had been accused of making improper advances. Luckily the interview had taken place at the police station so the exchange had been recorded. Nevertheless, it had made him nervous about conducting interviews on his own with women who might behave inappropriately. He decided to approach her discreetly in public on the museum floor. It was too late to do so that day.

Unable to get through to Bev, he hadn't arranged to pick her up at the train station that evening. Refusing Ted's offer of a drink after work he went straight home. He expected to find his wife there but the house was empty. He tried her mobile again but she didn't answer. Faintly worried, he called her parents' house. Her mother answered the phone.

'Bev's not here. She'll be back later.'

She was surprised when Ian said he had been expecting her back that evening.

'Didn't you get her message?'

'No.'

'She's staying for a few more days.'

'When is she coming home?'

'I think she said Wednesday, but you'll have to ask her.'

Ian sighed. There was no point in complaining that Bev never answered her phone. His mother-in-law would never accept any criticism of her daughter from him.

'Tell her I miss her,' he said and rang off.

Chapter Fifty-two

UNUSUALLY EVERYONE STOOD around in silence on Tuesday morning, before the briefing. As they waited uneasily, a constable attempted to crack a joke about cutting the atmosphere with an axe. The response was barely even half-hearted. Another officer told him to shut up. This was no laughing matter. Ian looked around at the sombre faces. Worse than dejected, he was worried. A demoralised team didn't work well. Somehow the team needed to rekindle the outrage that had energised them at the start of the case. Since then, the shock of two more brutal murders seemed to have overwhelmed them all. Not only that, but teams of officers drafted in from Northallerton and the surrounding area had altered the atmosphere in the station, which felt both more professional yet less focussed at the same time.

Eileen arrived looking flustered. That wasn't an encouraging start. Any hope of good news evaporated at the sight of the grey pouches under her eyes, and the droop of her shoulders. She seemed to have lost her customary confidence. Her opening words were low key. Ian sighed. There was no doubt Eileen was dedicated and thorough. With detailed knowledge of the procedures, she was unlikely to ever put a foot wrong, but her demeanour was that of a woman facing defeat. What they all needed was someone to psyche them up.

'This man we're looking for can't be that clever,' Ian said, remembering how his school rugby coach had found encouraging words even when the team was being totally thrashed. 'We can do this. He's not going to outwit us for long. He's bound to make a mistake, leave his DNA somewhere, or someone who knows him will come forward.'

For a moment no one answered. They all understood what he was doing. It didn't make any material difference, but he thought one or two of the young constables looked more cheerful.

'That's all very well,' Eileen said, 'but so far we've got nowhere.' At least she sounded angry rather than defeated.

To Ian's surprise, Naomi piped up in his defence. 'Ian's right. Someone somewhere must know something.'

There was another pause. The hope that someone somewhere would tell them something wasn't much to go on. Ian hesitated to speak again.

'Let's focus on the murder weapon,' Eileen said. 'It's unusual, distinctive anyway. Where is he keeping it? Why has no one seen it?'

Eileen wanted the papers to run a picture of it again, and Yorkshire Television channels to show the image with an urgent request for any member of the public who had seen it to come forward.

'I know we ran this before, but let's have a real push, get this image out everywhere. If anyone in the UK has seen this axe recently, they need to be alerted to the fact that we're looking for it. We have to find it.'

They were going over old ground but, if there was the slightest chance that another appeal might yield results, they had to go all out for it. They were all desperate for a break, no one more so than Ian. Bev was due home that evening and he would have given anything to get the case wound up before her return. Of course that wasn't going to happen. Even if they caught the killer, there would still be a mountain of paperwork to get through to ensure a conviction. But at least his wife would have his attention while he was at home. Until the killer was apprehended, even when he wasn't at work, witness statements would keep repeating themselves in his mind, as he sifted through searching for inconsistencies.

At half past nine, Ian set off for Jorvik. Instead of buzzing himself into the upstairs offices he joined the short queue and paid to enter. By the time he reached the front desk, the queue had built up behind him. He wandered in and crossed the large first chamber, passing an excited group of children on a school outing. He found Sophie standing at the boarding point for electric carriages that took visitors on a journey through a reconstructed Viking village. The corridor was not well lit. He had a disturbing feeling she might fling herself at him, but she merely smiled shyly as he approached. She was wearing a long pinafore, belted at the waist. Loose fitting, the outfit contrived to look attractive, perhaps because it emphasised the curves of her body. Her blonde hair was concealed beneath a complicated white headscarf wound around her head.

'Do you want to go for a ride?' she asked, peeping up at him from beneath her head gear and blushing.

'Actually, I'm here to see you.' He winced at the unintended ambiguity of his words. 'I wanted to check a few details with you.'

'We could go somewhere quieter.'

'No, this is fine. I won't keep you long.'

There was no mistaking her peeved expression. Behind him Ian could hear the gleeful shouts of the school children. He spoke hurriedly.

'You said you were at home with your flatmate three Sundays ago, when the first murder took place, and on your way home from work the following Wednesday. I just need one more detail from you. Where were you last Thursday evening, at around nine?'

'You mean you're asking for an alibi, after I've done all I can to help you?'

She seemed sad, rather than angry.

'For the process of elimination,' Ian said.

She screwed up her face. 'Nine o'clock on Thursday I would have been at home.'

'Can anyone vouch for that?'

'I don't know. You can try my flatmate, but she might have been out. I don't keep a record of when she's in.'

The fact that Sophie's response wasn't conclusive only made it more credible. Ian sighed. Unlike alibis in fiction, those in real life were frequently vague. Unless they had an appointment or had booked something specific, most people couldn't remember exactly what they had been doing a few days earlier, at a particular time. Faulty and false memories resulted in a great deal of speculation. Such incomplete information was never helpful, and was frequently misleading.

Chapter Fifty-three

SOPHIE'S FLATMATE WORKED at a restaurant in York. Tall and gangly, her bleached hair was streaked with various shades of pink and purple. It wasn't clear whether the multicoloured effect was deliberate or if the dye had faded inconsistently. Ian wasn't surprised to see the top edge of a tattoo on her neck when she flicked her long hair back behind her shoulders.

'Sophie? Yeah, I know Sophie. We live in the same flat.' She didn't refer to Sophie as a friend, or even a flatmate. 'She in trouble then?' she added incuriously.

'We're just eliminating her from an enquiry.'

'Oh, OK then.'

'Can you confirm that she was at home on Thursday evening?'

The girl shrugged one skinny shoulder. 'I don't keep a diary of her comings and goings.'

'Does she go out a lot?'

'I couldn't say, really. I mean, I'm hardly ever there in the evenings. If I'm not working, I'm out with mates. Sophie and me, we share the bills but that's about it really. I'm in the kitchen before she gets home from work, if I'm not eating here, and she cooks in the evening when I'm working, so we kind of work around each other, you know? I hear her clattering about in her room sometimes, but mostly you wouldn't even know she was there. It's not like we're best friends. Like I said, we just share the bills. She's in her own room most of the time, when she's not out at work. I mean, she keeps herself to herself, but that's OK. Suits me fine. We do our own thing. I'm hardly ever there anyway.'

'So, last Thursday evening?'

The girl frowned. 'Thursday? Yes, I know. I wanted an early night before the weekend so I went straight home after work and I remember she was in because I heard her music in her room. It's OK, she doesn't play it loud.'

Ian thanked Sophie's flatmate for her help and left. It didn't seem that Sophie had been out on the streets hunting for victims to hack to death. Another line of enquiry, albeit an unlikely one, had drawn a blank.

He set off early that evening to meet Bev at the station. Her train came in on time. He recognised her short blonde hair and bright red coat before she saw him. With an involuntary grin, he hurried towards her.

'It's all right, I can manage,' she laughed as he seized her case. 'I'm not an invalid.'

On the way back to the car, he suggested going out for a meal.

'It's a lovely idea, Ian, but I'm really tired.'

'No worries. I'll drop you at home and then go and get a take-away, if you like.'

'Sounds great. Just give me time to shower and throw some clothes in the washing machine. I'm starving!'

'You look great,' he told her as they sat down at the kitchen table later.

It wasn't an empty compliment. Her oval face had a healthy glow and she had put on a few pounds. He hesitated to mention it, knowing she was justly proud of her figure. She tucked into her korma with a will. If he told her she had put on weight, she might not want to eat so much, and she was clearly enjoying her dinner. It was good for a person to have a healthy appetite. He didn't care if she was putting on a few pounds. She was still the most beautiful woman he had ever seen. He told her so and she blushed.

'Stop it, Ian.'

'I can tell you how beautiful you are if I want to.'

She laughed then, and put her head in her hands. He realised she was crying.

'Bev? What is it?'

'I'm just tired. I'm sorry. I'm so sorry.'

He stood up and went round the table to her but she pushed him away and blew her nose vigorously.

'We need to talk.'

Her serious tone made him uneasy.

'What is it?'

'Sit down. There's something I need to tell you.'

'Are you ill?'

All at once it struck him that she was about to announce she was leaving him. He took a deep breath, too shocked to speak. She looked up, her eyes streaming with tears. Her next words took him completely by surprise.

'Pregnant?' he repeated wonderingly. 'You're pregnant?'

She dropped her head in her hands and began to cry again. For a second, Ian felt as though he couldn't breathe. They had never had a serious discussion about when they might start a family. It was something they had only talked about in very general terms. Swallowing his amazement, he forced a smile.

'That's wonderful news, Bev. We should celebrate.'

'What is there to celebrate?'

'Bev, you're going to be a mother. I'm going to be a father. We're going to have a baby.' He injected as much enthusiasm into his voice as he could. The conversation felt unreal. He had no idea why she was crying, but he supposed it was her hormones making her emotional. 'There's so much we need to talk about. When are you due?'

'Not now, Ian. I'm so tired. I just need to get some sleep.'

'Have you told your parents?'

'No. I wanted to tell you first. But we mustn't tell anyone yet. It's early days, and it's bad luck to tell anyone until the first three months are over. Promise me you won't tell anyone. Promise me, Ian.'

Overwhelmed by the news, Ian agreed at once. He would have agreed to anything. As she left the room, carrying his child, he realised he hadn't asked her when she had found out, or how long she had known. This was not the time to start bombarding her with questions. A few seconds later he heard her going up the stairs. He didn't know what to do, but she had said she was tired so he decided it was best to leave her alone.

Doing his best to ignore his excitement, he opened his laptop. He had a new incentive to do well at work, a new future to plan. With a burst of energy he logged on and set to work.

'I'll protect you,' he whispered, as though his wife was still in the room and could hear him. 'I'll soon have this crazy bastard behind bars. The streets will be safe again for you and the baby.'

He hoped it wouldn't take long. Bev needed him more than ever now.

Chapter Fifty-four

BEV WAS ASLEEP when Ian took her tea in bed in the morning. She stirred when he went in the room. Leaning over the bed, he told her softly that he was going to take care of her from now on, but she didn't wake up. He stood quite still for a moment, watching her, filled with an overwhelming love, stronger than he had ever felt before. They were joined now by so much more than their marriage vows. Promises were easily broken. A child was for life. Gently he put the cup of tea down by her side in case she woke in time to drink it before it was cold. Then, with a fatuous wave, he left.

It was hard to concentrate on the investigation. His thoughts kept returning to his wife. Until Bev was ready to share the news with other people, the baby would remain their secret. No doubt she would want to tell her family first. Until she had done so, he could not tell anyone about it, even though the baby was his too. He still couldn't believe it. In his break, he didn't go to the canteen. He would probably bump into one of his colleagues there, and he wanted to be alone. He wasn't sure he could trust himself to hide his emotion and Bev was adamant she didn't want him to tell anyone. It was all right for her, sitting at home. He was at work, sitting on the most exciting news he had ever heard. On impulse, he jumped up and strode out of the building. He wasn't sure where he was headed but found himself outside the pub a few doors along from the entrance to the police station. Hoping he wouldn't see anyone he knew, he went in and ordered a half and a sandwich. It was unusual for him to drink at lunchtime when he was on a case, but this was no ordinary day. He was going to be a father. As he sipped his beer, he couldn't stop grinning to himself.

There wasn't much he could do for now, but he was determined to attend every single antenatal class. He was going be at her side to witness the birth. In the meantime, he would give his wife everything she could possibly need. They would have to decide on a name together but there was nothing to stop him thinking about it as he had his lunch. Idly he found a website and looked through a list of boys' names. The site gave the derivation of the names, and he scanned through the meanings as well. He already knew that Ian meant Gift from God. That was all very well if you believed in God. Looking further down the list he discovered that Ralph came from Old Norse, meaning wolf-like. Staring at the screen, he felt a sudden wave of excitement and struggled to catch his breath.

George the profiler had suggested the killer might be acting out a fantasy of being a Viking warrior. Obsessed with Vikings, he might even work at Jorvik. Now Ian had discovered that one of the staff there had a Viking name. Not only that, but according to Jimmy, Ralph was obsessed with Viking weapons. Ian checked his notes. 'Ralph knows all there is to know about the weapons. He's the expert. He gives them all names and talks to them when he thinks no one's listening.' That had struck Ian as significant at the time. Now it seemed to fit with George's theory. Leaving half his sandwich untouched, he hurried to Eileen's office.

'You think he's a killer because of his name?' Eileen repeated, frowning.

Ian flinched at her scathing tone. He had to admit it sounded ridiculous, but when he tied his theory to what George had said, the detective chief inspector began to look excited. 'A Viking name? Go on. Bring him in,' she barked. 'Let's see what he has to say for himself.'

Ian hesitated over how to approach the suspect. It might be better to string Ralph along for a while. He might be more inclined to talk if he had no idea that he had become a suspect. Once arrested, he might clam up. Instead of arresting him, Ian invited Ralph to accompany him to the police station on the pretext of helping the enquiry by answering a few more questions.

Ralph agreed cheerfully enough. 'If you're quite sure you can't speak to me just as well here.' He didn't sound worried, but that could be part of his delusion, that he was untouchable.

Once they were at the station, Ian questioned the unwitting suspect about his name. If Ralph was surprised by the question, he didn't show it.

'Yes, it's my name. Well, that is, it's my middle name, really. My first name's Jason. I don't mind it, but I prefer Ralph.'

'Why?'

'What?'

'Is there any particular reason why you choose to use your middle name?'

Ralph shook his head. He was beginning to look irritated. 'I just like it.'

Ian skirted around the main purpose of the interview for a while without making any headway.

'Where were you last Thursday evening, at around nine?'

Uncertain where this was leading, Ralph seemed rattled.

'What? I was at home, where I always am in the evening.'

'Did you go for a drive?'

'No. I haven't got a car. What are you talking about?'

'Did you hire a car, or borrow one, last week? There's no point in lying, Ralph, we'll trace the records. Did you drive out towards Leeds last Thursday?'

Ralph's expression changed from annoyance to indignation as he realised what Ian meant. His squint seemed more pronounced than ever.

'Are you kidding me?'

However hard Ian pressed him, Ralph insisted that he was mistaken.

'You're crazy to even suggest I had anything to do with those murders. It was some sicko. You've got nothing on me. The whole idea's crazy.'

'It's crazy all right,' Ian muttered. 'Your alibis aren't that clear for any of the times of the murders.'

'And that's supposed to be proof of guilt, is it?' Ralph laughed, but he looked terrified. 'I'm not going to say any more until I've spoken to a solicitor. Jesus, are you really so desperate to pin this on someone, you're prepared to accuse me just because my alibis aren't a hundred per cent watertight? Is that really how the justice system works? And why me? I don't get it. Anyway, I'm not going to say another word until I have a solicitor.'

They couldn't afford to leave questioning Ralph again until the next morning. The time for holding him without a formal charge was running out. Resigning himself to the fact that he would be home late again, Ian phoned Bev. At last the solicitor arrived but he only slowed down the questioning process. It made no difference. Ralph remained adamant that he had nothing to do with any murders, and he knew nothing about the replica Viking axe that had been used to kill three people. Every time Ian tried to press him, the lawyer raised the same question.

'Do you have any evidence against my client?'

'If he's guilty, we'll find the evidence, don't you worry about that.' Ian leaned forward across the desk, glaring at Ralph. 'You won't get away with this.'

'If,' the solicitor repeated laconically.

Chapter Fifty-five

IT WAS A MILD evening as he set off, Biter in hand. This time he went in the opposite direction to the usual one, away from the town. His fame was spreading so rapidly that the streets in the centre might be too dangerous for him to risk another raid there. Where he was heading, there would be no jewellery stores but he might come across someone on their own. Easy pickings. He strode past a couple of boats out on the river, and turned his head away from a man with a dog, several cyclists who jingled their bells at him to get out of the way, and a couple of joggers. He wasn't interested in them.

Leaving the tow path, he passed an old church, and entered a residential estate. He crossed the road to avoid a small shop and a pub, for fear of being seen, but the pavements were deserted. All he could see was row after row of houses. He had never considered breaking into a private property. Looking around, he wondered whether that might be a good idea. The trouble was, he had no way of knowing who was on the other side of the doors. The wolf could destroy a guard dog with a few snaps of his powerful jaws, but there might be more than one person to contend with in addition. It was too risky to enter unknown territory. He walked on.

As the daylight began to fade, he heard footsteps tapping a light rhythm on the pavement behind him. It sounded like a woman in high heels. Passing a side street, he slipped round the corner and waited for the pedestrian to appear. A moment later she came into view, a slight girl of about twenty with long hair that swung from side to side as she walked. She was wearing a short green coat and high-heeled shiny black shoes. Silently he glided after her. His feet barely touching the ground, he stole along with Biter concealed under his cloak, waiting for an opportunity to strike.

The woman trotted on, seemingly unaware that she was being followed. His heart pounded with the thrill of the chase. He was closing in on her. The trouble was there were houses all along the street. Someone could be watching through a window. He needed a deserted spot that wasn't overlooked, so that he could pounce. He was ready. He padded after her, his eyes flitting from side to side, checking for watchers. All at once, she turned and hurried up a path. Instead of going straight to the front door, she slipped around the corner of the building and he saw that there was a second front door at the side of the house. She must live in a maisonette on the first floor. The doorway was like an answer to a prayer, hidden from the road. The young woman thrust her hand into her bag, feeling for her keys. If he didn't act swiftly he would lose her. With one bound he was on the path. Another few steps and he was close enough to touch her. She heard his approach and looked round in surprise.

He looked into her eyes and saw her fear. Before she could utter a sound, Biter struck. It was like the first attack all over again: her eyes widening in terror, lips parting as though to scream, the only sound the impact of his blade as it struck bone. Her skull cracked, unable to withstand the momentum of his swinging arms. Blood spurted from a gash in the side of her head flowing through her hair and down her arm. With a muffled cry, she fell on to her back and lay across the path without moving. Scarlet rivulets trickled down her front door. He jumped sideways but couldn't avoid the spray completely. It reached the edges of his cloak. He suppressed a smile at the badge of honour. It was never going to be long before his new cloak was bloodied in combat.

There wasn't much risk of being spotted from the road. More pressing was the danger that there might be someone in the house, listening out for his victim's return. They could have seen her walking down the path, and heard her footsteps outside the front door. At any second the front door might be flung open, and there could be half a dozen people in there. It was unlikely, but possible. He had to work quickly to fill his bag and make his escape. The blood was flowing steadily from her head but no longer spraying around. It was safe to approach. Her eyes were shut, her lips parted. If she wasn't already dead, she was unconscious. He had no time to find out which. He didn't care anyway. It made no difference.

Deftly he slipped his gloved hand into first one pocket of her coat, then another. Both were empty. He swore softly. She had fallen on top of her bag. He tried to pull it out. The clasp had fallen downwards so that it was impossible to reach without pulling the whole bag out from under her body. Each time he pulled at it, her body jolted. Suddenly her eyes flew open. She reached out with both hands. Finding his cloak, her fingers clutched convulsively at the fabric. He abandoned his search. All he wanted to do was get away from her grasping fingers. White eyes glared at him from her blood-streaked face. Panic swept through him like a blast of cold air, making him tremble. With a muffled grunt he wrenched himself free and fled, empty-handed. He had reached the church before he realised he had left Biter behind.

All too soon they would discover the dead woman and be on his trail. He cursed the gods that had led him into this trap. He couldn't risk going back. Blindly he ran along the river path. Whatever shape he took, dogs might still be able to track him. Forcing himself to calm down, he ran towards the river. The boat was his only chance of escape. Making his way to the gap in the wall, he forced himself through, shoulder first. For once heedless of the rough edge of the wall scraping at him, he felt around for his boat and pulled it over the wall and on to the path. Panting, he dragged it down the steps to the bank and into the water. With a final effort he leaped on to the boat and let the current carry him away. He gazed out over the dark water as the boat floated out to the middle of the river. The gods had taken Biter, but he had survived. He would never be caught.

Chapter Fifty-six

EILEEN WAS VERY keen to make a formal charge but she decided to wait until the morning, hoping some useful evidence would turn up by then. Meanwhile teams of officers were working through the night, hunting for proof that Ralph was guilty. A search team were busy at his flat. So far they had found nothing. Once, Ian would have gone to Ralph's flat to check on the progress of the search, keen to be on the spot in case any evidence turned up, but the focus of his life had changed. Now he only wanted to be with his wife. Leaving instructions that he was to be contacted straight away if the search team found anything incriminating, he set off home. Bev might be asleep, but his place was still with her. He had left her alone for long enough that evening. He almost hoped evidence wouldn't be found before the morning.

Bev was dozing on the sofa when he reached home. He went into the kitchen as quietly as he could, but she woke up and called to him.

'I'm just making a cup of tea,' he replied. 'Would you like one?'

Replacing the bottle of beer he had just taken out of the fridge, he put the kettle on.

'Have you eaten?' she asked, coming into the kitchen.

'Yes. Don't worry about me. You go and sit down and I'll bring your tea in to you. Would you like anything with it?'

She laughed. 'I'm pregnant, Ian, I'm not an invalid.'

But she went back in the living room.

'How was your day?' she asked when he took her tea in to her.

He smiled. 'We're about to make an arrest.'

'Shouldn't you be getting on with it then, if you know who it was? It's not like you to miss the action.'

'Don't worry. He's safely locked up, waiting to be charged. It's one of the people working at Jorvik.'

'You always said it would be, though I don't see why.'

'It was just a hunch. If the killer's obsessed with the Vikings . . .'

'Obsessed with the Vikings? How do you know that?'

He sighed. He was tired, and she wasn't really interested. 'We don't know. Like I said, it's just a hunch. It doesn't matter.'

They sipped their tea in silence for a moment.

'How was *your* day?'

She shrugged. 'I'm pregnant. What do you expect? I was sick this morning so I went back to bed. Then I felt better so I got up and cleaned the kitchen. And that's about it, really. I was sick and I cleaned the kitchen.'

She sounded so wretched that he felt guilty. In an attempt to cheer her up he suggested they pay someone to help her in the house, just while she was pregnant. They could afford it.

'And then what am I supposed to do all day? You're never here. There's no point in making dinner because I never know if you're going to be home in the evening . . .'

He switched off from the familiar complaint. From now on things were going to be different. He didn't need to tell her. She would see the change in him for herself. The thought of having a baby scared him. He wondered if she felt the same, and what their lives would be like from now on. He looked away, embarrassed by his confusion. Bev needed him to be strong now. Her whinging stopped and a moment later he heard her snoring gently. She was still holding her cup. He crept over to the sofa and lifted it gently from her hand. She opened her eyes.

'I wasn't asleep.'

He didn't mention her snoring.

'So, when do the classes start?' he asked, sitting next to her.

'What classes?'

'The antenatal classes. You know I'll be there with you whenever I can.'

'Whenever you can?'

'I do have a job.'

'I know.'

He put his arm round her, drawing her close.

'Let's not fall out. Not now. I know it's been rough for you, moving here. Maybe it was a mistake coming here. We could think about moving back.'

She twisted round so that she could look up at him, her face troubled. 'Really? Do you really mean that?'

'Of course. Why not? If that's what you want. Look, assuming all goes well, there's no reason why I shouldn't be able to put in for another promotion in a few years. We could settle nearer to your parents. They could babysit . . .'

'A few years? Thanks, Ian. I know you're trying to be nice but you're not helping.'

She was crying again.

'Why don't I make you a fresh cup, and fix us a snack? Do you want anything? Anything at all?'

She blew her nose. 'There's a bottle of Pinot Grigio in the fridge.'

He held back from telling her she ought not to be drinking alcohol, afraid she would become aggressive again.

'You look all hot and bothered. I'll get you some water.'

As he stood up, his phone rang. Bev's head jerked upright, and her fists clenched.

'Leave it. You've got your killer. You don't have to go out now. Leave it. They can speak to you in the morning.'

'I have to answer. Don't worry, I'll tell them I can't go out again tonight.'

But as he listened, he knew he would have to let his wife down. He rang off and turned to face her.

'There's been another murder.' Struggling to curb his impatience, he added, 'they've found the murder weapon.'

'Ian you've only just got home. Don't go out again.'

'Bev, I have to go. You know I can't ignore this. The killer's still out there.'

'You told me you'd got him locked up.'

'We thought we had, but it seems we got the wrong man. We've had to release our suspect.'

'Great!'

'But now we're going to be able to trace the right one through the murder weapon. We're about to crack it, Bev. I have to be there. You must get the significance of the find.'

'Yes, all right, I get it, I get it. But it's down to the forensic people to examine it and come up with something. There's nothing

you can do. You're going because you want to go, not because anyone needs you there.'

The phone rang again.

'I'm on my way,' he said, standing up.

He leaned down and gave Bev a kiss on the top of her head. She
turned away.

Chapter Fifty-seven

THE DEAD GIRL lay across the path that led beside her house to a back garden or yard. The only illumination on the path normally would be a faint glow from the street lamps on the road running past the house, and any light that reached it from the moon. Tonight the area was lit up by bright lamps. White-clad scene of crime officers flitted around, ghostly in the unnatural light. More lights had been set up inside the forensic tent. Crime scenes out of doors were always difficult to manage. One end of the tent was open to the elements, allowing a scene of crime officer to examine the front door to the property which was spattered with blood. He leaned forwards, intent on his work, and took no notice of the bustle of activity going on behind him. Across the centre of the narrow tent lay the body, her face a mess of blood. More blood had seeped into the cracks of the paving stones beneath her. In the bright lighting, Ian could see one side of her long dark hair was streaked with red. It had stained her coat, scarlet blotches against green fabric. Beside her on the path lay a bloody axe. Ian's breath caught in his throat as he gazed at the murder weapon that had taken four lives, possibly more. He had seen similar axe heads at Jorvik, where they were called bearded blades because of the curved lower side designed to hook over enemy shields, and a rounded cutting edge.

'Some of her blood must have sprayed on the killer,' a scene of crime officer said. 'It went everywhere. Look.' He pointed at the ground where a bloody smudge was visible. 'It's only a partial, but we might be able to get something off it. And there's that.' He nodded at the axe.

Ian stared first at the blurry footprint left by the killer, and then at the axe that must surely yield up his identity. After weeks of casting around helplessly, the net was finally closing in.

Another scene of crime officer came over to tell Ian that a doctor was on the way. A brown leather handbag dangled from his arm. It was stained with blood.

'We retrieved this from underneath the victim. The strap was still slung over her shoulder. It must have swung round behind her as she fell and she must have landed on top of it.'

Ian took the bag. Fumbling with gloved fingers, he opened the zip and pulled out a fluffy pink purse. Inside it were a couple of ten pound notes and a handful of change. The killer had not had time to steal the girl's coins before running off. Obviously he had left in a panic, or he wouldn't have left his axe behind. Ian wondered what had disturbed him.

'Something rattled his cage all right,' a scene of crime officer commented, as though he could read Ian's mind. 'Wish I knew what it was. We've got a right crazy here.'

Ian examined the contents of the bag. Apart from a make-up case and a pen, he found a bank card in the purse, and a door key. A quick check of her bank details revealed that the dead girl's name was Andrea Shelton. She was twenty-two years old and she had been killed on her own doorstep. Someone must have passed by, or shouted out, for the killer to rush off in such a hurry. They needed to find that witness. It was possible someone inside the house had heard something, although no one had contacted the police. Manoeuvring his way past scene of crime officers, Ian rang the bell. No one answered. He hammered loudly on the door but there was no response from inside. It didn't look as though anyone in there had frightened the killer away.

After banging on the dead girl's door, Ian went to check with the adjoining properties. The victim had lived in a first-floor maisonette. To start with he tried the people who lived downstairs. A man in his early thirties came to the door. He said he was at home with his girlfriend and claimed to have no inkling that a tragedy had been unfolding just outside his home. He told Ian they had been watching television in their living room at the back of the house. They hadn't heard any disturbance outside. His girlfriend came to join him. Short and blonde, she was clearly shocked to hear that her neighbour upstairs had been murdered.

'But she was so nice,' she burst out, 'who would have done that? Who?'

She was shaking. Her boyfriend put his arm round her as Ian explained what appeared to have happened.

'Oh my God,' the girl kept repeating, over and over, 'oh my God.'

Having established that they could tell him nothing that might help move the investigation forward, Ian left. He gave them each a card and asked them to contact him if they thought of anything that might help discover the identity of the killer. The neighbours on both sides of the property were similarly shocked, but unable to offer any useful information. Ian returned to the tent, deep in thought. If none of the neighbours had interrupted the killer, someone else must have gone past to disturb him at his grisly work. The police would have to put out an appeal for witnesses. That could be a longwinded task, inviting all sorts of cranks to come forward with false information. It was a pity none of the immediate neighbours had noticed anything. He tried the properties over the road, but no one had seen anyone go past. As before, the killer had disappeared without a trace – except that this time he had left his axe behind.

That was enough.

A doctor arrived and gave the body a quick examination. Thin and fair-haired, she scowled up at Ian as though he was to blame for dragging her out to look at a corpse. With a grunt she rose to her feet and dusted her knees with the back of a gloved hand.

'Well, she's dead,' she announced.

'Time of death?'

'It's difficult to be precise, with the body being outside, but I'd say about two hours ago, between eight thirty and nine thirty.'

She looked surprised when Ian asked if she could tell him anything about what had happened.

'I would have thought that was pretty obvious. Now I really need to get going.'

Without another word she spun on her heel and walked away.

Before the axe was removed for close forensic examination in the lab, a police handler arrived with a tracker dog. With luck, it would lead them straight to the owner of the weapon. The handler was concerned that the blood on the axe might put the dog off the scent they wanted it to follow, but he was ready to give it a try. There was a chance it could work. Ian watched the animal sniffing at the axe. It was a surreal scenario that seemed to take ages. At last the handler seemed satisfied the dog had picked up the scent.

'Let's hope it's the right one,' Ian muttered as he followed the handler down the path beside the house, back to the street.

After sniffing around on the pavement for a few minutes, the dog set off up the road. The handler hurried after it with Ian following. As they reached the end of the road there was a clap of thunder. The dog didn't even pause in his stride as it began to pour with rain. The handler had come prepared in a waterproof jacket. Ian swore. He wasn't wearing a coat.

'It's taking us back to the river!' the handler called over his shoulder.

The dog began to trot faster as they approached the river path. They were returning to the location the dog had led them to once before. Ian was convinced they were on the right track, even though it would probably only take them to the water's edge again.

Chapter Fifty-eight

THE DOG STOPPED abruptly, then ran round in circles sniffing the ground. Once or twice it looked up at the handler. The two men waited. The dog went over to the wall that ran alongside the path and stood beside it for a moment. Then it put its head back and howled softly.

Ian turned to look at the handler. 'What does that mean?'

'I don't know. Something happened here.'

Ian nodded at a constable who was accompanying them. 'We need to search this area. Maybe he stopped and threw something over the wall here.'

'Yes, sir.'

'Yes. Something happened here. You can trust him. Come on, boy.'

Understanding the signal, the dog moved away from the wall and took a sharp turn down the narrow steps to the river. It stood on the bank, snuffling at the water. It was the same spot where it had brought them before. Ian swore. All the tracks led to the river. The dog had been casting around. It pulled his handler up the steps again and loped along the path towards the town. The two men hurried to keep up. Reaching the railway bridge the dog stopped and began its routine of sniffing again.

'He stopped here,' the handler said.

Ian nodded. That made sense. The killer was running away. Under the bridge he would be out of sight, concealed from every direction. He might have paused to gather his breath. Maybe he had a stitch. Or he might have stopped to remove a disguise, his cloak perhaps.

'How long did he stop for?'

The handler shook his head. 'I don't know. He could tell us everything, if he could talk.' He stooped to pat the dog's head.

At a signal from the handler, the dog set off again, back towards the steps where he had lost the scent before. All tracks led to the river where the dog couldn't follow him. Nor could the police. Yet again the killer had vanished into the night. It wouldn't be easy to conduct a search of the area in the dark, but Ian couldn't afford to wait until morning. With every passing hour the killer might be moving further away. He would have realised that he was no longer safe in York and must be planning to slip away from the city as soon as he could. He might already have gone. In six months, or a year, they might read about a psychopath hacking people to death with another axe in another county. Another police team would set to work, looking for the axe killer from York, while more people were murdered.

There was nothing more for the tracker dog to do. With a nod at the handler as he left, Ian was on the phone organising a search team to check the river path, inch by inch. In the darkness they had to find something that would reveal the identity of the mysterious killer who had slipped away from them yet again. It didn't help that the ground was wet. The rain had stopped, but the earth was sodden. Despite the darkness and the wet, they had to press on. This time they would leave no loopholes. Not only the path, but the river itself would be closed. The killer would not escape that way again. Everyone who lived along the river would be questioned first thing in the morning, before people left for work, in case anyone had noticed a figure, or a boat, in the night. Beside the path a whitewashed wall fenced off a ditch, beyond which a steep grassy incline led up to the railway line. The wall would be taken down, panel by panel, starting opposite the steps leading down to the river. If the killer had left even one hair there, Ian wanted it found. With four murders committed, he could call on almost unlimited resources to aid him in the search. Every available officer had been drafted in to assist the investigation, and now they knew where to focus their efforts. Sooner or later they would find what they were looking for. They could only hope they would discover the killer's identity in time to prevent anther death.

'This time he won't get away,' Ian muttered down the phone.

He wasn't sure if anyone heard him. It didn't matter. He was talking to himself.

With impressive speed the path by the river was illuminated beside the narrow stairs leading down to the water, where the killer had twice evaded capture. Beyond the circle of brilliant light, uniformed officers were scouring the path and the bank below with hand-held torches. There was an atmosphere of quiet industry on the ground. Overhead the fluctuating roar of a circling helicopter rose and faded as its powerful beam of light swept across the area. Ian was standing beneath a tree on the slope near the steps, water dripping gently from the branches above his head. He considered going to wait under the nearby railway bridge but stayed where he was. His hair was already wet. It was hard to keep still, but there was nothing he could do. In the light of his torch he studied the bark of the tree, gnarled and rough. Light from the helicopter shone intermittently through a mist that hung eerily over the water, spreading in pockets across the surrounding land.

Even in March the night air held a hint of winter. Ian wasn't dressed for a chilly night vigil. Preoccupied with Bev's complaints, he had left the house in a rush without stopping to grab a coat. It hadn't been raining then. Worse than his damp clothes, his shoes weren't waterproof. Damp had seeped through the seams before he reached the river path and pulled on shoe covers. His hair was wet. His socks were wet. His feet felt like blocks of ice. He stamped on the ground, and wrapped his arms round his chest, pressing his hands against his sides with his upper arms. It was hard to remain optimistic when he was so cold.

On the path in front of him a couple of young officers paused in their search. He couldn't hear what they were saying but one of them must have cracked a joke because they both laughed before turning back to their work. Isolated, Ian waited in the darkness. He seemed to be standing there for hours before a voice rang out, disturbing the muffled sounds of the night search.

'Over here!'

His cold feet forgotten he dashed across the path, splashing through a puddle as he hurried towards an officer waving at him in the light of a torch. Several panels of the wall had been taken down. The dazzling beam of light illuminated a gap in the wall just opposite the steps where dogs had twice lost the killer's scent. Red-faced from his exertions, an excited officer accosted him as he reached the space in the wall.

'The panel was broken here, sir. There was a gap. When we pulled the panel, there was enough room to get through. So we got the lads to take it down completely. SOCOs are examining the bit of wall they took down. And bloody hell, sir. Just look at what we found on the other side!'

In the glare of the lights, Ian gazed towards the muddy ditch on the far side of the wall.

'Bloody hell,' he echoed the officer's words.

Chapter Fifty-nine

THE FIRST RAYS of the sun were beginning to appear, burning off the night mist. With the daylight, the air instantly seemed warmer. Ian felt his temporary depression vanish with the mist. It was hard to believe the sudden change in the atmosphere along the river bank. The search continued, with officers inching their way along the path, scrutinising the ground. Ostensibly nothing had changed. But the muted voices sounded livelier. Word might have spread about the killer's lair in the ditch, or it could have simply been in response to the dawn, the end of a long, cold night. Either way, the mood among the searchers was almost cheerful.

Pulling on fresh shoe covers, Ian approached and stared down into the ditch. Beside a large blue plastic bucket half a dozen tins stood in the muddy water.

'Metal polish, machine oil, linseed oil,' the officer told him, following the direction of Ian's gaze.

Ian nodded. Several filthy rags lay spread out on the earth, above the level of the water, together with a large, clear plastic bag containing packs of sandpaper. Stepping closer, he saw a few leather gloves inside the bucket, together with what looked like a carbon steel brush. There was an orange plastic bag beside the bucket.

'What's in the carrier bag?'

A scene of crime officer replied. 'A file. Looks like it was used on metal. We'll bag it up and send it off to the lab as soon as we've finished with the photos.'

'Looks like he brought a vice with him and clamped the weapon to a tree root. Here.'

He pointed to a large root protruding from the earth scored with deep incisions. Some instrument with straight sides had cut into it several times. Ian nodded.

'And here again.' The officer indicated further markings on a fence post.

The whole set-up would have looked bizarre had they not known what had taken place there. As it was, the scene made perfect sense. The killer had brought his axe there to sharpen it. Perhaps he had kept it stored there when he wasn't using it. The makeshift outdoor workshop raised some telling questions. Clamping his axe head to a tree root was hardly ideal. They were so close to the end, but the investigation wasn't over. They couldn't afford to become complacent. The DNA that must be plastered all over the area might not yield a match. Carefully stepping away from the makeshift outdoor workshop, Ian took out his phone.

Back at the station, Ian discussed the night's findings with Eileen and Ted. Before Andrea's body had even been examined, they had a lot of new information to weigh up and disseminate.

'There must be a reason why he felt unable to sharpen his axe indoors,' Ian said.

'That's what I was thinking,' Eileen agreed. 'It suggests he doesn't live alone.'

There might be a flatmate who noticed he had been away from home whenever a murder had been committed. A blacksmith had confirmed the opinion of the scene of crime officers, that the axe had only been sharpened behind the wall once. Before that it must have been done elsewhere.

'Maybe he started doing it at home but then something got the wind up him and he decided that was too risky.'

'Perhaps he just didn't want to take it home any more,' Ian said. 'Once the papers reported the murder weapon was an axe, it would have been risky for him to walk around carrying it. That could be why last night's attack was carried out close to the river, away from the centre of the town. He had been keeping the axe at home – wherever that is – but it became too dangerous, so he moved it, along with all the gear he used to sharpen it. And he turned away from the town for his next attack.'

Eileen and Ted nodded. What Ian was saying made sense.

'That stacks up in theory,' Eileen agreed.

Ian sighed. He understood what she meant. They needed something more concrete than a theory. While Eileen brought the rest of the team up to speed, the forensic lab worked on the axe found at the crime scene and the equipment that had been discovered in the ditch. Ian returned to Andrea's street. The mortuary van was just leaving, taking the body with it for a post mortem. Ian hoped it would be done that day. If not, it might have to wait until after the weekend. Meanwhile, Ian had set up a team to question people living in sight of the river. It was possible someone had glanced out of their window and seen a figure running along the path or dragging a boat into the water the previous evening. The Royal

Mail had a depot along the river. An officer was sent there to ask if anyone had been working after nine o'clock who might have seen someone out on the river path, or in a boat. As well as questioning local residents, notices were posted along the river path, beyond the cordoned-off area. Drivers of trains that had passed over the railway bridge after half past eight were tracked down and questioned, in case they had seen anyone walking on the river path below the bridge the previous evening. While this massive information gathering exercise was taking shape, blood tests and DNA samples were being processed from the crime scene and ditch by the river.

Ian set off with renewed enthusiasm. Something had to result from all this activity. He was kept updated by phone. The wall panel had yielded a lot of useful information. Tiny threads of black fabric had been caught on the rough edge of the wall panel where the killer had forced his way through. There was fleeting excitement when traces of blood were discovered on the wall, until it was found to match Andrea's. Identifying her blood confirmed that the killer had been there, but they already knew that, really. Still by the river, numerous splinters of wood had been picked out of the water in the ditch. Analysis suggested they came from a boat as water from the river as well as rain water had been detected in their chemical content. But there was still nothing to indicate the identity of the killer.

Chapter Sixty

IAN HAD SPENT the afternoon talking to people who lived in Andrea's street, without learning anything new. No one had noticed a stranger in the area, or heard anything unusual. Andrea's flatmate, Julie, had spent the evening in the nearby pub knowing nothing about Andrea's fate until she had arrived home shortly before eleven. Finding her flatmate dead on the doorstep, Julie had called the police. Ian had spoken to her himself and was convinced she had seen no one on her route home. In any case, the killer must have disappeared a couple of hours before she had left the pub.

By seven o'clock, Ian was worn out. After the excitement of discovering the killer's hiding place that morning, they were still waiting to find out anything definite. All the neighbours and residents of the riverside properties had been approached. It had been a door-to-door enquiry on a massive scale which had produced no results at all. There was nothing more to do but wait for the results of the forensic tests. Ian drove back to the police station with Ted, intending to pick up his own car and go home to Bev. There were any number of statements to scan through, but they could wait until the morning. All he wanted to do was write up his own notes and get some sleep. Sitting at the desk in his little office, he called his wife.

'How are you feeling?'

'Yes, I'm OK. Did you come home last night?'

'No. I'll explain when I see you. It's been a rough night, but it was worth it. We've had a huge break through.'

'Does that mean the case will soon be over and done with?'

'Oh yes.'

'So when are you coming home? I mean, am I going to see you later?'

'Yes, that's why I'm calling. I've got about half an hour to do here, and then I'm coming home.'

'Great. I'll put some dinner on. What would you like?'

All he wanted to do was go home and fall into bed, but he didn't say so.

'Whatever you do will be great. Don't go to any trouble.'

'It's no trouble . . .'

'I mean, I'm tired. I really need an early night.'

'I'm not surprised if you've been up all night,' she retorted, but she sounded cheerful.

He settled down to complete his log. Before he had finished, his phone rang. It was Avril, calling from the mortuary to tell him Jonah had finished carrying out a post mortem on Andrea.

'That was quick.'

'Well, we had an idea it might be kind of urgent.'

'That's great. Is he still there?'

'Yes, he's waiting for you to come and see for yourself.'

'I'm on my way.'

He had wanted to go home, but the pathologist was waiting. Reluctantly, he called Bev. To his relief, she didn't remonstrate too much.

'Oh Ian, you said you were coming home.'

It was a half-hearted protest. He was relieved, but slightly disappointed that she accepted his change of plan so readily. If she had remonstrated strongly enough he might have been tempted to send Ted to the mortuary instead of going himself. Instead, she merely mumbled that she hoped she would see him later. With a sigh Ian heaved himself off his chair and set off.

Avril wasn't there. Jonah himself let Ian in when he buzzed.

'See how dedicated I am?' the pathologist greeted him with a smile. 'It's getting on for eight o'clock and here I am, doing your bidding. I just hope you appreciate how lucky you are.'

'I do, I do,' Ian grinned. 'Now, what have you got for us?'

Returning Ian's smile, Jonah led him inside.

'Where's Avril?' Ian asked.

'Alas, Avril has deserted us for a hot date. She seems to cherish the illusion that she's entitled to some sort of life away from this place. You and I both know that's not possible, of course. Not when we're dealing with something like this,' he added, as he opened the door to the room where Andrea's cadaver lay waiting for them. 'The only date we have right now is with this young lady.'

Jonah smiled ruefully at Ian. Thinking about Bev at home, Ian didn't answer. He stared past Jonah to the body lying flat on her back on the table, her body scored with more incisions than the killer had made.

'What can you tell us?'

'Injuries are consistent with those sustained by the other three victims,' Jonah replied.

'So the same weapon was used in all four attacks?'

'I'd say that's possible. Yes.'

'Is that a definite?'

Jonah hesitated. 'It was the same weapon, as far as we can tell. If it wasn't the same, it was one exactly like it.'

Jonah ran through Andrea's injuries. She had been killed with one impact from a sharp blade that had cracked her skull.

'Does that tell us anything about the killer? I mean, would it have required much strength to do that?'

Jonah shook his head. 'Not necessarily. If the axe was swung with enough speed and momentum it might not have taken a particularly powerful person to strike the blow. Don't forget the killer uses an axe, so all the force is concentrated on one sharp edge.'

Ian nodded despondently. They were gathering so much information, but none of it had so far led them to the killer. Ian tried to hide his dejection as he thanked the pathologist.

'I'm sorry I can't tell you anything more,' Jonah replied. Usually cheery, he seemed to share Ian's dejection. 'I'm sure you'll catch up with him after this. You've got the weapon now, haven't you?'

Ian nodded. The axe should give them the owner's DNA. Even if there was no match on the database, a DNA sample would offer information about the killer, maybe enough for them to make an arrest. It was hardly likely that the killer had never touched the axe with his bare skin, or even breathed on it. All they needed was for him to have coughed or sneezed just once, one brush with his hand, one scrape of skin as he was sharpening the blade, and they would have the evidence they needed. But first they had to find a sample they could use. Eileen was fuming with impatience. Ian was too tired to care that it was taking so long to find the killer's

DNA. Evidently he had been careful to wear gloves when handling all his equipment, from the axe itself to the bucket, tins and files. Even the bloodstained rags had only yielded up DNA from the victims. The forensic team would find what they were looking for, but it was taking longer than any of them had anticipated. They had the murder weapon, but not the murderer. Not yet.

Wearily Ian drove home. It was late. Expecting Bev to be in bed he went straight upstairs, but she wasn't there. He went back downstairs. The light was on in the hall but the rest of the house was in darkness. He opened the door to the living room but she wasn't asleep on the sofa. He switched on the light and glanced around. The room was empty. With a growing sense of unease, he checked the kitchen. She wasn't there. He was frightened now. He put the light on and saw an envelope on the table, addressed to him, propped up against the salt and pepper pots

There was no greeting, just a simple message to let him know she had gone to stay with her parents again. He wasn't sure whether to feel guilty at having left her on her own so much, or angry that she had gone away without letting him know first. He had no idea what time she had left, but it must have been hours earlier. It was too late to call her. They would have to speak in the morning. He felt slightly sick and his legs ached. He went to bed and fell asleep almost at once.

Chapter Sixty-one

THE FORENSIC TEAM were making slow progress, partly because the killer's hiding place was out of doors in a waterlogged ditch at the bottom of a muddy slope, and partly because the axe itself had been smothered in Andrea's blood. There had been a flurry of excitement when a trace of someone else's blood had been discovered on the handle. It had turned out to be Beryl's. The axe had evidently been thoroughly cleaned after each murder and sharpened as well, removing most of the earlier blood stains. Ian sat at his desk fiddling around with files, rereading statements, thinking about his pregnant wife. It was tempting to jump on a train down to Kent. He would have to change in London but he could be in Tunbridge Wells in under four hours. The trouble was, if anything new came up it could take him a lot longer to get back, depending on the times of the trains. If he was needed after the last train had gone, he would have to drive home and that could take up to six hours, depending on the traffic. He couldn't really afford to be so far away in the middle of a case. Far better to persuade Bev to come home. He wanted her with him. He picked up his phone.

'Bev, it's me. Please call me when you get this.'

He wasn't sure what he was going to say to her when she called back. He was excited at the idea of becoming a father, if scared, and prepared to cut her as much slack as possible. In spite of his determination to be tolerant, he didn't relish the prospect of a hormonal wife dragging him along on an emotional roller coaster. Bev could be difficult to deal with at the best of times. He wasn't thinking about her any more when she rang later that afternoon.

'Ian, it's me. We need to talk, face to face. That's why I've come home. But I'm not staying.'

'What?'

'I'm at home. Can you come home and talk? I'm not staying long.'

It was hardly an encouraging start, but at least she was home. He promised to be there within the hour.

'My wife's not feeling too well,' he explained to Ted. It wasn't too far from the truth. 'She's pregnant,' he added, feeling he needed to excuse his absence at such a critical time.

'Congratulations! Why didn't you say something?'

'It's early days so I'd appreciate it if you didn't tell anyone just yet.'

'Sure. It's not my news to tell anyway.'

'So can you and Naomi hold the fort while I'm away? I know Eileen's off at a meeting all afternoon and won't be back until tomorrow, but I'll just be at home if you need me.'

'Naomi went to talk to Sophie. It was Eileen's suggestion. Sophie might know something without realising it, and Eileen thought she'd be more likely to talk to Naomi than any of us. Both being young women and all that. But don't worry. It's not as if there's a lot going on right now. Apart from the waiting.'

Ian thanked his sergeant and dashed off home. Bev was waiting for him in the kitchen. She was pale and there were grey pouches under her eyes. He could tell she had been crying. At the same time, he registered her raised chin, and the determined expression on her face. Despite her miserable expression, she had lost the hangdog air he had grown accustomed to since their relocation. Before he had a chance to greet her, she blurted out that she was leaving him.

'What?'

'I'm leaving you.'

'You've only just got back.'

'No, I'm leaving you. For good. I'm not coming back. It's over between us.'

'Bev, what's got into you? Sit down. We need to talk about how you're feeling right now.'

'There's nothing to talk about. I just came back to tell you that I'm leaving you.' She dropped her head in her hands and began to cry. 'I couldn't tell you over the phone, could I?'

'Sit down.'

She sat, and he drew a chair up to the table beside her.

'Bev, I don't know why you're talking like this. Whatever's making you unhappy, we can sort it out. We've had difficult times before but we've always worked things out. You can't talk about leaving me, not now, not ever.'

He leaned to put his arm round her shoulders but she drew back.

'It's not yours.'

'What?'

She looked at the floor, her hands fidgeting in her lap. 'The baby. It's not yours.'

Ian sat up and stared at her in disbelief. Close up he could see her cheeks and lips were unhealthily pale, and her eyes were bloodshot. She must have been crying a lot. Pushing the thought from his mind he spoke very calmly and quietly. Only his years of training enabled him to retain his self-control.

'What do you mean, it's not mine?'

Her words cut like a razor. 'I've been having an affair. The baby's not yours. That's why I'm leaving. I can't make it any clearer. I don't know what more I can say. I'm really sorry it's worked out like this. I never meant for it to end like this. Please don't make it any harder for me than it already is.'

'Hard for *you* . . .?'

He turned away to hide his bitterness. Just a few seconds ago he had been looking forward to becoming a father, now he had lost not only the prospect of fatherhood, but his wife as well. He could quite cheerfully have strangled the life out of the man who had been screwing Bev.

'Who is he?'

'You don't know him.'

'It's the manager where you used to work, isn't it?'

'What difference does it make?'

While he was struggling for words, his phone rang. Bev laughed, her eyes bright with fury.

'Go on, answer it. You know you want to.'

He shook his head, pleading. 'Bev, don't do this. We can work it out.'

She stood up. 'It's too late, Ian. I'm leaving.' She was crying so hard he could barely understand what she was saying. 'Let's not have a scene. We can be civilised about this.'

'No!'

He tried to take her arm but she shook herself free. Helplessly, he watched her walk out of the room.

Chapter Sixty-two

As Bev disappeared, Ian jumped to his feet. He flung open the kitchen door. Ignoring the muffled ringing of the phone in his pocket, he ran after her and caught up with her at the front door.

'Bev! Wait! We can work this out.'

He put his hand against the door to prevent her from opening it. In his pocket his phone kept ringing.

'It's too late, Ian. I don't want to stay here any more. It's over. I'm sorry.'

Sobbing, she ducked under his arm, wrenched the door open and shot past him. Stopping only to grab his keys, he ran after her in time to see her opening the door of a taxi that was waiting for her. As though paralysed, he watched her through the taxi window, gliding away from him. He ran to his car, intent on following her to the station. His phone rang again.

'I can't talk now,' he gabbled, before he realised it wasn't Ted but someone from the forensic lab.

'You wanted us to call you with any updates. Well, first of all, the axe head is made of iron, with an edge welded on made of

EN42 steel that has been sharpened more than once. But that's not all. We discovered female DNA at the crime scene. To begin with we assumed it belonged to the victim. Well, we've tested it, and it's definitely not hers. We found the exact same DNA on the axe-sharpening materials, the file and the rags and the polish and so on that you found in a ditch by the river. It's identical, so we think we have the killer's DNA. We'll be sending a report, but you said you wanted to be notified straight away if we found anything.'

Ian felt his spirits lift. At last they had come up with something. Even if they didn't have a match yet, finding the DNA was certainly a move in the right direction. It could only be a matter of time now before they had the killer behind bars.

'That's great. Thanks for letting me know.'

'It's certainly a step forward.'

'You say you haven't found a match?'

'No, we're working on it but there's nothing yet. We'd love to be able to give you the killer's identity, but we just don't have it.'

'So what *can* you tell us about the killer?'

'Other than that she's a woman, you mean?'

'A woman?'

The scientist had mentioned finding female DNA at the crime scene. Distracted by Bev's departure, he hadn't realised the significance of the information straight away. The killer was a woman. Ian's thoughts raced. One woman had appeared fascinated by the case all along. Sophie had deliberately lied about Frank to lead the investigating team astray. Ian had thought she was affecting an interest in the case as an excuse to see him. It now appeared that her interest might have had a different motive. She had been checking on his progress to find out if he suspected her. He needed to report his suspicions to Eileen urgently. But first he had to get to the station before Bev and persuade her not to leave York. As he pulled away from the kerb, he remembered something Ted had said.

Naomi had gone to talk to Sophie on the off chance that Sophie might know more about the killer without realising it. Only now it seemed that Sophie not only knew a lot more about the elusive killer than anyone else, she could be the axe murderer herself. Although it was hard to believe that such a delicate-looking girl could be responsible for so many brutal murders, at the same time it made sense. Jonah had told them a woman could have slashed the victims, given a sharp enough blade. The murder weapon had been regularly sharpened. The more Ian thought about it, the more convinced he became that Sophie was the killer they had been looking for.

He tried Naomi's number. There was no response. He called Ted who answered straight away.

'Where's Naomi?'

'I thought I already told you she went to question Sophie. She went a while ago but she's not back so she must have gone home after seeing the witness. I think she did mention she wanted to get to the shops later. Something about friends coming for dinner at the weekend.'

'Has she called in a report?'

'No, not yet, but I'm sure she's working on it.'

Ted was evidently anxious to cover up for his colleague who had gone off without phoning in to say where she was. Ian had a far more serious worry concerning the constable's whereabouts.

'Did she go to speak to her at Jorvik?' he asked.

Nothing too drastic could happen to Naomi at the museum in front of other people. If there had been an incident, a report would have reached Ian by now. Ted said he would check, and Ian set off in pursuit of Bev. Before he reached the station, Ted called back. It seemed Naomi had gone to the museum but Sophie wasn't at work that day. After turning up and asking for her, Naomi had left Jorvik without telling anyone where she was going. Ted supposed she had gone to Sophie's home address.

This was no time for talk. Ian spun his wheel.

'Meet me at Sophie's flat,' he told Ted. 'I'm going there now. I think Sophie's the killer.'

'What?'

As briefly as he could, Ian explained what he had learned from the forensic lab. It would be easy enough to check whether the DNA found at the crime scene matched Sophie's. She could be quickly eliminated, if Ian had jumped to the wrong conclusion. But first they had to find her, and check that Naomi was all right.

'She knows how to take care of herself,' Ted said.

He didn't sound very confident. The best trained officer could be overpowered if they were taken completely unawares. Naomi was going to question Sophie as a potential witness, not a suspect. There was no reason why the constable would enter the property prepared to defend herself against a violent attack. Although she no longer had an axe, if Sophie *was* the killer, she might have other potential weapons to hand, kitchen knives and scissors, if nothing else. In the wrong hands, ordinary household items could become lethal weapons.

'I'll be there in five minutes,' Ian barked. 'Join me as soon as you can, and alert any patrol cars in the vicinity. We need to get there as quickly as possible. Go now!'

Ian put his foot down.

Chapter Sixty-three

WITH BITER HE HAD been in control of his life. Without his trusted weapon, he was vulnerable. He struggled to know what was happening. He needed to understand why the police woman had come to see him. She was only a woman, but she looked strong enough to put up a fight. He was nervous. This was not his normal way of working, not least because she had come to him. He didn't like that. Out on the street, in the dark, he had the benefit of surprise on his side. Here, the police woman was watching him. There was no way he could creep up on her unawares.

He smiled at her standing on his doorstep. He didn't want her to suspect he was afraid. Hiding his fear, he smiled and allowed her to enter. There wasn't much else he could do after she had invited herself in. At the same time he was wondering what she was really doing there. She couldn't possibly have seen through his disguise. He had been so careful. The police had been to Jorvik several times, and he had seen this detective constable before so he knew who she was, even before she introduced herself. He wanted to yell at her to get the fuck out of his home. Instead he led her into the kitchen and invited her to sit down.

Outwardly calm, he offered her a cup of tea, pretending he wasn't bothered by her unexpected appearance at his front door. He had no idea what she was thinking, but she didn't know what was in his mind either. Biter was merely his instrument. He was the killer. The wolf in his head panted to tear her flesh.

'How can I help you?' he asked, ever so politely, when they were both seated on kitchen stools.

She had refused a cup of tea. Just as well, as he had run out of milk. He dropped his eyes to the floor under the intensity of her gaze. When he looked up again, she was looking down at the floor. In the instant before she raised her head, his eyes flicked to the knife rack beside the sink. He weighed up his options. If it was necessary to silence her, the opportunity would arise. A warrior never hesitated. But he had to be clever as well as bold. The trouble was, if he struck her with a knife, her blood would spray all around the kitchen in the flat where he lived. It would be impossible to clean up completely. The police were bound to redouble their efforts to find him if he killed one of their own. He would have to find a way to get rid of her without spilling a drop of her blood. It wouldn't be easy, but he had never been one to shy away from difficulty.

'How can I help you?' he repeated, trying to keep his voice steady so he wouldn't betray his feelings.

Beneath the mask people were animals, able to sense fear.

'We've narrowed our search down,' she replied. 'We're pretty sure now that the killer we're looking for works at the Jorvik museum.'

He raised his eyebrows. 'Really? What makes you think that?'

She was lying. She had to be. The police couldn't possibly know where he worked. He had been far too careful for that, covering his tracks so that no one could find him. The river had offered him escape and protection. Even their dogs couldn't follow him across the water. Somehow she knew more than she was letting on. He didn't understand what trickery this was. He bitterly regretted having let her in. He took a deep breath. He needed to think clearly. If he panicked, he was lost. She had no idea who he was, or she would never have turned up alone. Growling, the wolf in his head hunkered down. All he had to do was negotiate his way around her questions and she would leave, no wiser than she had been when she arrived.

'I wish I could help you,' he lied.

She returned his smile. The stupid bitch had no idea who he was. He burned to reveal himself, but this was not the place for such a display. He would have to content himself with imagining her surprise if she could see his true identity. He tried to focus on her words as she reiterated that the police suspected the axe murderer could be connected with Jorvik.

'We're questioning everyone who works there to see if anyone can offer us any further information at all. Anything you can tell us might be useful. Anything at all. Nothing is too small to be of potential interest to us.'

She enquired whether he had noticed anything unusual in any of his colleagues, any strange patterns of behaviour, flaring tempers or signs of stress. He shook his head, thinking, wondering when this was going to end. She seemed to have been sitting in his kitchen bombarding him with questions for hours, when they were interrupted by her phone ringing.

The wolf growled. He couldn't control it. Her eyebrows rose a fraction at the rumbling in his throat. He coughed and her features relaxed.

'Frog in my throat,' he muttered.

He struggled to control the beast.

'Can I get you some water?'

'No, no, I'm fine, really. Thank you. I'm fine but actually I'm not feeling too well. Is there anything else I can help you with?'

It was her hint to leave. As she stood up, her phone rang again. She reached into her bag for it. As she listened, her expression altered. Her eyes met his. In that instant he understood. She had been sent in advance to keep him talking so he didn't leave, and he had fallen into the trap. The police were outside waiting for her to open the door. The phone call had been her signal that all was ready. The flat was surrounded by police officers poised to rush in and capture him as soon as she opened the front door. But first she had to reach it.

With a snarl, the wolf leapt.

Chapter Sixty-four

IAN WAITED A FEW doors away from Sophie's flat, tapping his fingers impatiently on the steering wheel. He tried again but Naomi still wasn't answering her phone. She was probably in a supermarket by now, as Ted had suggested. With no phone signal, she was busy shopping for her weekend. That was fair enough. Her shift was over. There was no reason for her to have returned to the police station at the end of her day. It was just unlucky that they were worrying about her when she had no phone signal.

The side street was quiet. If it seemed unlikely that a brutal killer was living in one of those ordinary-looking houses, it was still harder to believe in the identity of the axe murderer. Still, this wouldn't be the first time he had tracked down an unlikely suspect. Whatever he might think about it, the DNA evidence was conclusive. Now that the forensic lab knew what to look for, they had been able to confirm that samples of the DNA found on the axe had also been present in Tim's shop. That in itself wasn't proof that it belonged to the killer. Traces of a lot of different DNA were discovered in the shop. Nevertheless, taken in conjunction with the DNA found on the axe and on the materials discovered in the ditch, there was no longer any room for doubt. The killer was a woman. She had naturally blonde hair and blue eyes. Everything pointed to the one person working at Jorvik they had overlooked. It would be easy to confirm that the killer's DNA matched Sophie's, but right now Ian had to focus on Naomi.

He felt as though he had been waiting for hours when Ted drove up. The sergeant parked badly and leapt out of his vehicle. Ian could see the anxiety on his face before Ted reached him.

'She hasn't been back to collect her own car. She's still out somewhere in an unmarked vehicle,' Ted gasped as soon as he was close enough to be heard.

Naomi wasn't shopping for the weekend. She was working, her last known destination Sophie's flat. Ian jumped out of his car and joined his sergeant on the pavement.

'Do you really think all those murders could have been committed by a woman?' Ted asked.

'Insanity is no respecter of gender.'

'But would she have been strong enough?'

Ian remembered what Jonah had said. Sophie wouldn't need to be especially strong if she was using an extremely sharp axe. However unlikely a suspect Sophie might have appeared at first sight, there was no longer much doubt about it. They had discovered the identity of the axe murderer. But before they moved in, they had to consider that Naomi might be in danger.

Sophie rented a room in a house where she shared a kitchen and bathroom with a flatmate. Now there were two of them, Ian and Ted agreed they would go ahead and enter the property as quickly as possible, even if they had to smash their way in. If Naomi was in there, the sooner they could reach her the better.

First they rang all the door bells except for the one labelled 'Flat 3'. After a moment, they heard footsteps approaching. The door was opened by an elderly man who peered up at them. He was wearing a threadbare grey cardigan and trousers that were too big for his shrunken frame.

'Go away!'

The old man shuffled sideways and began to close the door. Ian put his shoulder against it and brandished his warrant card in the other man's face.

'Police!' he snapped. 'We need to gain access.'

'Not bloody likely,' the old man retorted. 'I wasn't born yesterday.'

There was no time to remonstrate. Ian elbowed him out of the way. He knew this was the kind of behaviour that gave the police a bad name and resolved to return with an apology when the case was over. For now, he was focussed on rescuing Naomi, if she was there. He turned to the old man who was cowering against the wall.

'Don't hit me.'

'No one's going to touch you. I told you, we're police officers. We need to find Sophie James' flat. Which floor is it?'

The old man shook his head.

'Which one is it?'

'Number three, on the first floor. I'm calling the police,' he called after them as they ran to the stairs. 'You won't get away with this.'

They ran up the stairs and found number three. Ian knocked. They waited. There was no response from inside. Not being an external entrance, the front door to the flat was relatively flimsy. Ian knocked again. After a moment, he stood back and turned to Ted.

'Break it down.'

Ted stared at him, his face taut. 'Back-up is on its way . . .'

'We can't wait. We need to get in there now.'

With a nod, Ted braced himself. 'Stand back from the door,' he yelled, 'we're knocking it down. Stand back from the door!'

With a loud grunt, he kicked the door. It shuddered. He tried again. At the third impact it burst open with a crash. Ian stepped into the silent flat with Ted at his heels. All at once, Ian raised his hand. They listened. Nearby they could hear muffled whimpering. Ian jerked his head towards one of the doors.

'Come on,' he whispered. 'It's coming from in there.'

Ian tried the door but it was locked.

'Stand back from the door!' Ted yelled again.

Almost at once they heard an answering shout from the other side of the locked door.

'Will you stop kicking doors down? It sounds like Armageddon out there. Jesus, give me a chance. Didn't you hear me shouting?'

Ted stepped back, frowning.

'Was that Naomi?' Ian asked.

Chapter Sixty-five

THE DOOR FLEW open. Naomi stood in the opening, her face flushed, her hair a mess. Her eyes looked wild. On one side of her head strands of hair were tangled and matted with blood that was seeping from a wound in her neck. Staining the collar of her white shirt, it was barely visible against the dark fabric of her jacket, making it impossible to see how much blood she had lost.

'You're injured,' Ian said, starting forward.

She glared at him. 'Yeah, thanks for pointing that out.'

'How bad is it?'

'I'm not a fucking doctor.'

Ian understood the constable was in shock, but he needed to get past her belligerence as quickly as possible and ascertain the extent of her injuries. She was still standing upright and talking coherently, but he was concerned about her loss of blood.

'Let me take a look.'

She stepped back.

'Stand still, constable,' he snapped. 'That's an order.'

'Yes sir,' she replied, with a sarcastic emphasis on his title.

She didn't move as he lifted her hair gently off her neck and examined four deep scratches. They looked like flesh wounds, not very deep.

'She did this with her finger nails?'

Naomi nodded and held out her right arm. 'The fucking bitch bit me. I'm not sure she broke the skin through my jacket but it hurts like hell. She's a lunatic.'

'Where is she?'

Naomi half turned so that Ian could see into the room. Behind his injured colleague, Sophie was crouching on the floor on her hands and knees, snarling like a dog. Her palms were flat on the floor, her wrists manacled together.

Ian went up to Ted and spoke very softly. 'I'll hold her down while you put cuffs on her ankles. We want her immobilised. But be careful. She's likely to kick. I don't want a second officer injured.'

Taking care to avoid her gnashing teeth, Ian grabbed hold of Sophie, pinning her to the ground, with one of his hands firmly pressing her head into the carpet. At the same time, Ted seized hold of her legs and snapped cuffs on her ankles. She wriggled and groaned, but without the use of her arms was incapable of resisting the strength of two men.

With Sophie rendered powerless, Ian led Naomi over to a chair. 'Back-up will be here soon. We need to get you to a hospital and get you checked out.'

'I'll probably need a bloody tetanus jab, thanks to that maniac.' She jerked her head towards Sophie, and winced as she moved her neck. 'Talk about a head case. There was absolutely no warning or I would have stopped her in her tracks. One minute we were sitting chatting, the next minute she just leapt at me, growling like a fucking animal, biting and scratching. Honestly, it was unbelievable. Don't ask me how I did it, but I managed to get my truncheon out of my bag.' She paused, frowning. 'The funny thing is, as soon as I flipped the truncheon open, she fell on the floor like a limp lettuce and let me cuff her hands without so much as a squeak. It was weird. I tell you, if she hadn't stopped with her biting and scratching, God knows what might have happened.'

Hearing footsteps charging noisily up the stairs, Ian joined a team of uniformed officers outside Sophie's flat to stop them trampling all over the carpet. The flat hadn't yet been searched. Treating it as a crime scene might yield useful evidence. The officers were accompanied by a couple of paramedics who arranged for Naomi to be taken to hospital.

In the midst of all the kerfuffle, Sophie's flatmate turned up.

'What the hell's going on here?'

'Who are you?' a uniformed officer asked.

'I'm Fiona Greenway. I live here. Let me in.' When Ian stepped forward and explained she would not be able to go in the flat until it had been searched, her face went red and she started shouting. 'What are you talking about? I live here. You can't stop me from going into my own home! You might not believe it but I pay good rent for this shithouse. Now let me in . . .'

She broke off as Sophie was carried out, strapped to a stretcher.

'What the hell are you doing to her? Let her go! What have you done to her? Why have you tied her up like that? This is – that's it.' She pulled out her phone and took a photo of her flatmate. 'This is going online right now. You can't do this to people. We're not living in a police state yet. You'll never get away with this . . .'

'Put it online and tell people they can walk the streets safely now because the axe murderer has been caught,' Ian interrupted her sharply.

'That's ridiculous!' Fiona said.

Ian hesitated before allowing her to approach her flatmate.

'Be careful. She bites,' he warned her.

Fiona stepped forward.

'It's all right, Sophie,' she began.

Sophie's eyes focussed on her flatmate. With a sudden jerk of her head, she snapped her teeth at Fiona who leaped back just in time.

'What the fuck? She tried to bite me!'

Quietly Ian explained that the police had reason to suspect Sophie was a dangerous maniac who had been committing murders on the streets of York.

Fiona's eyes grew wide with alarm. 'You mean she's really the axe murderer?' she whispered.

'That's for a jury to decide,' Ian replied, 'but we have evidence that suggests she is the axe murderer.'

'Was,' Ted corrected him. 'She won't be doing any more of that where she's going.'

Recovering from her outrage, Fiona agreed to go and stay with a friend for a few days, until the police had finished with the flat.

'To be honest, I'm not sure I'd want to come back here,' she added. 'But at least I suppose I could sell my story to a magazine.'

'Your story?' Ian repeated.

'Living with an axe murderer! Not that I knew she was, of course.'

Ian sighed. With all his experience on murder investigations, people still amazed him. Selling a story like that would have been the last thing on his mind if he had been in Fiona's situation. It made sense, of a kind.

'Young people don't think the way we do,' he muttered to Ted who looked at him in surprise.

They went downstairs. Sophie was being thrown in the back of a police van, snarling and snapping like a dog. Ted looked pale and Ian wasn't sure if his colleague was trembling slightly.

About to ask the young sergeant if he was all right, Ian changed his mind. 'Oh well, that's what you might call a good day's work,' he said instead. 'That was a bit hair-raising, wasn't it?'

'It certainly was. What a nutcase!'

'A dangerous nutcase. You OK?' he added, as though it was a casual remark.

'I'm fine,' Ted said.

On the way back to the station to write up his report, Ian thought how lucky he was with his colleagues. Although he had struggled to deal with the crazy killer, Ted had coped, and Naomi had conducted herself with admirable professionalism. Ian was proud to be part of the team that had caught a dangerous murderer.

Chapter Sixty-six

IAN WENT INTO work late on Saturday. Ted arrived in the canteen about half an hour later. From beneath his lowered brows the sergeant's eyes squinted as though he was dazzled by the light.

'You look as hungover as I feel,' Ian greeted him.

'I feel terrible,' Ted said, sitting down and sipping a mug of coffee. 'I'm so hungover it's not true.'

'Me too.'

Ted frowned at Ian who was tucking into a plate of egg and sausages with beans and mushrooms and fried bread.

Seeing his colleague's expression, Ian put his fork down. 'Best thing for a hangover,' he assured Ted. 'The more you eat, the more you soak up the alcohol.'

'That's bollocks. It's far too late. Once your brain is fried, you can't unscramble it.'

Ian laughed. 'The way you talk, it sounds like your brain's made of eggs, fried or scrambled, but I'm telling you, you'd be far better off eating them.' He scooped up a forkful of egg. 'Food and lots of it. It's the best cure for a hangover.'

He raised his fork. Runny yolk dripped on to his plate.

'If I swallowed a mouthful of that shit, I'd throw up,' Ted said.

Ian nodded cheerily. 'That's another way to cure a hangover.'

'Thanks for that. You're in a good mood.'

It was true. Ian thought for a moment. Instead of feeling devastated by the breakdown of his marriage, he felt elated.

'We caught the killer,' he said at last.

'And you're going to be a dad.'

Ian paused, fork in mid air. 'Oh, that,' he replied as carelessly as he could. 'No, that's not going to happen. At least it is, but I won't be there to see it. We're not together any more.'

'What?'

'She left me.'

'But she's pregnant . . .'

'It's complicated.' Ian leaned forward. 'I'd appreciate a bit of discretion here, but the truth is – well, I don't know what the truth is.'

As he was speaking, it occurred to Ian that his hangover hadn't hit yet. He was still drunk. He probably shouldn't have driven into work that morning. All at once his mind began darting around, out of control. The thought of Bev giving birth without him at her side was unbearably sad. She would be all on her own. Worse, another man might be there in his place. She had told him the baby wasn't his. That meant she was seeing someone else. He shook his head, forcing a mental shutter to close out the disturbing thoughts. He had believed he was fine with it, but he wasn't ready to think about losing Bev yet. None of it seemed real: her pregnancy, their split, her affair – it was all like a horrible dream. He wanted to cling to his state of disbelief for a little longer. He regretted having confided in Ted.

'Don't mention this to anyone at all, ever,' he said fiercely.

'Silent as the grave.'

They sat for a moment without speaking.

'So, how was your evening?' Ian asked at last, with forced good humour.

'Oh shit. I'm sorry – it's not the best time to be saying this, but Jenny and me are engaged.'

Ian couldn't help laughing at his sergeant's stricken expression.

Scowling, Ted pushed his chair back and stood up. 'I'd better get to work.'

'Sorry, I didn't mean to be rude. To be honest, I'm still a bit pissed.'

What he should have said was 'congratulations,' or 'commiserations,' but he just laughed again. He couldn't help it.

'Do you think there's a kind of balance in the universe?' Ted asked, sitting down again, Ian's apology clearly accepted. 'You lost a wife, I gain one. Almost like there's a finite number of marriages possible in the world.'

'Stop talking shit and go and write up your report, if you're not prepared to do something sensible like join me for breakfast.'

Grumbling that he never should have sat down to watch Ian eat, Ted left. Ian finished his breakfast and made his way along the corridor to his office. Scene of crime officers had finished examining Sophie's room. Ian wasn't surprised to learn the search team had discovered a hoard of small metal objects, mostly coins and jewellery, hidden under a loose floorboard beneath Sophie's bed. Some of the jewellery matched the description of Beryl's rings. When it was all over, and evidence could be released, he would make sure Beryl's rings were returned to her husband. It would be a paltry comfort. Apart from a few cheap pieces, the other jewellery came from Tim's shop. It was a slight comfort to know that all of the identifiable property in Sophie's stash was accounted for. There was nothing to suggest she had killed anyone else.

Ian and Ted faced Sophie across a table. The preliminaries had been dealt with. It was time to start the formal questioning. Ian was glad the interview was being taped, not filmed. Unshaven, with slightly bloodshot eyes, Ted looked as though he had been sleeping rough. A faint sprinkling of dandruff on his shoulders added to his unkempt appearance. Straightening his tie, Ian noticed a patch of crusty yellow on his creased shirt where egg yolk had dripped. By contrast, Sophie looked surprisingly fresh-faced and clean despite having spent a night in a cell. An uninformed observer might conclude that she was the professional police officer, questioning a pair of dodgy characters.

With enough evidence to secure a conviction, they should only need to go through the motions. Their job was made easier by Sophie's refusal to be represented by a lawyer. All the same, Ian was on his guard. Even at this late stage in the proceedings it could all go terribly wrong if he failed to adhere to strict procedures. The Police and Criminal Evidence Act had tripped officers up before on cases that should have resulted in straightforward convictions. Regulating police treatment of the public was necessary to make sure officers didn't exceed their powers, but it made interviewing suspects a minefield. In this instance it would not only be a travesty of the justice system if Sophie were released on a legal technicality, it would let a dangerous psychopath loose. Eileen was away or she would have been present. As it was, the future safety of the streets depended on two hungover detectives. Ian took a deep breath and began.

Chapter Sixty-seven

'SOPHIE, YOU'VE BEEN arrested on suspicion of the murders of Angela Jones, Timothy Granger, Beryl Morrison and Andrea Shelton. Do you understand?'

Sophie gave a nonchalant shrug. 'I didn't know their names, did I? I mean, what difference does it make what they were called? It never made any difference to me, and it makes no difference to them now, does it?'

'Are you saying you admit to killing those people just mentioned?'

'Well, I don't know, do I? How do I know who Angela Jones, Andrea Shelton, and all those others are? I've never heard any of those names before in my life so there's no point in even talking about them.'

She leaned back in her chair and folded her arms across her chest as though to signal that she had nothing more to say. Ian drew four photographs out of a file and placed them side by side on the table in front of her.

'Do you recognise these faces? We can sit here as long as you like but you'll need to look at them sooner or later. We can wait all day if you want to carry on playing games, but it won't help your cause.'

'Oh all right, keep your hair on. Jesus.'

'The photographs,' Ian repeated quietly.

It was hard to believe the laid-back young woman facing him across the table was the snarling beast they had arrested the previous day.

Sophie glanced at each of the images in turn. 'Very nice.'

'Do you recognise these people?'

'Difficult to say, really.'

Ian placed the axe on the table. He was careful not to nick a hole in the plastic evidence bag protecting it from any risk of contamination. He had been warned that the blade was sharp. Sophie's eyes lit up at the sight of it, the first indication that she really was the insane perpetrator of a recent spate of horrendous murders.

'Have you seen this before? For the tape, I'm showing the suspect the murder weapon.'

Sophie hesitated.

'The axe had your DNA all over it. Your breath, your sweat, even your blood where you must have cut yourself. So, I'll ask you again, for the record, to confirm that this is your axe.' He paused before asking whether she wanted to reconsider legal representation.

Sophie reached out and touched the plastic on the handle with one finger. Her features softened in a smile, making her look young and vulnerable. Ian reflected ruefully how wrong his initial impression of her had been.

'This is Biter,' she said softly, ignoring his suggestion that a lawyer be present to advise her.

'So you admit you've seen it before?' He waited. 'I need an answer, Sophie. Have you seen this axe before?'

'This is Biter.'

'It's yours, isn't it?'

She didn't answer.

'Why Biter?' Ian asked, adopting an oblique approach in the hope of drawing her out. 'Biter's an odd name for an axe, isn't it?'

'It's a perfect name for an axe.'

Ian watched her gazing at the murder weapon. From her expression she could have been watching a kitten. He felt a sudden flash of rage, but he spoke in an even tone.

'You used that axe to hack four people to death.'

She didn't even look up.

'It's hard to believe anyone could do that, let alone a delicate woman like you,' Ted chipped in.

He couldn't have chosen a better way to provoke a response. Sophie looked at him and laughed.

'That shows how stupid you are. You're all stupid. All of you. You believe I'm a woman, but I'm not. Not really. Not at all. Sophie is just one of many shapes I can assume at will. I'm a shape shifter. I can change into any shape I like. This is my true shape.'

She pushed her shoulders back and sat up very straight, seeming to grow in height. With a rigid frown on her face, she looked surprisingly fierce for such a slight woman.

'Now do you understand?' she roared in a deep voice that seemed to reverberate round the room. She rose to her feet with a triumphant laugh. 'I am a mighty warrior. That puny woman, Sophie, is just one of my disguises. I am a fierce and mighty man, a warrior hero and I will never be conquered so long as the gods protect me. I can escape your thraldom any time I like, because I can adopt whatever shape I please.'

'Including a yapping dog?' Ian asked, remembering what Naomi had said.

'I am a wolf.'

She dropped to the floor, her hands still cuffed, and crouched there howling like a wild beast.

'Get up.'

Ian nodded at two uniformed constables standing by the door.

'For the tape, the suspect flung herself on the floor, pretending to be a wolf. She is being returned to her chair.'

'In battle I'm a bear,' she shrieked, writhing as the constables picked her up. 'I can break out of these chains with superhuman strength. You can't keep me locked up. I'll smash you and your cells to pieces. You can't keep me here. The gods will strike you down with thunder and lightning.'

She was raving, her eyes rolling wildly, her hands clawing at the air. Ian glanced sideways at Ted who was watching Sophie, mesmerised by her performance.

'Do you think she really believes it?' he muttered to Ian.

Ian shook his head. It was difficult to know what to say. At least she had admitted the axe belonged to her.

'So you are a fierce warrior,' he resumed, when she had quietened down enough to be returned to her seat.

'My prowess in battle is renowned. I am a glorious hero. My fame has spread. I am a legend in my own lifetime. Poets will still be singing about me a thousand years from now.'

'A great warrior would never have been beaten in combat, and by a woman.'

She bristled. 'No one has ever beaten me in battle. No one.'

'Naomi did.'

'Who's Naomi? Is that someone else I'm supposed to know? Because I don't.'

'That's the name of the female police constable who came to your flat. The one who slapped you in handcuffs.'

Sophie gave a cunning smile. 'I know better than to fight with a volur.'

'What do you mean?'

'As soon as she took out her staff, I knew she could overpower me with one flick of her wrist. I'm not a fool. I'll take on anyone in a fair fight – and win – but I'm no match for her.'

'What the hell are you talking about?' Ted asked. 'You must have been in with a chance. One on one. You might have disarmed her.'

'With what? I'm a shape shifter, not a sorceress. I have no power against the magic of a volur.'

Ted muttered something about a nutcase. Ian vaguely recalled Sophie telling him about women known as volurs who were sorceresses. They used a sort of magic wand. The Viking belief in magic made the volur powerful enough to control strong warriors. When Naomi had flicked open her truncheon, Sophie had submitted to her superior power, in the mistaken belief that Naomi was brandishing a magic wand.

With the mystery of Sophie's surrender resolved, Ian was curious to know what had triggered Sophie's killing spree. He asked her about it directly.

'Isn't it obvious?' she replied, reaching out to touch the handle of the axe again inside its plastic cover. 'The gods sent me a sign when they placed a weapon in my hand.' She looked up earnestly. 'The gods must be obeyed.'

Ian ended the interview, advising Sophie that they would continue in the morning. It was only a formality from now on. They had all the evidence they needed, backed up by her confession that she had used the axe to kill people. Her ignorance of the identity of her victims wasn't important. They had more than enough to secure a conviction.

He switched off the tape and leaned forward. 'We're going to work a different sort of magic for you,' he said softly. 'It's a magic that will see you locked up for the rest of your crazy life.'

Sophie laughed. 'You're no sorceress,' she said, 'and I know you're not a shape changer. There's no magic in you.'

'We'll see about that.'

Ian stood up and nodded to the uniformed constables at the door. 'Take her away, and keep her under twenty-four-hour surveillance. She's completely insane, crazy enough to try anything. We need to get a mental health assessment done as quickly as possible and, in the meantime, make sure she can't do herself an injury.'

Eileen asked about Naomi when she phoned to congratulate Ian on a satisfactory outcome. He wondered how she had heard about the dangerous situation Naomi had faced. He hoped it wouldn't count against him, as the superior officer in Eileen's absence.

'There was never any problem, Ma'am,' he assured Eileen. 'Naomi's an extremely competent officer.'

He was minimising the danger Naomi had faced only partly to cover his own back. He was also protecting the constable from a reprimand for taking an unnecessary risk. Privately, Ian thought his colleague had had a lucky escape.

Chapter Sixty-eight

IAN HAD ALL HIS notes ready for typing and checking, but that could wait until the morning. The hard work that lay ahead was just a formality, although crucial if they were to secure a conviction. The uncertainty was over. After a day spent in an interview room with Sophie, he was mentally drained. The rest of the team were going for a drink to celebrate the arrest. Ian finished tidying up his desk, and went to join the others in the pub. He had nothing to rush home for. As soon as he had finished his reports, he would take a few days off and go to Kent. He had no idea what he was going to say to Bev. They had been together for so long, he couldn't envisage life without her. He didn't even want to think about it yet.

The normally quiet pub was packed and rowdy. Many of the officers who had been drafted in from the surrounding area had already gone home, but there were enough left to fill the place. Ian struggled towards the bar where a harassed-looking landlord was pulling pints as quickly as he could. His lips were moving, but it was impossible to hear what he was saying. Ian found Ted and Naomi in the melee.

'DCI's at the bar,' Ted shouted. 'What are you having?'

'A pint,' Ian mouthed.

Ted turned to an officer standing behind the detective chief inspector and called out something about a pint for Ian. A moment later, Eileen looked round and raised a hand in acknowledgement. George was with her. He also turned and grinned at Ian.

'It's mad in here,' Ted yelled.

Ian nodded. With a pint in his hand, he followed Ted to the side of the room, where there was a little more space. Naomi joined them. They didn't attempt conversation. Ian gazed around at his colleagues, many of them single or divorced. Perhaps it was inevitable that so many relationships failed. Bev had never been happy with what he did, but he would never give it up. The adrenaline rush of the chase was addictive, as was the satisfaction of achieving a result. He had dedicated his life to the service of justice, stopping the guilty and protecting the innocent. It was partly down to his efforts that a demented killer was behind bars, and no longer prowling the streets hunting for a victim. Four people were dead. There could have been more. Bev herself had been at risk, along with the rest of the public. Yet she refused to understand that he was protecting her as well as everyone else.

Although he hadn't wanted to go home to his empty house, he didn't stay long at the pub. There were a few speeches, which no one could hear, and a lot of cheering and drinking. He left while the orgy of self-congratulation was in full swing. He didn't feel like celebrating. Driving home, he realised he was hungry, but he couldn't be bothered to stop for a takeaway. Somehow it wouldn't be the same without first phoning Bev to ask if she wanted anything. He played the familiar conversation in his head as he drove. He would enquire if she was making dinner. She would want to know why he was asking, although they would both know that she knew what was in his mind. He sighed and pulled up outside the house, empty-handed.

Indoors, he had to stop himself from calling out to her, or looking for her in the living room. It crossed his mind that she might have thought better of her decision, and he shouted her name with a sudden rush of hope. There was no answer. He flung himself into a chair and dropped his head in his hands. He always felt horribly deflated at the end of a case. For weeks all he had thought about was the axe murderer. He had spent every waking minute reading statements and searching for clues. He had dreamt about the victims at night, when he had been able to sleep. Now it was over and, in spite of his relief, there was a void in his life. He had nothing to occupy his mind now, except his failed marriage.

When his phone rang, he nearly didn't answer it. He wasn't sure he could cope with any more emotion just then. Steeling himself, he picked it up.

'Ian, it's Geraldine.'

He was pleased to hear from his former colleague. Geraldine had no idea that she was probably his closest friend. At least she understood the horrible flatness he went through at the end of a case, when people who hadn't experienced it might expect him to be feeling triumphant. That was one more thing about him that Bev had never understood.

'I thought you were sounding a bit down,' Geraldine said, when he had told her about the arrest.

Soothed by her understanding, he blurted out that Bev had left him.

'What?'

'She's left me. Gone back to Kent. For good.'

'Oh my God, I'm so sorry. Do you want to talk about it?'

She knew that he did. Why else would he have mentioned Bev, before she had even asked about her. But having brought the subject up, he didn't know what to say.

'There's not much to tell you, really. She left me. Went back to Kent.'

He realised he was close to tears and hoped his voice didn't betray his wave of emotion.

'She was never exactly supportive, was she?'

Her sympathy surprised him. He had always believed he was to blame for his marital problems.

'Was it just the move, or is there someone else?'

'I'm not sure.' He paused. 'Well, yes, there is someone. The thing is, she's pregnant . . .'

'Oh, Ian!'

'Only she says it's not mine,' he added, speaking very quickly. He wasn't sure why he was telling Geraldine all this. 'I'm telling you that in confidence. All of it.'

'Of course.'

'The thing is, I'm not sure whether to believe her when she says it's not mine, and I don't know what to do. It's all such a mess.'

It was a relief to share his bewilderment. Not only was Geraldine a woman, but she had been his inspector when he was still a sergeant. It felt natural to turn to her for advice.

'Pregnant women are often all over the place. I know my sister is.'

'Is she pregnant?'

'Yes.'

There was a pause.

'Talk to her, Ian,' she said at last, realising he was waiting for her to speak again. 'She must be unhappy. She always resented moving, didn't she? Talk to her. Try to sort it out with her.'

The more reasonable Geraldine was, the more angry he felt.

'She said the baby's not mine.'

'That might not be true. You said yourself you don't know whether to believe her or not.'

'Then why say it?'

'It could be a desperate cry for attention. She's telling you loud and clear that she doesn't want to stay in York. That could be all it is. If you want my advice, for what it's worth, I think you should talk to her. You don't even know if there's anyone else involved. That's the first thing I'd do, if I were you. Find out if she's been seeing anyone else. Oh, Ian, I'm so sorry if she *has* been cheating. But you know what to do. Find out all the facts before you reach any conclusions.'

In spite of his unhappiness, he smiled. Geraldine was so predictable.

'It's not a police investigation.'

'You'll sort it out, one way or the other. Things might not be as bad as you think. But you need to find out what's behind it all, before you can work out what you want to do.'

She was right. He was in a state of limbo, unable to think straight, because he didn't really know what the hell was going on. Once he got to the bottom of it, he would decide what to do.

Geraldine was speaking again. 'Congratulations on getting that axe murderer. From what you've said, it sounds like you did a great job! I'm really proud of you. I always am.'

It was typical of Geraldine to be more concerned about his case than his personal life. He couldn't help smiling again. Now Sophie was safely behind bars, he had time to pursue Bev. Geraldine was right. As soon as his reports were written up, he would follow his wife to Kent and find out exactly what was going on. Reaching that decision made him feel more positive. He glanced at his watch. There was nothing he could do to salvage his failing marriage that night but there was still time to go back to the pub and raise a glass to the arrest of the axe murderer. He said goodbye to Geraldine, and picked up his car keys.

Glossary of acronyms

DCI – Detective Chief Inspector (senior officer on case)

DI – Detective Inspector

DS – Detective Sergeant

SOCO– scene of crime officer (collects forensic evidence at scene)

PM – Post Mortem or Autopsy (examination of dead body to establish cause of death)

CCTV – Closed Circuit Television (security cameras)

VIIDO– Visual Images Identifications and Detections Office

About the Author

LEIGH RUSSELL is the award-winning author of the Geraldine Steel and Ian Peterson mysteries. She is an English teacher who lives in the UK with her family.

www.leighrussell.co.uk
www.witnessimpulse.com

Discover great authors, exclusive offers, and more at hc.com.